BANKING ON DECEIT

A Toni Jasper Murder Mystery

B. J. Dandro

This book is a work of fiction. Names, characters, corporations, institutions, events and locations in this novel are products of the author's imagination. Any resemblance to a real person or company is coincidental and used fictionally.

To the actual Ed Bradbury: my dad and the person I most admired

.

Acknowledgements

My gratitude for inspiration and constructive criticism extend to my
Writer's Group led by John Chaplick: Golda Brunhild, Kathryn M. Dorn,
and Albert Lucas. Thoughtful and candid readers and advisors include
Terra Askar, Zoe Athans, Ken and Marylyn Cantrell, Brenda Ciecieznski,
Natalie J. Ciecieznski, Onyx Haran, Jon Michael Miller, and Sarah Sagaro.
Special thanks for medical fact verification go to outstanding nurses Ernest
McKinney, Greg O'Brien, and Mark Stultz as well as dental hygienist
Priscilla Barreiro and dentist Rafael Palaganas, D.D.S.

BANKING ON DECEIT

Chapter One

"No. No. No," said Mike Milner, handsome editor and publisher of the well-read *Woodlands Gazette*. In the small town of Seminole, Florida, he was *the* eligible bachelor. He leaned back in his chair and at the same time raised his X-crossed fingers in a feigned effort to dispel the "evil" force he saw approaching. The determined persona of Toni Jasper embodied that so-called force.

Toni's energized personality set the tone for her business meetings, though she regarded any face-to-face with Mike as part business, part attempted conquest. Focused on her goal, she peered over Mike's desk, far enough to allow her long, chocolate-brown waves to reach down and caress the computer screen. Silver teardrop earrings sparkled through strands of hair, and her blue-green eyes twinkled with a tinge of mischief.

"What?" Mike barked with a sly grin creeping across his face.

"Oh, Mike, it's so nice to see you too," Toni quipped with a coy smile as she moved around the desk. Depositing herself in the adjacent chair, she leaned toward him, still smiling in her disarming way.

Any chance to visit with her former editor invigorated Toni Jasper. A year ago, she'd hesitated to quit her reporter job partly because it meant not being around Mike every day. But the challenge of a new career beckoned, and Toni couldn't refuse her dream. She thrived on tackling new situations. And today, Mike's attitude needed tackling.

"No time to chat, Jasper. I've got a bank robbery to deal with. And Pasco County Sheriff's Department just announced the discovery of a body. We've got news."

1

"I see. The morbid war correspondent returns. Tell me more about that bank. And what does a gruesome find in another county have to do with this little paper? Could it be someone I know?"

"Hold on. You left this *little paper* and decided to branch out with your own advertising firm. So this is *my* news. I can say that the bank robbery's local. Under a rock about ten feet from the Pasco victim, detectives found one of our Seminole Plait Gym guest passes. It'd been there a while, but the lamination kept it pretty much intact. Who knows if or how it's linked to our little city?"

"Yeah, that's seriously big news," Toni acknowledged with a mental note to find out more later. Still determined to get the publicity she'd come to snag, she said, "But my news involves a major new client for me: PinCo Bank. It was a tough sell, but I've got a nice P.R. campaign. I promise they'll place some ads, too."

"Promises, promises. That's all you give me." Though his head was stationary, Toni noticed his quick scan from her head to toes.

Her impeccable fashion sense made the most of her slim, yet curvaceous, five-foot four-inch figure, wearing dark denim that hugged her lean legs and gracefully flared at the bottom. With an antique-white silk blouse under a deep-red, tailored faux leather jacket, Toni knew her head-turning presence was right for this encounter with Mike.

"They're having a community open house on Monday," Toni continued. "Since people don't understand why they have to go *into* a bank, this PinCo branch is giving them a reason to come and meet them, the community bankers."

"That's the best pitch you've got?" Mike said with a half-interested expression.

"Hey, we need good space to announce this event. See." Toni pulled her prepared press release from her portfolio and placed it securely on the desk in front of her former editor. "It's an appreciation party and would balance your bad news bank heist."

"Hmm. Party? Like food? Band?" Mike grabbed the press release, although Toni had already emailed it to the publication. She was confident he had seen it. But he pretended to view the material as if it were a fresh revelation.

Eyebrow arched, he scanned the lines. "Ahh . . . what? No nice, crisp, free fifty-dollar bills as giveaways? Okay. I'll take a worn-out one."

Toni understood that Mike's favorite pastime was to keep her in suspense. Rarely did the ruse work, but Toni knew he enjoyed it. She usually played along.

"Milner, this time, I'll ignore that lame attempt at humor."

"So . . . what else is new?"

"I haven't asked for a favor in a long time."

"Of course. Not since last week."

Toni knew Mike truly liked her and respected her talents. When she worked as his features editor and reporter, he would grill her to be sure that her story facts were exact. His goal after he came onboard as executive editor was to produce more substantial local interest stories. Working together, the Milner-Jasper team had been a masterful newsroom combination.

At over six feet tall, the man had a powerful presence, but his demeanor was charismatic and mesmerizing. Leaning in, Toni studied his normally piercing, deep-blue eyes that revealed a softer expression.

Mike straightened in his chair and smoothed his neatly cropped pitch-black hair.

"Okay," the editor said. "I can give you the front-page lead corner as well as an inside announcement. The car dealer who usually has that *paid* spot just pulled his ad, so the space is available at the last minute. Might as well have something in there. Just don't get used to preferential treatment." Mike slapped the press release down on his desk with a genuine smile aimed at his former reporter.

Toni grinned and relaxed her shoulders. She wanted to impress her friend Emily Phillips, the bank's local branch manager in charge of the campaign. This choice front-page ad just might do it. Toni regarded Emily as a type of control freak, not one to let any circumstance affect her professional demeanor.

Still seated next to Mike's desk, Toni found her reverie cut off when she heard her name bellowed from down the aisle. Her eyes rolled as she forced a grin to greet the man marching toward her.

"Hey, P.R. person," said Paul Delaney, the forty-year-old aggressive ad manager. "What're you working on now?" He stared down with his automatic smile. "We need money for ads, not free P.R."

Typical Paul, she thought, *always on the lookout to wheel and deal.* Toni believed a lesson in subtlety might serve Paul well. However, he had increased advertising revenue every year.

"Paul, I *am* working on new ad business," Toni answered. "I'll get with Sue as soon as I have a schedule."

"Who's the new client?" As if he didn't know, Toni realized.

"PinCo Bank. They're making a big push for new business in the local branch. Weren't you talking with Emily at the chamber lunch yesterday?"

"Yes," Paul said, "we conversed at length. She mentioned her big event. So get some ads in ASAP, Toni. You don't want to disillusion the client with grandiose hope of P.R. success. Place a big ad. Reserve the double truck. This client needs a big splash. After all, it's a bank."

"Working on it. I'll let Sue know when I have an ad."

"Good. Just get her off the phone," Paul said, shaking his head. "That new boyfriend of hers monopolizes her time, for God's sake."

Toni made a mental note to find out more than just Paul-gossip about that situation. An appointment with her advertising account representative Sue just became a priority. Whom had she met after her decree to swear off men? Toni's inquiring mind was dying to know.

When Sue came to the paper a year before Toni left, the two work pals developed a warm friendship. Sue's ability to listen and communicate contributed to their excellent rapport.

And Sue needed a friend after her deceitful, cheating husband deserted her. So now a new boyfriend. Hmm, Toni wondered.

Toni turned back to Mike with her lips stretched and eyes shining. He seemed to squirm in response, almost uncomfortable in his well-padded executive chair. *Good grief: will he ever ask me out instead of wriggling in that chair?*

"That's all I need for today," she said. "Thanks. Emily will be thrilled. See ya later, Milner."

"Yeah. Have a good weekend, Jasper," he said, refocusing on his computer. Toni stood and pivoted. As she walked through the newsroom, she knew Mike was still within view. So she planted each step of her burgundy Bootie heels, engineering her stride to please the audience.

Since she no longer worked for the paper, Toni knew that they *could* date. For now, though, Mike exercised his editorial privilege to give in to her with merely a free, prime-placement ad. And that was all.

Chapter Two

Most customers regarded PinCo Bank's Seminole branch as a welcoming venue, in a hotel décor sort of way. But today, police loitered while tough, expressionless men and women in jackets labeled "FBI" strode in and out, stirring up the normally docile ambiance. Fortunately, the entry was not blocked. Not that a barricade would have stopped Toni Jasper.

She hesitated after one step across the threshold, scanning the interior for evidence of a crime. Spotting her good friend, eighty-three-year-old Chloe Ford, with a dejected expression exacerbated by a slumped posture, Toni darted over to her.

"I've been robbed," Chloe cried. "I came here to get my special sapphire and diamond ring, you know, the one my husband gave me. And it's gone."

Dropping into a seat next to her, Toni took her friend's hand.

"What happened?"

"I don't know. I remember putting it inside of my safe deposit box a few months ago."

Toni yearned to get the whole story. Even though she wasn't a reporter anymore, her inquisitiveness kicked into gear. Besides, she wanted to help her special pal.

Suddenly, bank-manager Emily charged out of her office, clearly frazzled. She peered down at the sad senior citizen.

"You're still here. Didn't you give your statement to the investigator?" Emily barked with a scowl at Chloe.

"Whoa," Toni said, glaring into the manager's eyes. "Obviously, she's in shock. I'm here to help."

"Thank you, dear," Chloe stated with affection directed toward her friend—strategically ignoring Emily.

"When you're done, Toni, come to my office," Emily retorted. "We have a meeting scheduled." The manager's heels clicked on the gleaming marble floor as she stomped to a hostile beat. Toni frowned at Emily's retreat. *She must be disappointed about this negative turn of events for her bank.*

Turning back to Chloe, Toni asked, "Are you okay to drive home?"

"Yes, I'm fine. I'm glad you were here." Chloe squeezed Toni's hand.

***

A bit ill at ease with federal officials hovering over most of the bank's staff, Toni stopped outside of Emily's door. The still-strident tone of her voice was hard to miss. So Toni averted her eyes, pretending not to listen.

"We'll talk about this when I get home," Emily growled. "I've got to go. The advertising woman's here." The irate manager slammed the phone down as Toni calmly waved to her from outside of the office.

"Come in," Emily ordered.

Toni sank into a cushioned seat in front of the mahogany desk.

"No one can believe this happened," Emily began, standing but leaning with her fists supporting her. "That Mrs. Ford thinks her ring was taken from the vault. Don't worry. We'll find the answer." In a quickly rediscovered professional tone, Emily assumed her on-stage persona and an erect stature. "Any news from the paper? Are they printing the bank's open house information?"

"Yes. I couldn't be happier," Toni answered with excitement, "especially since Monday's open house will be featured in the front-page corner. We don't even have to pay for it, which is a genuine break. They'll also run the complete event information inside. It's better than I hoped for."

"Excellent. What invitations do we need for the mayor, city council and anyone else important? My boss wants them all to be here. He's put a great deal of pressure on me, Toni. As I mentioned, we don't have a large budget. So we need to work smart."

7

"Let me draft some personalized letters for the city's VIPs and key local business owners. After you approve them, we'll print each one on your stationary and get your signature. Peggy and I will deliver them—just to be certain they get into the right hands. Businesses will be urged to bring their employees. That'll help the turnout."

"Perfect. When can you email me the letter? I need to run it by my superiors, and legal will want to sign off. You'll make the content similar to the press release that they already approved, right?"

"Yes. I'll send it from my office in a few hours. Will you be here all afternoon?"

Emily nodded. "I'll watch for that email."

"Good. Thank you, Emily. With your caterer and the nice giveaways, people will rethink their *personalized* banking experience and want to come *into* this bank."

Toni recognized that being the manager of a financial institution fit Emily's personality and talent. She enjoyed power, control and a fat salary, as she had told Toni—several times. Having grown up in a poor family, Emily said she drove herself to live a different life, one without monetary fears.

Two years ago after her promotion to an executive position, she and her husband bought their three-thousand-square-foot dream house. Emily got a two-carat diamond ring as well. She flaunted her gem in front of Toni and anyone else within sight in an effort to appear like she had "made it big"—even as a bank manager.

Toni glanced at Emily's jeweled hand as she rose to leave. *Yup, the ring's still flashy.* Just outside of Emily's door, she turned back.

"Oh by the way, those mugs we've ordered with the bank's logo were promised for Friday, so they should be here in the afternoon."

"Good. I meant to ask you about them. Thanks, Toni."

***

Chief investigator and liaison between the Sheriff's Office and local Seminole City officials, Detective Alan Dietz paced near the FBI huddle just outside the bank's front door. His distinguished salt-and-pepper hair added to his air of authority. When it came to commanding attention, his six-foot-three, slightly paunchy build didn't hurt.

Toni caught his eye and nodded. "Good morning, Alan. No one saw anything?"

"Do they ever?" he asked. "Look, Jasper, I don't have time to talk. Are you here on official business or merely checking on local crime?"

"Oh, you know me. I came for *serious* snooping. My friend Chloe Ford told me her precious sapphire and diamond ring vanished from the vault. Apparently, it was appraised at over ten thousand dollars."

"Yeah," Alan said. "Just when we assumed one place remained safe in this little burg. I can't believe this story's already been tweeted or something, and now it's all over the local TV news."

"It's on Twitter, Alan. I'm just glad you can operate a cell phone. How did you communicate in that big city?"

"Funny. Hope you didn't leave your fingerprints anywhere or the FBI'll have to drag you in for interrogation."

"Fingerprints *are* needed to get into the vault."

"Yes. That method *should* secure the entry." Detective Dietz lowered his voice. "Obviously, it's an inside job."

Toni whispered, "Inside job? Who in the world could access a vault that requires a personal code plus handprint set-up? And each box has its own key."

"Good points. Stay tuned."

"But I have a big open-house event for the bank on Monday. We need this cleared up ASAP—for publicity's sake. This bank's a top client for my agency."

"Yeah, right. Your company's needs are top of everyone's mind. You know that tomorrow, no one will even give this robbery a second thought."

"Except Mrs. Ford. I know her. She may come across as pretentious, but she's quite delightful, funny and sharp. Everyone loves her. I better go see what I can do for her."

Alan nodded. "Good idea. Just get out of the crime scene, Toni. Go away. I need to check in with the FBI."

Chapter Three

Toni revved her car up to full legal speed. The smooth engine hummed in contrast to the discord in Toni's brain.

This open house was supposed to be a no-brainer. Easy. Organized. Now FBI, a possible theft and God knows what else might interfere.

A few miles away, the well-manicured lawn surrounding the paver-brick driveway of upscale Pine Oak Place seemed to reach out and welcome Toni's moderately classy vehicle. She stepped out of her car and braced herself for a not-so-pleasant encounter with Chloe Ford.

The manager and marketing director for the "active, graceful lifestyle" assisted living residence, Bob Wolfe, strode ahead of Toni in the lobby.

"Hi, Bob," she said.

The man rotated his well-fed torso. The top button of his narrow, lapelled brown business suit was fastened, though strained as if it might pop in a heartbeat. Though his clothes were tailored, several strands of curly dark brown hair hung over his forehead, in an attractive yet relaxed fashion.

"Nice to see you," he said. "What's up? I didn't see your name on my schedule?"

"No meeting today, unless you want to plan an interim mailer to support that six-color newspaper insert."

"Good try. No. You've got plenty of this month's budget already."

"Actually, I'm here to visit my friend Chloe Ford. Do you know what happened at the bank today?"

"Of course. Our *shy* Chloe has informed almost everyone. She's convinced half of our residents to examine their safe deposit boxes. Who knows what will be left in that bank when she's through?"

"Is she upstairs?"

"No. Last I laid eyes on your Mrs. Ford she sat alone in the solarium. She needs to grieve for her lost jewels. Personally, I think she forgot the ring in some drawer in that large apartment. Besides, who else could get into her vault box?"

"Good question, but Chloe's as sharp as a tack. She wouldn't have misplaced her ring. I'll see what I can figure out. Talk with you later."

Toni and Chloe were, as Toni put it, nontraditional "BFFs" or Best Fashionable Friends. Last year, Toni had helped Chloe with a fundraiser fashion show at the city's new recreation center. When the event raised more money for the local children's hospital than either of them had anticipated, Toni became Chloe's personal hero.

Chloe's late husband had donated to the hospital even though they never had children of their own. She wanted to increase the annual contributions made in his name. After all, she whispered one day to Toni, "I wouldn't have this marvelous lifestyle if not for my hubby's success."

Toni crossed the threshold of the solarium and headed for her BFF. Engulfed in an overstuffed chair reflective of her plump five-foot-four body, Chloe stared out the floor-to-ceiling double-paned window toward the serenity of the "active lifestyle's" picture-perfect garden. Brutus, her Shih Tzu-poodle, lounged on her generous lap. Dog and owner spun around in unison at the tapping of Toni's heels.

"Hey, Chloe," Toni said.

She bent down to scratch behind the dog's ear and cooed, "Brutus, you good doggie." Brutus glanced up at Toni. *Amazing, the pooch always smiles.*

"Just checking on your bank episode recovery. I believe you put your ring in that vault."

"Ha." Chloe's long, desolate countenance contrasted the abrupt syllable. "You may be the only one. Even the FBI guy thinks I'm wacko. Toni, you know how I guard my jewels. Yes, I put the ring there a while ago. But someone stole it—I know they did."

Toni pulled up a flowery ottoman and leaned forward, elbows on her knees. "I want to know what happened. Of course, I'm not

11

allowed into the bank's inner sanctum, but I promise I'll see what I can find out. Okay?"

"I trust you, so please do what you can."

"I will. Tell me again. Is your large sapphire ring the only item missing?"

"Yes. And it can't be replaced. Frank had it made for my fiftieth birthday. Since our big dinner party is this month, I wanted to wear it."

"I realize this is heartbreaking. But I can't understand how anyone could have gotten into your safe deposit box."

"Good question. FBI agent wants me to look through the contents again to see if any other items are *misplaced*. He'll send his car back to pick me up."

"Good. But don't you think you should go to the hospital? I heard someone at the bank say they were worried when you fainted."

Chloe glared at Toni. "Are you kidding? That place's full of sick people. No way. And don't you ever take me there either. Do you hear me?"

"Yes, Ms. Feistiness." Toni acquiesced to Chloe with palms in the air. They were truly kindred strong-willed spirits. "Don't Fence Me In" could have been their personal theme song.

"Okay, when will the car be back?"

"After lunch, about one-thirty or so. This time, Brutus will go with me. If those nitwits don't believe me, I'll have him chomp on their ankles."

"Yeah. Like Brutus would ever do that. An attack dog he's not."

"That's what you think. He's on good behavior around you."

Toni chuckled, shaking her head. "You beast, Brutus." *Again that wet nose and silly grin. Fierce only in Chloe's fantasy.*

Toni bid her BFF farewell and wove her way through the resident group huddled in the lobby. The room reverberated with chatter about a conference with the bank's officers to quiz them on security. Toni knew that most of the residents entrusted their funds to the sacred financial fortress located close to their assisted-living facility. Now confidence seemed to be waning, to say the least. She smiled at those she recognized, their faces taut with concern.

Back in her car, Toni considered her options. She had promised to get an invitation-letter draft to Emily, yet felt compelled to go back to the paper to see what Mike knew. Only eleven- thirty. Maybe she could con him into taking her to lunch.

Toni steered her car toward downtown, or what they called a downtown in this normally uneventful bedroom community. The one-and two-story building cluster comprised the official heart of the town, housing the police station/mayoral office, post office, library, community center and newspaper offices. The only other big draw was the new Seminole City Center, a "dynamic and unique retail development" as the promotion materials boasted.

Toni figured a little "Mike interrogation" over a midday meal from a local eatery would provide more time with her favorite ex-editor, a chance to gather information and enough calories for the rest of the day. She had agency work and critical sleuthing to do and needed energy to dive into both.

In her reporter days, she'd ferreted out story facts no one thought were obtainable. Her responsibilities mainly involved being a news and features writer. But her research into the behind-the-scenes facts, as well as cost analysis in her reporting, had helped the publication's circulation numbers rise.

Mike liked when the revenue figures leaned more toward readership and circulation over ads as a result of what he deemed her pushiness. But now, did he miss her? She wanted more, career-wise *and* love-life-wise. If she could sweep Mike off his feet with a bear hug and a deeply-planted kiss in the middle of deadline, she would do it.

Chapter Four

The newsroom buzz exceeded decibels rarely known in an office setting.

"Unbelievable. The FBI's in town for some old bat's misplaced jewelry?"

Toni heard the bitter line from an unfamiliar voice as she approached Mike's corner of the large newsroom. She reacted in her own not-for-debate tone.

"That woman's not a bat. She didn't misplace anything."

"Come on, come on." Mike raised his voice as though he hadn't heard her. "Just do it, Harry. Get the story. Sarasota had bank robbers in the news last month. Maybe it's our turn. You're a reporter. Go and report."

Harry, Mike's new hire, marched away. But Toni was not about to leave.

"Okay, Jasper. What're you doing here? I got rid of you already for today."

"Look, about that bank robbery, the missing ring belongs to Chloe Ford, one of the sharpest senior citizens I know. She swears that ring was in her safe deposit box. And I believe her."

Toni aimed her mascara-lashed eyes to captivate her prey, or at least his attention. With lunch at stake, she made sure her eyes met his.

"Great. You believe her. I'm impressed," Mike said as he shuffled papers.

"Well . . . we could talk about it over lunch. Don't you buy today?"

"Damn it, don't I always buy our business lunches? Not today. Some of us have a deadline to meet." He frowned at her. Toni assumed he was still irritated over Harry's irascible behavior.

"Mike, come on. No one has to starve through editorial deletes and transposed words. Besides, accounting loves your expense account. Your ability to proofread needs nourishment. Won't you do a better job if you take a break on such a stressful day?"

Toni angled herself toward the Mike Milner wall of obstinacy. She watched him stare pensively at his desk. *Man, this is more difficult than landing a million-dollar client.*

"Okay."

His eyes relaxed and focused back on hers.

Victory.

He said with resignation, "You know I hate it when you're right."

"Did anyone ever tell you what a lousy liar you are? Where're we going?"

"The Bistro's close. I've got to get back soon."

***

Their round table hugged a wall just inside the door of the cozy local eatery. Art deco surroundings begged for loud discussions, and the open-pipe ceiling added to the big-city atmosphere in a traditional family-dining town.

Toni knew Mike didn't need a menu. He always knew what he wanted—or so he thought. She perused the menu and opted for one of her favorites.

Their waiter approached with his happy-service expression. "The usual, Mike?" Mike nodded with a seriousness that only a newsman could bring to lunch.

"And you, Toni?"

"I'll have the Blackened Shrimp Salad. Blue cheese on the side, Alberto."

Toni watched the waiter amble off to the kitchen. Without extra ears around, she was eager to bounce ideas off Mike. Something about the gem heist bugged her, more than her faith in Chloe's memory. She couldn't pinpoint what. After all, inquisitiveness made her a good reporter. As opposed to Harry, she thought. *What in the world had motivated Mike to hire him? Today, he wasn't even agreeable to do his job and check out a big story.*

"So, what did you see in that Harry when you hired him?" she asked.

Toni's question broke Mike's faraway gaze. "Huh? Oh him. He looked good on paper. Came from a large, daily publication."

"Came? Or was tossed here?"

Mike smiled. She knew her transparency was one of the things he genuinely liked about her, so she felt comfortable to speak her mind.

"Now this robbery—" she continued.

"*Alleged* robbery," he corrected.

"Okay. I'll humor you for the sake of objectiveness. It just doesn't make sense. Who the hell could've gotten into that safe deposit box, let alone the ironclad vault? Chloe swears her expensive sapphire ring *was* in the vault."

"That's the only item taken?" Mike said. "Well, the FBI needed to be involved anyway."   "The agent wants Chloe to look through her entire box again. When she saw her priceless ring had vanished, she collapsed. I'm sure she felt mortified to have fainted in front of everyone. You know what a classy lady she is."

"Yes. I remember meeting her at that darn fashion fiasco you dragged me to and robbed me to boot."

"Fiasco my ass. You had a great time and you know it. Besides, your frugal contribution went to a very good cause." Toni pouted at him. Then saw the glint in his eye.

"I donated one thousand hard-earned buckaroos, madam fleece-my-account."

Toni knew he enjoyed teasing her and happily played into the banter. She leaned toward him and said, "We aim to fleece."

Mike chuckled and leaned back, his eyes gazing into hers.

After a quiet minute, Toni persisted in her quest. "I spoke with Alan Dietz at the bank, and he thinks it's an inside job."

"You went to the bank? In FBI company, no less. And . . . they let you go?"

"Very funny. I had an appointment with Emily. By the way, she's grateful for the front page ad. She's been quite concerned about their big event. I've never seen her quite this frazzled."

"Someone *allegedly* robbed the vault. And lurking FBI agents don't present a welcome-mat tone to bank patrons or employees."

"I'm serious. People at the bank have master keys to the vault. What if an employee did get into Chloe's box without authorization? And that assumption certainly begs the question of how *did* they get past the handprint entry?"

Plates of succulent shrimp perched on crisp romaine lettuce and a hot hamburger with steamy fries were placed in front of them. With her focus on their discussion, Toni had not even noticed Alberto's somewhat covert approach.

"Looks good," Toni said.

"Thanks, buddy," Mike uttered. "This is good, Jasper." He nodded as he chomped into the bun-clad burger. "You were right. I needed a break. No typo will go undetected this afternoon."

"You need a lot of things."

"Hey," he retorted. "Listen to who's obsessed over this bank thing? You need to worry about your own job. Law enforcement will manage criminal activity. You're not a reporter anymore. Your business needs you."

Toni was pleased that Mike supported her new business.

"Right. And you've got Harry. How could I have forgotten?"

They munched in silence for a few minutes. Then Toni continued, "People I work with and care about have been affected by today's news. I want to know what happened."

"I know. You're a caring person. But this isn't an area to waste your time on. Let the FBI handle it—if it's a robbery. For now, I'll give Mrs. Ford the benefit of the doubt. It could be a big deal."

"Exactly. Besides if there's any way I can help Chloe or Emily or both, I want to."

As they finished their meal, Alberto slid the check onto the table. He smiled with a nod toward Mike and a slight bow for Toni. The editor snatched the receipt and dug into his wallet.

"Your nosiness surfaces no matter what," he said as he stood up. "Come on, Jasper. Some of us have a real job to get back to."

Toni kidded, "I've had just about enough of you, too, Milner."

Mike deposited a large bill on the table. The ever-vigilant Alberto called his thanks.

"Have a good one," Mike responded.

They walked with brisk strides back to the newspaper building.

"I'm not letting this go," Toni asserted as she turned toward her car. "There's something weird going on. I can feel it in my bones."

"Then get a good chiropractor. This is a federal matter. Seriously, it's a wild goose chase at best."

"I remember when you supported my hunches."

"That was then. Not now. Besides, as you continue to point out, I have Harry—whom I better go investigate myself."

"Thanks for lunch."

"You're welcome. Now go away." Toni saw Mike's warm smile as he turned away from her. She loved his lighthearted wit.

That's the second person to tell me to "go away" today. It must be a sign that I'd better get my best sleuthing brains in gear. This investigation needs me.

Chapter Five

In spite of her curious mind eager for input, Toni headed for her office, her paying job. She knew if she wanted to maintain a salary, her clients required attention. The two-room ad agency "headquarters," as dubbed by Toni and her part-time associate Peggy Conway, housed three desks, a copy/scan/fax machine, several filing cabinets, a storage cabinet and a small conference table—just what the duo needed to run an efficient business. On occasion, one of their freelance artists or clients would occupy the spare desk.

The coffee machine rested on a small shelf just inside the main office door. Neatly lined up beside it, regular sugar, brown sugar and utensils were in reach. The nonfat milk, water bottles and cheese snacks resided in the Igloo mini fridge on the floor.

As Toni waltzed in, Peggy hung up her phone. "Press proofs are ready for the Pine Oak Place newsletter," she said.

"Terrific. Can you go to the printer and check them out? Watch that there's no goof-up with the color on the text like last time. The photos usually come out nice. But Meredith told me they got new equipment, so look through all the pages."

"Will do. Precision Printing's expecting one of us by three o'clock. They want to print the job tonight. Anything new for the bank event? Any brochures, flyers or ads?"

"Emily is sticking with mugs. I have to get the community officials' invitation letter emailed to her right away. We did get the *Gazette's* front-page lead corner for free."

"Excellent."

Toni sat in front of her computer. Pulling up the bank's file, she re-read the letter draft she'd written several days before. No typos. Click. Upload. Send.

"Your favorite editor, I assume," Peggy said with certainty after Toni's computer clicking ceased.

"What?"

"The free ad."

"Got that right," Toni said. "I stopped by the paper this morning before I went to see Emily. Did you hear about the robbery?"

"What robbery? I haven't turned on the radio."

"At our bank of all places, PinCo. Emily's pretty edgy about the whole thing. On the other hand, she still wants to proceed as if nothing's happened. I don't know. It's strange."

"Ya think? Robberies are usually upsetting, not our everyday activity."

"I mean something else. My gut feeling is a bit off-kilter."

No one understands what I mean. I should focus while I'm here. But the bank scenario is so weird.

"Toni, you're not a reporter anymore. What was taken anyway?"

"Chloe Ford's one-of-a-kind sapphire and diamond ring," Toni said.

"One ring. That's a pretty picky robber. How'd they know it was gone?"

"Poor Chloe went to get it for a special dinner. Apparently, she fainted in front of God and the world. Poor thing. And no one believes her claim that it was stolen, so she's pretty annoyed. Even the FBI thinks she misplaced it."

"Did you see her at the bank?"

"Yes, then I went to Pine Oak to talk with her. I saw Alan at the bank, too. But he wouldn't tell me anything. Or couldn't with FBI agents all around. But Emily waved me in for our meeting, almost like normal."

"So no other items are gone?"

"Not yet. The FBI agent in charge wants Chloe back at the bank for a full inventory of her belongings."

"Not yet," Peggy echoed. "What the hell does that mean?"

Peggy's petit, slim figure and loose-curled auburn hair did not portray her true strength, physically or character-wise. Together in several study groups in graduate school, Toni and Peggy had developed more than a professional friendship. They stood by each other in projects, yet could easily butt heads. In the end, the outcome landed them both in a better position.

With Peggy's two young children in school, Toni had the perfect assistant. Not too many hours so not too much financial expense. In the office during the elementary classroom timeframe, Peggy proved to be as invaluable an asset as any partner. Since she valued Peggy's input and skills, Toni delegated important tasks to her. Peggy always came through.

"It means," Toni said, "I'm going to go and support Chloe at the bank. Maybe I can pick up some more information while I'm there."

"They'll let you in the vault?" Peggy asked.

"Absolutely. I'll be with my pal. She may be there now. The FBI car picked her up at one-thirty. Gotta run. I'll swing by the deli's office afterwards. They should have this month's direct mail information ready."

"Glad you remember we run an ad business here. We're not P.I.s."

"Other people have mentioned that already today. Et tu Brute?"

"Can't take a hint? Alright. Go and sleuth. I'll run the show—your loyal part-timer."

Toni caught Peggy's eye. "Sarcasm truly is your best quality," she said with a failed attempt not to laugh.

"Very funny."

As she closed the door behind her, Toni saw Peggy's smirk. Their ribbing made the tough days good and the good days better.

I'm lucky to have you, Peggy, don't I know it.

Chapter Six

Toni spotted the plain, glossy black vehicle occupying the bank's "reserved parking" spot. By now, Chloe, Brutus and the FBI investigator had to be deep in their analysis of her safe deposit box contents.

Toni maneuvered her little car into the end spot and jumped out, ready to help her friend through her jewelry-analysis process. No law enforcement officials guarded the entrance.

As she walked up the sidewalk, Toni spotted Emily at the corner of the building in animated conversation with her brother-in-law, Jesse Morton. The high volume suggested a disagreement, but Toni was unable to make out the words. Jesse's large-boned frame, jet black hair and angry expression manifested an ominous look, though Toni imagined that Emily could hold her own, even at ten inches shorter.

I wonder why, after his ex-wife Debra divorced him almost a year ago, Jesse chose to relocate here, close to Debra's brother, Jon and his wife Emily? It just seems odd that Jesse should be so close to Jon and Emily after what happened.

Toni recalled Emily's story about the sudden divorce and Debra's subsequent refusal to communicate with her brother. Rumor was that no one had seen or heard much from Debra. Only a couple of postcards had been mailed from Orlando.

Okay. It's their business. Then again, if Debra's as close as Orlando, wouldn't she want to see her brother? Of course, families don't always get along.

Once again, Toni's super-sleuth gut gripped her as her suspicions rose, parallel in intensity to the pair's vocal tones. Toni knew Jesse handled some electronic security for the bank. But he wasn't an employee. Emily had hired him as an independent contractor.

Could Jesse be connected to the bank robbery? Does Emily know? Did Debra realize he was up to no good even a year ago? Did she want to get away from him?

As she walked through the lobby, Toni could hear Chloe's insistent verbiage emanating from the inside the vault. "I am not imagining it."

"Hello," Toni called as she approached the steel door. Two heads—one senior woman and one FBI man—snapped toward the door. Attached to Chloe's wrist by a loose tether, Brutus lounged close by on the floor. The pooch watched Toni approach but uttered no sound.

"Praise the lord. Get in here. Agent Nelson, my good friend Toni Jasper can vouch for my sanity."

"Ms. Jasper. I'm Special Agent George Nelson assigned to assist Mrs. Ford," said the blond, six-foot-two lanky federal official as he extended a hand. Hardly the appearance of high-level authority, the agent possessed a boyish, upturned nose and light-blue eyes. Toni perceived him as easy prey for her tactics though she noted the official badge hanging from his jacket pocket.

"Assist?" Chloe said. "All I hear is accusations, young man. I did not remove or misplace my ring. I put it in here a few months ago. After our Easter dinner. I'm positive."

"Mrs. Ford, you possess a number of valuable pieces of jewelry. Can we go through recent events once more?" The FBI agent's voice remained calm and steady as he lowered the velvet hammer of interrogation.

"Young man, I am not senile. Granted you are somewhat polite, but my patience is on thin ice. My sapphire ring is unique and special. I know I put it in this box. I only wear my valuable jewels during the holidays or for special events. Therefore, that ring should have been in this box. Why in God's name isn't it here?"

Though a recent addition to the FBI, Agent George Nelson had a reputation of a trusted official who possessed a natural finesse to handle delicate situations. Perhaps, Toni assumed, the agent figured he'd get an admission of forgetfulness out of the spry octogenarian. So far, no success. Chloe held strong.

"Do you have an inventory sheet?" the agent asked. "Some type of record as to what you brought with you last time you were here? The log states that you last entered your box in April. That's five months ago, ma'am."

Toni reached around Chloe's plump shoulders with a comfortable embrace while her cheerful wide eyes focused on the agent's serious ones.

"I have worked with Mrs. Ford on complicated projects," Toni said. "If she absolutely affirms she put her ring in this box, then I believe her."

"It's not that we don't believe Mrs. Ford," Agent Nelson pleaded. "We have to verify. At this point, little evidence suggests a robbery. Nothing confirms that any another person entered this specific safe deposit box."

"I don't care what the log shows. Mrs. Ford is quite proud and possessive of her gems. She wouldn't misplace any of them."

Chloe's head turned from the short Toni to the tall government man as the two talked about her. "I'm right here, you know. And I'm tired of this babbling," she said.

Both agent and ad exec looked at Chloe without a response.

Turning to the FBI agent, Toni asked, "Who else have you talked to?"

Toni Jasper has her own version of interrogation. Just ask my suppliers if I let them get away with shoddy work. I can ask tough questions, too, buddy.

"We're speaking with everyone involved."

"That includes just whom?" Toni fired back.

"Everyone present in the bank when it opened today."

"Such as—"

"Ms. Jasper, the FBI knows how to do its job, myself included. I've been assigned to help, as I pointed out. Please allow me to do what I need to do without any further interference."

"I'm here to help, too." Toni was determined to stand her investigative ground. "I mean, how well do you know Chloe Ford? Are you familiar with this bank branch? In various capacities, I have worked with the branch manager and vice presidents for years."

"And what capacities are those?"

"For one, as a news reporter for the paper."

"The *Tampa Bay Times*? I don't recall your byline."

"No, the *Woodlands Gazette*. But in any case, I can feel that some fact is missing."

Obviously exasperated, the FBI authority took a step back. "I can see we're not making progress here. Mrs. Ford, can I give you a ride home?"

Chloe turned an inquisitive face toward Toni.

"I'm sorry. I have quite a bit to do. I'm sure Agent Nelson will be happy to drive you."

Chloe uttered a low but audible grunt. Toni lent a hand to slide the large box back into its slot, then hugged Chloe.

"Thank you, Agent Nelson," Toni said offering a farewell hand shake.

***

Toni decided to hang around the bank and pick up clues. After all, she thought, some evidence had to be there. So what if the FBI didn't have it yet? Toni's gut feeling was often on the mark. She figured Ray must have a clue.

Ray Edwards, long-time bank vice president and Chloe's personal investment banker, stared at his computer screen, picking up his coffee without even a turn of the head. Toni marched up to his cubicle.

"Hi, Ray," Toni said, stepping just inside his cubicle.

Ray's shoulders made an abrupt and small shudder. After a few quick taps on his keyboard, he swung around in his chair and sent an exaggerated smile in Toni's direction.

"Toni," he chimed with his enthusiastic yet classic nobleman manner. Ray exuded courtesy and friendliness in an old-fashioned way. His expensive navy-blue suit, snow white hair and strong facial features completed the refined impression. He stood and rounded the table to pull a plaid-upholstered chair out from its spot tucked under the desk.

"I saw you come in. Have a seat. How is our Chloe doing?"

Positioning herself on the edge of the chair, she leaned toward the executive.

"You know Chloe. Unsinkable despite any FBI over flow." They both chuckled. "I'm surprised that you weren't in the vault with her just now. I came for extra support. I thought you'd be alongside her as usual."

"I'm always here for Chloe. This time, I presumed the FBI agent would handle the situation just fine. I didn't want to be in the way."

"Very thoughtful. Now what're they doing now to find Chloe's ring?"

"Well," Ray turned on his best southern charm. "Chloe is a lovely person. But she is getting on in years."

"What the hell does that mean? Good God. You've worked with Chloe for the last two years. I can't believe you think of her as *old*."

"It's hard for younger people like you to see. But I'm closer to Chloe's age even though I'm about twenty years younger. The mind begins to cloud up a bit."

"Are you crazy? You know that's bull. The woman is one of the sharpest people I know for any age. What the hell's going on?"

"Toni, calm down. I want to make an effort to be realistic—"

"Yeah. Right." Toni stood with a force that nearly toppled the chair and turned toward the door. "When you come to your senses, let me know."

"Just let it go," Ray said with a somber tone.

Toni's loud heel clicks echoed through the bank's pristine lobby. The tellers and loan officers operated as if all was back to normal. Was it? Toni's gut suspicions now gnawed at her brain. But an appointment with one of her freelance artists forced her to delay further sleuthing. Not that her thoughts didn't race ahead.

After a jump into her car, she sped toward her office without a glance at the speedometer, her mind still on the oddities of the day's events.

I have to focus. I have a deadline for the hospital billboard. Peggy's super but the business won't run itself. Thank God she's got plenty of patience with me.

Toni had already figured out the approach for the board's art and the message. She needed her artist, Brad, to pull it all together. The deadline would be here soon, and the billboard company required almost a week to produce the vinyl banner.

She hopped out of her car in her usual parking spot and gasped to see Detective Alan Dietz staring at her from inside his unmarked police car.

"Alan, aren't you the sneaky type," she said.

"Do you have any idea how fast that little car of yours flew here?" His long, drawn-out words left Toni speechless. "I know you're upset about your friend and the bank. But you still have to drive like a good citizen."

"I've got a lot on my mind."

"That line's your new and improved excuse? Lord, help us."

"Okay, okay. Will you apprehend me, Detective?"

"No. But you're on alert. Just cool it. Everything's fine for now. Our good citizens are safe."

"Fine? For a law enforcement guy, your inquisitive powers amaze me."

"Come on. The FBI's handling the investigation. It's not my jurisdiction."

"Investigation? And that includes harassment of an honorable woman like Chloe Ford?"

"Just go up to your office and work. If anything develops, I promise to keep you *out of the loop*." The police investigator looked up at the petulant woman and spoke with a loud voice to emphasize his point.

"You're not a reporter anymore," he continued, "go advertise or publicize or whatever it is you do in those rooms."

"You know, Alan, you used to be a nice guy—for a cop."

"Have a lovely day, *sweetie*." Alan's boyish smirk reflected his mischievous intent.

"I'm not your sweetie and don't you forget it," she called as he drove away.

Toni almost smiled but acted her part of the offended female. She made people aware, in particular the esteemed City of Seminole investigator, that she regarded herself as nobody's sweetie, hon, dear, or any other demeaning name. But she knew Detective Dietz liked to rattle her when he could.

That Alan. Maybe he's right. I should give up my quest. Heck no, he's not right. But I do have a business to run. Damn, I'm late for the appointment.

Alan saluted as he turned out of the parking lot. Toni gave into a little smile. He deserved at least a pleasant look for not issuing her a ticket. But she'd catch up with him later for more information. In the years Toni had known Alan Dietz, she'd regarded him as a by-the-book guy, yet fair when regulations needed slight bending. And for that, she was grateful.

Chapter Seven

Outside of Toni's office door, Brad (short for Ed Bradbury) appeared to support the door jamb as he leaned on it with his six-foot, muscular body. The man's usual brawny yet artistic appearance included disheveled light-brown hair, a tie-dyed t-shirt and well-worn jeans punctuated with holes as if to confirm his creative image. As much as Toni loved her designer jeans, she couldn't imagine buying a pair that already looked worn out. And paying a high price to boot.

"About time." Brad said with a grin.

Toni had known Brad for a couple of years from the chamber. He'd started working with her when she began her agency. At first, she worried how to fire him if his graphic art ability didn't demonstrate the talent she needed. But his creativity was evident and he strictly adhered to deadlines—just like now. Brad stood at her door, right on time.

"Sorry. Peggy's off with her eagle-eyes to scour press proofs for significant misuse of color. I had to do a little digging at the bank."

"Digging? Is that a new business strategy? Or is it nouveau P.R.?"

"Good thing I didn't hire you for your wit." They laughed while taking their places at the small conference table.

"The hospital construction is well underway," Toni said. "Have you driven by lately?"

"Not in a few days. But last I saw, it seemed like it was headed in the right direction."

"Good. So, time for the next billboard to announce the medical specialties that are re-locating into the new wing. Here are the notes from my last meeting with their P. R. director along with my ideas. She liked what we did for the first board, so carry on with the overall theme. Can you email me a design in two days? I'll need another few days to get it approved even though the overall theme is the same."

"Not a problem. Do they want the same colors for the specialties? I'd like to reserve the hospital colors just for the logo. Then do a bright design that is a bit wild to denote the specialties."

"I like it. Just remember, these are conservative medical types. They've given us some pretty good leeway so far. I want to keep them in 'yes' mode."

"Got it," Brad said. "But remind them that change needs to *seem* fun for those concerned, employees *and* patients."

They both knew how these particular executives had suffered through two years of the first phases of the building's construction. She figured they were chomping at the bit now to have it all done.

"I know," Toni said. "They appear to have their panic attacks under control. If not, they can add a relaxation room and inhale deep breaths." They both grinned.

"Thanks. I'll call to confirm my appointment next time."

"I knew you'd be here. I even risked a speeding ticket to get back to the office. Didn't you see Detective Dietz outside in lecture-mode with me?"

"No. Darn. I always miss the good stuff. Oh well. Take it easy."

***

Toni closed the door and headed for her desk. The phone rang as she pulled up her chair. "Jasper Advertising and P.R." she answered. "This is Toni. How can I help you?"

"It's Chloe. I'm home now. And I must say that I'm more than frustrated."

"I understand. But I don't know how to help since the FBI is in charge. Have you spoken with your insurance company?"

"No. I'll call them now. Can you come for dinner tonight? It's friends and family night in the dining room. And you're the best friend I have right now."

"Sure. I'd be delighted. What time?"

"Come over at five. Don't expect gourmet but the food's pretty good. About the same as the lunches you've had."

"I'm easy when it comes to food. I'll meet you in the dining room, okay?" Toni's little food fib would do for the evening. When it came to edibles, she was quite particular.

"Perfect," Chloe said and hung up.

Toni pulled out the agency's weekly job list and scanned down to check the status of all production and client meetings. *Good. Under control, for the moment.*

After she completed calls to set up appointments for the next week, Toni updated the office schedule. She made the requisite copy for Peggy and placed it on her associate's desk. Locking the office, Toni headed for a pleasant evening with her friend—or as unstressed as she could make it. *Maybe I can lift Chloe's spirits.*

Chapter Eight

The stylish dining room at Pine Oak Place seated one-hundred-and-fifty seniors and their guests. Classic Parsons chairs with deep purple and sea green print covers surrounded square tables. When Toni approached, a low hum of conversation with laughter interjected every few minutes told her most of the diners had already arrived. She scanned a wide area for Chloe and saw a hand beckoning. Toni smiled and stepped forward toward the table.

"Just a minute, young lady." A short, stocky, bald man grabbed Toni's elbow. "Aren't you that reporter?"

"Hi, Walter." Toni stopped, recognizing the man. "I'm not a reporter anymore. I own an advertising agency now."

"Yeah, but your news stories were good. I used to read them. You got to the bottom of things. I liked that."

"I know. You told me before, and I appreciate it." Toni wanted to get over to Chloe who stretched and craned her neck to see what delayed her friend in the middle of the room. Toni tried to pull away, but the man held tight.

"My wife and I are not usually here in September. We stay up north until January so we can have Christmas with the grandkids."

Toni nodded. "Glad you're here early, Walter."

"But that's the point. Our schedule's off. We know what happened to Chloe Ford. My wife and I swear we put our stuff in our safe deposit box, and now some of it's missing. You must be on the case." His grip stayed strong. Toni couldn't break free.

"Truly, I'm flattered. But the FBI is handling everything. I am not an investigator anymore." Toni hoped he wouldn't detect her hesitation. "I *do* need to go. Chloe is expecting me. See." She pointed as she emphasized, "Chloe's waving at me." Over the sea of gray heads and ornate, brightly-covered chairs, an animated hand beckoned.

"Okay, okay," Walter said and loosened his grip, "but we're not done here. My wife and I are seated at this table." Toni glanced over Walter's shoulder, smiled and nodded toward the diminutive, white-haired lady. "We want to talk to you. Tonight. Got it?" Walter's insistence left Toni with an uneasy feeling.

"That's fine. When dinner is over, I'll come back. I'd be happy to speak with you both. But right now, Chloe needs me. I don't mean to be rude, but I promised I'd have dinner with her."

"Just promise that you'll come back in an hour or so. We go to bed early. And this is important."

"I promise," Toni reassured the man as she moved on, at last free from his ironclad hold.

After a quick hug with her BFF pal, Toni took her seat next to Chloe. "Sorry. Walter's a pretty strong guy. I had a heck of a time after his death grip took hold."

"He ran a large business, so he knows how to get his way. Fitness centers, I believe."

"No kidding. He's pretty fit, I can say that. What does he want anyway?"

"An answer. They're concerned about the theft. In fact, several other residents want to speak with you. I told them you're on the case."

"What?" Toni said. "What case is that? You realize I own an ad agency now. Besides, I get stonewalled every time I ask a question."

Toni could feel the blood rushing to her face. *I have to become a better fibber.*

"I knew it. You *are* snooping—as you used to say in your reporter days."

"I am *not* snooping." Toni almost choked on her words. *I'm not on the case. I'm just asking questions. Curious.*

"We'll see about that. Besides, I've known you long enough to know when you're lying."

"Chloe Ford. I am not lying. Well maybe. A little." Toni smiled.

"Good. I hope you're hungry. I've ordered for both of us: stuffed fillet of sole with crab meat. If I can't beat that FBI agent, I might as well chew on something just like him. Stuffed and tough . . . with crabbiness thrown in."

Toni laughed. "You're mean. Agent Nelson had a job to do, and he tried to do it." *Well, tried is the key word.*

"Yes, I know. He tried my patience, and then you made me ride home with him."

"I had a meeting. In fact, I ended up being late for it."

Plates of broiled fillet of sole were laid on the table in front of them.

"Oh, thank you, Millie. Toni and I are in a heated debate here. I didn't see you walk over."

"Hi, Mrs. Ford," the server said, "I hope you win."

Toni shot a shocked look at the woman who grinned in return as she walked away.

"So you think you've got everyone wrapped around your pinky finger?" Toni asked.

"Only the special people. Seriously, we do have a problem. I'm not the only one who's had valuables vanish from the vault of this PinCo's branch. Now Walter and his wife have, too."

"Walter made his point when I walked in. I have to listen to him again in a few minutes. But they've been away for months. Are they positive they didn't leave these things up north?" *I need facts. Evidence.*

"To think I used to believe in you, Toni." Chloe sat back shaking her head.

"All right. I will give them the benefit of the doubt. But only two are questionable out of how many safe deposit boxes?"

"For now. The whole thing stinks, and I bet snooty Emily is in on it. She never did give me much time, always too busy and so utterly official."

"She's fine, just has a lot on her plate. I was surprised Ray didn't go into the vault with you. He's usually glued to your side whenever you're there." Toni knew that Ray was dedicated to his customers. But Chloe appeared to be his favorite.

"He did greet me when I got there. The FBI shooed him away."

Toni shook her head. She and Chloe picked up their forks, aimed at their tiramisu cake slices and savored every bite. With each forkful, Toni realized the pow-wow with Walter and his wife got closer.

I'm not an investigator. So why the hell am I so curious? Keep denying the crime, Toni. Run your damn business, Jasper.

After a little more chit chat, Toni and Chloe rose from the table. "I'm ready to go home," Chloe affirmed. "You can handle Walter by yourself. Just be nice to him, Toni."

"Yes, ma'am." Toni saluted in military fashion.

***

Even though their empty plates had long since been cleared away, Walter and his wife hadn't budged from their seats. The table held only their water glasses and the bowl of sugar substitute packets. Toni took her seat in the chair next to Walter. She didn't want to seem adversarial by sitting and staring at him from across the table. She said hello to his wife, and then looked directly into his eyes.

"Here I am as promised, Walter. What's up?" She didn't want the couple to think that she was there to *investigate*, so she hoped to keep the mood somewhat light with Walter, if possible.

"I'll tell you what's up," the former executive growled. "Robbery. And not one of those bank officers seems to care."

"From the bank vault, right? Can I ask what items were taken?"

"Yes. Valuable items I know I put in my safe deposit box. Just like Chloe. I told the FBI agent, but the guy thinks I'm a nut as do the bank execs."

"You spoke to Agent Nelson? He is doing his best." *Another fib. I should've said trying his best.*

"Best? Whose side are you on, missy? My bonds are gone. And my social security card. I never take that out. And I put those bonds in there before we went home for the summer."

"Walter, I don't doubt you. But are you certain?"

"Yes, I am absolutely convinced," he emphasized.

"What's the FBI's plan of action to find your bonds?"

"Not a damn thing that I know of. They need to be redeemed but don't mature for another two years. I want to get 'em back before some sleazeball impersonates me."

"I'd like to help both of you, but I don't see what I can do," Toni pleaded with as much empathy as she could muster. In reality, her blood pressure seemed to climb to a new high.

This can't be a coincidence. Valuable bonds? A one-of-a-kind, expensive ring? What's going on?

Toni looked from Walter's wife, who never uttered a word, back to Walter. "If I learn of any developments, I'll let you know. You have my word. Just remember, I'm not a reporter anymore. The FBI is running this investigation."

"Some investigation," Walter stated with a snort. "Where's the forensics team? They didn't even fingerprint Hilde and me for the elimination record." The frail non-talkative woman on the other side of Walter only nodded sheepishly.

Toni bid farewell to the Walter team. She passed the Pine Oak front desk guardians as she strolled to her car, hardly aware of her surroundings as the night's revelations reverberated in her head. Driving home, Toni felt her brain ache with the day's events weighing her thoughts. She couldn't wait to get home to Tylenol and a hot shower.

Fortunately, her meeting schedule had been kept open for the next day. She needed time on Friday to handle anything that came up before the bank's event on Monday. She'd have to check that the logo-engraved-mug delivery arrived at her office in good condition and was transported to Emily's office. The UPS online link had assured her of a definite Friday delivery. Now she realized how opportune the situation had become. Some snooping time could be worked in. Since she'd been appointed by Emily to act as the greeter on Monday, she could truly keep an eye on any suspicious activity.

A familiar cell ringtone blared just after Toni pulled into her condo complex. Peggy. *Why in the world would she call me at this hour?*

"Hey, Peggy. What's up?"

"You won't believe it. On a whim, I checked the office email, and the bank has cancelled Monday's open house. The email came from the bank's executive office. We're screwed. The mugs, the caterer. Before I left today, I spoke with the Stuffed Onion and guaranteed our order."

"What? Good God. Okay, relax. The bank will still pay for the mugs. They can use them anytime. Call the caterer first thing. Maybe they'll let us all off the hook. I don't think they've made those little sandwiches yet. What'd Emily say?"

"I didn't see an email from Emily."

"That's strange. She communicates pretty well. This certainly should be one of those times. Don't worry about it. But hey, thanks for your diligence and the call. Seriously, what would I do without you?"

Toni hung up, worry surpassed curiosity. The number of inconsistencies had now grown beyond the point of coincidence, and she felt uncomfortable with her increased anxiety.

***

After a dash to the kitchen cabinet at the far end of the room, Toni grasped the knob and opened the door. The tight top of the Tylenol bottle almost proved too big a match for the pained ad exec.

The hell with curious. I'm way beyond worry. Now, I'm mad.

She charged up the steps to her loft, sat in front of her laptop and signed on. She scrolled down to the email from the bank. Peggy told her it came from one of the home office bigwig execs. Not a positive read, it only made her head throb more. She looked for something—anything—sent from Emily. Nothing.

Toni rested her arms on the desk, fingers frozen over the keyboard. What now? She pondered assessing the options. Should she call Mike? Could she call him? He'd be home by now.

Oh damn. What would he say? But I want answers even at this hour.

After fifteen minutes of exhausting all possible alternatives, Toni decided on a shower—a long one. She always came up with her best ideas in the shower.

Chapter Nine

After hours of on and off sleep, Toni climbed out of bed and peered into her closet. Friday's former agenda called for another casual-dress day. But now, the landscape had changed. The situation required an inquisition and a brightly-colored suit. Those bankers might dress in black and blue, but her attire would make a statement. Don't mess with Jasper.

Her current corporate finances rested on whether the bank agreed to pay the caterer's cancellation fee. How dumb. She hadn't thought to amend that stipulation in the contract. But businesses didn't cancel their social events in sleepy Seminole, and this bank shouldn't have either. Not when their image was at stake. Of course, the so-called robbery precluded the air of festivity.

After taking extra time with her makeup, Toni donned a crimson, tailored pantsuit. An off-white blouse with a neck bow completed her corporate look. She swept her long hair into a stylish low knot. Gulps of orange juice helped her swallow a daily dose of vitamins and supplements. Ready in the refrigerator, her iced coffee provided the requisite caffeine hit. After several big spoons of yogurt with a few blueberries tossed in, she was ready. Toni grabbed her black faux-leather shoulder bag and headed out on her mission.

***

"Morning, sunshine." Toni strode toward Mike's desk, medium coffee cups clutched in both hands with a Dunkin' Donut munchkin box hanging from an unoccupied finger.

"Jasper. Bribing again?" Mike reached for a munchkin. "Good. You can have *anything* today. I'm starved. Is that my coffee?"

"Yup. You seem to be in a good mood. What gives?"

"The sheriff up in Pasco County may be closer to identifying the body they found yesterday."

"Closer?" Toni echoed.

"Yeah, but they're not revealing any specifics. Hey, push those little donut devils over here."

"And nothing stops your appetite. Was that Seminole Plait badge significant?"

"Toni, what about 'not revealing' is unclear?"

"Mike, it's me."

"I know. You are not my reporter anymore."

"Okay, okay. But I'm glad your Friday's fantastic, at least in Milner style. Want to hear my news?"

"Another fashion show? Count me out this time." Mike slurped his coffee while attempting to hide a smile. But Toni caught it.

"No," she stated flatly. "But I detect an eager expression of runway anticipation. Seriously, the bank cancelled Monday's open house."

"Yeah, I heard."

"What? You knew?"

"Yeah, someone from the corporate office cancelled the press release. No explanation, though. What's the reason they gave you?"

"Not much of one. Our corporate email explained that due to scheduling conflicts with personnel, they had to postpone. I didn't get an email from Emily either last night or this morning. My next stop is the bank."

"Fine. Thanks for breakfast." Mike turned back toward his waiting computer screen.

"Wait a minute. Last night, I had dinner at Pine Oak. Other residents had items taken from their safe deposit boxes."

"I know. The FBI guy called me and asked the paper not to print any of these unsubstantiated allegations."

"You knew that, too?" Toni asked, exasperation elevating her tone. "So, is he concerned?"

"No. Just fed up. He's going back to the Tampa office today. No more questioning."

"He can't do that."

"Actually, he can and he did. Geez, you don't sound like an ad exec today, but you look terrific. Who're you conning for lunch today?"

"Humph," Toni grunted. "I'm getting to the bottom of this bank heist. At least two safe deposit boxes were violated and an event Emily and I had planned for weeks was abruptly cancelled. Doesn't something—anything—about this seem suspicious?"

"Hasn't coincidence crept into that brain of yours? People forget stuff, especially senior citizens." Mike's hand went up in response to Toni's abrupt look of protest. "I understand your Chloe Ford is quite the sharp exception. But, Toni, let the crime beat go. Talk to Emily. My money's on her rescheduling soon."

"On my way." Toni pulled out her cell phone and punched a code to unlock the screen. "Still no email from her. Good grief. Bye."

Toni stood and headed for the door. "Hey, thanks again for the munchkins." Mike called after her. She barely heard. Her gut feeling reared its ugly presence again.

Maybe the top brass took the vault violation seriously—ah yes, alleged vault violation. The bank has to be open by now.

Toni checked her watch. Nine o'clock.

Chapter Ten

Toni opened the tall, stately glass entrance and stopped to observe various areas of the bank's lobby and the adjoining offices. The branch manager's cubicle housed only the furniture. No papers on the desk. No Emily. Toni walked to one of the teller windows and asked if Emily happened to be in the building.

"No," the teller stated. She offered nothing additional.

"When do you expect her?" asked Toni.

"We don't know. And we're not supposed to talk about her. Can I help you with any bank business?"

"Not today. I need to speak with Emily as soon as I can. Do you believe she's at corporate headquarters?"

"Look. I can't say anything. Please," the woman whispered.

A teller who won't tell. At least something's secure at this bank.

"I understand. Thanks."

Toni turned to leave and walked slowly toward the exit. She had to think and analyze her next move. She realized that she'd better call Peggy to find out if any other major clients' jobs had collapsed in her own office. She stepped out to the parking lot and retrieved her cell phone from the side pocket of her purse.

"Hey. It's me. Any new disasters?"

"Wow, aren't you the cheery note I need to start the day? Of course, it *is* Friday. But I'm here. Isn't that good enough? And what perchance could be wrong?"

"Cute. Well for starters, Emily's not in the bank and her staff are sworn to secrecy as to her whereabouts."

"Maybe she fled Pinellas County."

"Yeah. Now you're the bundle of hope. Geez, Peg."

"In any case, the Pine Oak press proofs looked great. No text color errors like last time. And our printer didn't steer us wrong. The photos look crisper and bolder. Bob Wolfe has to be ecstatic this time."

"Hopefully. We need to keep him happy. Any other news? The physician group proposal?"

"Nope. I'll call that office manager and touch base right now."

"Good. See ya later."

Toni hung up and stashed her phone in her bag just as Ray Edwards pulled into his reserved spot. She waited until he closed the shiny navy-blue door on his sleek Acura.

"Hey, Ray, 'bout time you got here," she said with her sweetest smile.

"What the hell does that mean?" he barked in return.

"Just adding a little levity. Got to keep your endorphins up. I realize everyone's a bit stressed around here."

Ray snorted and marched past Toni. He pulled the large glass door open with determination and continued his trek until firmly seated behind his desk. Toni trailed behind.

"Look, I just want to understand what's going on. Did the bank have a robbery or not? And where's Emily?"

Ray stared at his desk. "Sit down. I'm not sure exactly." He sighed, stood and walked back around his desk to pull out the chair for her, not losing a beat of his genteel style.

"Not sure? What do you mean 'not sure exactly'? The robbery or Emily?"

"Emily's supposed to be out at corporate this morning. Apparently, a few of Chloe's compadres are up in arms about items apparently missing from their boxes. They've complained to upper management. So the ball's in the executive court. That's all I can say. My job is on the line, too. I've worked here too many years to let some wild claims ruin my retirement."

Toni sat there for a moment. She couldn't believe what she heard.

So Walter went to the top brass. Figures.

"Is there any way a bank official can get into the safe deposit boxes? Don't you have master keys?"

"No. Yes."

"No? Yes? What does *that* mean?"

"Look, Toni. I appreciate the fact that you have something at stake here. But I've got to get things done. I have clients, too."

"All right. But I believe Chloe and her friends. Something is wrong. I'm going to find out what happened."

"Is that *your* job? Just let it go," he said in a decisive voice.

Ray reached to move his computer keyboard closer. Toni muttered a goodbye and headed for her car. She couldn't believe he shut her out. Her car was ready to go, but her brain had to stop and run through the rationale.

How odd. "No and Yes"—what does that mean? Could someone other than the assignee get into a safe deposit box if they wanted to? But how? Damn, no Emily. And Ray is stonewalling my investigation. Hmm . . . maybe I am on the case after all. So much for self-denial. Whom should I hit up next?

Chapter Eleven

Toni gunned the engine and headed down the street. *Time for a visit to police headquarters.* Just her good luck as she observed Alan hunched down over his desk, poring over a report while he sipped a cup of steaming coffee.

"Another cup of coffee? I'm buying?"

"Huh?" Alan sat upright, pulled out of his aura of concentration. "Trying to be nice after your brush with the law? What're you doing here? Snooping, I presume."

"Hey, my business needs this bank as a client, but things are getting weird. Some of Chloe Ford's friends—you remember her, the one who discovered the theft—are also concerned."

"Alleged theft."

"Well, that's according to the FBI. Isn't that what you told me? Is that your professional opinion, too?"

"Right…not a reliable source."

"Who? You or the FBI?" Toni decided to interrogate the detective—Jasper style. Perched on the edge of the chair, she continued, "Come on, Alan. A few of Chloe's friends also lost valuables from their safe deposit boxes."

"And how did you discover that?" Alan leaned back in his chair, coffee cup in hand.

"I had dinner with them last night. They want my help."

"Great. Reporting and news writing to advertising to crime fighting. Be reasonable, Toni," Alan said, This is police business."

"But I thought the case belonged to the FBI?"

"It does, smarty. They're police, too. I've got to get through this report."

Toni peeked down at the papers lying on the desk. The Plait name stood out from the title, quite evident even if the type faced upside down from her vantage point.

"Is that about the body found in Pasco County?" she asked.

"Toni," the detective stated in a loud voice.

"Did the Pasco Sheriff ask for your help? The Plait Gym pass came from the Seminole location, right? Did it go with the victim? Did they get an I.D. from the badge code?"

Alan exhaled in exasperation. "Mike must have hated losing you—just when did you learn how to ask these probing, rapid-fire questions? I'm not giving in. Remember—police business."

"But doesn't this all seem odd for little old Seminole?"

"*But* aren't you jumping to conclusions? I'm reading a report here, not solving the crime. Now, go do what you should do."

"You know, Alan. You've definitely inspired me to find out more," Toni retorted and turned on her heels. "Have a good day."

"Yeah, right."

Back in her car (or as she viewed it, her mobile office), Toni punched Mike's number.

"Are you aware that our own Seminole detective is investigating that body in Pasco?"

"Is he?"

Toni knew that tone of voice.

"Don't you think it's likely and not some fluke that the I.D. *as well as* the victim came from here? That person must have been a Seminole resident."

"So far, it's an unidentified body in Land O'Lakes. Maybe someone from the Pasco Sheriff's command staff will make a statement later today."

"Land O'Lakes?" she echoed.

"Yeah. The body's location was Land O'Lakes."

"So the Pasco Sheriff's department is investigating?"

"Yes, Toni. Now go back to work. Bye." The phone went dead.

Okay, I can take a hint. Land O'Lakes isn't that far. Time for a drive.

Toni headed for her office. Her old press I.D. just happened to be squirreled away in the bottom desk drawer. She'd known better than to get rid of it—just in case. She could write a few copy blocks for the funeral home mailer and leave it for Peggy to finalize the client's approval. Afterwards, she'd have a nice evening in Land O'Lakes. Better yet, spend the weekend. Why not?

She hadn't been north of Tampa in a while. When the new village-style mall, The Shops at Wiregrass opened a few years ago, curiosity had motivated her to visit. She had figured a new outfit would be worth the trip. So, she drove the Suncoast Parkway, pulled off at the State Road 54 exit as the mall directions indicated, but took a wrong left turn.

When she found herself on a narrow road far from civilization, she retraced her trail and finally reached the destination. She also remembered Land O' Lakes, north of Lutz, as not being too built up at that time. More country and cows than in Pinellas County.

This time, the trip will be easier to navigate. And it'll be a treat after this week's calamities.

For now, Toni pulled the vehicle into its usual parking spot in front of her office. Reaching for her phone, Toni hit Google and searched for hotels in Land O'Lakes. *Okay, Priceline negotiator, I don't want Spring Hill or New Port Richey. Residence Inn Marriott Tampa in Lutz. That's close enough. Great. Three rooms still available. Got it. I'll be ready for a big day tomorrow.*

She bounded up the stairs, eager to share her plans with Peggy. She heard a door close as she rounded the corner and saw Peggy turn her way.

Toni stopped in her tracks. "Leaving?"

"Yeah, it's Brownie Troop night at my house. Fifteen short people about to wreak havoc in my kitchen with rice crispy creations. The clients are fine for now—well, so far. Not much should transpire this afternoon. But if you hear loud screams later emanating from the direction of my kitchen, come rescue me. I'll find the authority to make you an honorary Brownie."

"What I've always wanted. How did you know? You guys have a good time, and don't let those little Brownie bakers burn the house down because I won't be any help. I'll be in Lutz for the weekend."

"What the hell do you want to go to Lutz for?"

"Oh, I have a kind of lead."

"For *what*? You don't make proposals on the weekend. Are you still on that damn bank thing? Wait, what *is* in Lutz and where is it?"

"Lutz is just north of Tampa. A body surfaced just up the road in Land O' Lakes, and a Seminole Plait I.D. badge was lying on the ground near the corpse. If you do need me, though, I'll be at the Residence Inn Marriott Tampa in Lutz. Okay?"

"Oh right. All that makes no sense. What the hell are you talking about?"

"I saw Mike and Alan. Mike told me about the body. He's excited, of course. This could be big news for the paper. And then, Alan had a report on his desk mentioning a Plait badge at the scene that came from our Seminole location. Doesn't it seem odd, a bank robbery here and a body that could be from Seminole?"

"It's police business, not yours."

Ignoring Peggy's comment, Toni continued, "Next I went over to the bank. I couldn't catch up with Emily. She's supposed to be at corporate today. But I did see Ray. He's very worried about the bank situation. Apparently, it's not business as usual despite appearances. So with Ray's apprehension and Emily's anxiety, I believe there could be a connection between the bank and the body. Besides, no big romance looms for this weekend. Why not?"

"Okay, have fun, I guess. And don't forget your magnifying glass."

"What?" Toni turned the door handle while she glanced back at Peggy.

"Sherlock Holmes Jasper."

"I bet you think you have a sense of humor."

"I do. Bye."

Toni chuckled as she entered her office. After a quick look over her email and perusing the company job list, she got ready for her two-day jaunt. She pulled the out-of-commission press card from its secure spot in her desk's bottom drawer and stashed it deep in her purse. She needed to run by the ATM for some cash. Then she'd grab a few things for her little adventure and leave extra food and water for her cat. Bubbles usually slept while Toni was away from home anyway.

Chapter Twelve

Bags packed and car loaded, Toni's trek began. Though merely a short trip, she felt good having some activity to move the case along, if it was indeed a case. The frustration of the bank's cancelled event as well as the physician group's slow response to phone calls and messages provoked her need to explore.

To Toni, the bank heist (as etched in her mind) and the victim that could have lived in Seminole needed more of her attention. Patience did not rank high on her list of virtues, so she wanted to do her own probing into what seemed like more and more oddities.

Even though she had travelled only forty-five minutes away, Toni felt like she entered a new world for the weekend. At least one where she might get some satisfaction of an answer or two. *Time to check into the hotel and roam the area for a few hours.*

The front desk clerk smiled as she took Toni's credit card. Efficiently, the young woman finalized the process and handed over the room key.

"Thanks, Veronica." Toni said with a confident smile. "Actually, my paper sent me here to get information about that body found in Land O'Lakes."

"Oh. Yeah, what a shame. The traffic is light on that stretch of Highway 41. No wonder someone left that poor person there."

"Really? So who's in charge of the investigation? From our reports, U.S. 41 is the dividing line for two of the sheriff's three jurisdictions, or District One and District Two. When I left earlier today, we hadn't confirmed on which side of the road the body had been found." Toni slipped her room key into to her purse while making a point to let her press card fall onto the counter.

"Let's see. They closed 41 on the southbound side last night, so that would be the west side of the road. Yeah, Larry in the office said that. He had no trouble on the drive home to Connerton going north on forty-one. His neighbor drives up to Coleman every day. He had a hard time when he came home heading south."

"Excellent." Toni reached out to shake the girl's hand.

Nothing like a good source. It's a start.

After depositing her bags in her room, Toni took off heading east on State Road 54. How fortunate, she considered, that Highway 41 stuck in her mind as the wrong left turn she had made a few years back.

Now that mistake of a maneuver comes in handy. I'm headed in the right direction.

After a left turn onto U.S. Highway 41, she escaped the heavy traffic and construction of the state road. She encountered several stop lights on the divided road. A few more miles and the six-lane road narrowed to two lanes. Houses and stores dwindled. Only wide pastures, a few mobile homes and scattered groups of cows were in view. Then, a cluster of police and forensics vehicles broke the serenity of the countryside.

Toni pulled the press card out of her handbag and looped the lanyard over her head. She slowed the car close to the gathering, turned across the road and parked in a south-facing direction in front of the first forensics van in the row of official cars.

If they throw me out, I can make a quick getaway.

She approached with her arm extended, exuded her best "official business expression"—direct eye contact with a slight smile—and greeted the first deputy who seemed to be standing guard. "Hello, I'm Toni Jasper from Pinellas County. Heard you have quite a situation here."

"Yes," he affirmed and shook her hand without a direct introduction of himself. "This is a crime scene though, ma'am. I have to ask you to leave immediately."

"I realize that, Deputy Ragin," she responded, leaning in slightly to read the officer's name badge. "I'm with the *Woodlands Gazette* and need some information. That Plait Gym pass came from the club's location in my town of Seminole." With her feet planted, she had no intention of leaving immediately.

"Oh, I get it. You're here snooping for some local paper."

"Something like that," Toni murmured in reply to the officer's apparent disdain. She presented a determined countenance as she looked up toward the deputy's down-the-nose insolence. "If this unfortunate person is one of our fine city's citizens, we have a right to know." Toni's tone of resolve hung in the air as the deputy made no sound or move for several minutes.

"Yeah, the damn media leaked that badge bit. Okay, might be one of your neighbors, huh?"

"Yes, sir. I certainly hope not…well, not that I'm happy it's anyone else." Toni's empathetic expression had won over interviewees. She hoped it would work with the formidable Deputy Ragin.

"Look, we haven't positively identified the victim and notified next of kin but should have that done by tomorrow. The press conference is at ten in the morning in New Port Richey. Just be there if you want more facts."

"Excellent, sir. I'll be there."

"You got it, lady. Now you have to leave. Let us do our job."

Toni climbed back into her car and headed south on Highway 41. While checking into her hotel room earlier, she had seen a cafe on the map not too far away just east on S.R. 54. Now she headed in that direction. She could eat and plan her questions for the next day.

Toni pulled in and parked in the not-too-crowded lot. She ordered then toted her turkey chili and tomato mozzarella flatbread to a far corner booth. After fetching her mocha coffee she seated herself, ready for business. At the top of her phone log, Mike's number awaited her command.

"Hey, glad you're still at the office. Have I got news," she said.

"I hope you're not snooping."

"You realize I need to know what's going on with *my* client. Anyway, my gut feeling tells me somehow the bank thing and the body here in Pasco are connected. I mean that Seminole gym badge was so close to the remains."

"*Here* in Pasco? Where the hell are you?"

"Oh . . . I just took a little vacation and happened to end up in Pasco County for the weekend."

"Toni, have you lost it? What in God's name do you hope to get out of this venture? And why do I have to keep repeating that you do not work for the paper anymore. You've got your own business to run."

"Yeah, yeah. But this time, I need to have answers for my business—for my client. Aren't you curious about the body possibly being from Seminole?"

"I didn't say I wasn't. Of course I'm curious. But I want you to succeed in your agency. Being distracted won't get you more clients."

"I understand. I need to be sure this client will pay their bill. I got worried when the bank's corporate biggies cancelled the open house, and then Ray at the bank evaded my questions about Emily's next action—if she has one. Besides, the investigative techniques you taught me have to be good for something. How's an agent going to help her client if she doesn't take the time to understand said client?" Toni hoped her persuasive plea would get some traction.

Mike's silence at the other end of the phone told Toni that she had made a point– or at least he could be considering her point of view. Or not.

"So," Toni continued, "the Pasco County Sheriff will have a press conference tomorrow at ten in New Port Richey. And I'll be there."

"How will you get in?"

"I happen to have my old press card. See. Good planning."

"Good grief is more like it. Tell me what you find out. But this paper is *not* paying you. It's *not* an assignment."

"No problem. Thanks." Toni hung up before Mike had a chance to voice any further objections. She placed a small notebook next to her chili and alternated pen and spoon until she finished her dinner and had written what she considered to be good number of probing questions.

Toni felt eager and ready for the next day's press conference. Meanwhile, she took advantage of a fun opportunity to shop at the sleek Shops at Wiregrass nearby.

The upscale stores in that mall are just what this fashionista wants. I deserve a new outfit. And new information tomorrow. This will be a good trip.

Chapter Thirteen

Toni pulled into the Sheriff's Office, District One Patrol Division, at nine-thirty on Saturday morning. The two-story cement and glass structure stood as a formidable guardian of the law. The United States, State of Florida and Pasco County flags waved with respect atop a pole that reached far toward the sky.

For most events, Toni liked to arrive early to size up the room and the audience. She pushed through the double-door entrance with her press card dangling from her neck. From the lobby, she peered into the adjacent conference room but noticed only a few attendees had arrived. Toni greeted the officer seated behind the front desk with a confident smile and leaned on the counter.

"Not too many here yet?" Toni's knack to get others engaged in a conversation over trivial details had often paid off.

"This isn't breaking news, you know," the blond-haired woman confirmed with her chin at rest on her palm, her makeup flawless. "And I don't think they'll have much to say."

"Why's that?"

"Well, the body happened to be toast. They're having trouble with an I.D."

"Toast?" Toni heard herself echo. "What about dental records?"

"There aren't any. They'll share that much today."

"No dental records?" Toni's eyes widened and her eyebrows arched.

"No teeth," the woman confirmed.

"What do you mean no teeth?" Toni hadn't anticipated that detail. For what reason would the killer extract the teeth before burning the corpse?

"Yeah, I can't comment any more on that. You'll have to ask the sheriff during the conference."

This must be the work of a pro. A hit perhaps? But the gym card from Seminole? Carelessness or a plant to throw us off a trail?

Several other local reporters strolled in and seated themselves in the middle of the bland, almond-colored room. Toni ambled to row one of the folding chair line-up, not wanting to appear worried and surprised. The sensibly composed questions from her café sojourn last night took on an uninspired character. Her brain began to throb as she devised new questions. She couldn't probe about the person, the background, or anything. At bit annoyed, she could feel tension descending from her head to her feet. She took her seat with legs parallel and the soles of her shoes fixed solidly on the tan vinyl flooring.

She allowed her thoughts to find their own sequence. She'd handled other press conferences.

What can they reveal about the body? The person? I'll have to check missing persons' reports. Alan must have this information. Of course, he won't share it with me. I need to check out of the hotel and get back to Seminole. Damn, I haven't gotten a response from any of my texts to Emily. Where is she?

She glanced at the black and white round wall clock in the corner. Just a few minutes until ten. She didn't want any mental distractions no matter how non-newsworthy the announcement.

Toni's thought stream halted abruptly when the microphone resonated with a firm tap.

"Good morning, ladies and gentlemen. Thank you for coming."

Chief Deputy Colonel Geoffrey Huntington surveyed the room from his post behind the lectern. His broad shoulders, wide neck and buzz cut contributed to the man's embodiment of authority.

The sheriff cleared his throat and paused to check the position of the microphone. He looked around the audience and began, "We scheduled this press conference in the hope of revealing more about the identity of the body found yesterday about 60 feet west of U.S. 41 and roughly two miles north of State Road 52. Unfortunately, we do not have a positive I.D. at this point. The teeth had been smashed, making it difficult to use dental records for our victim's identity. Our forensics team is pursuing all avenues possible. I appreciate your coming today, but that's all I can say."

Toni's hand flew toward the ceiling as her voice projected. "Colonel Huntington, how long had the body been in that field?"

She'd gotten the name of the person making the statement so she wouldn't mispronounce it. *At least I sound like I'm still a reporter.*

"You are?"

"Toni Jasper, *Woodlands Gazette*, Pinellas County. The Plait badge apparently came from that facility in my town." *I'm not lying. I didn't say that I actually represent the Gazette.*

"Oh yes. That Plait badge. Well, Ms. Jasper, I have no comment other than it was found a short distance from the remains."

"How far was it from the body?" Toni asked. "And was the person a male or a female?"

"I didn't want to comment further. But since you brought it up, I can say this. The Plait badge was about twenty feet away near a rock. It may not even be relevant. Though the card was mostly intact, the bar code was unreadable." The Chief Deputy purposely raised his eyes from the front row to the rear of the room. "Mr. Napper in the back."

"Thank you, sir. Aiden Napper, *Tampa Times*. What means are you using to establish an I.D.?"

"So far, it's a challenge. This body was burned beyond recognition. And as stated, the teeth were smashed in an apparent attempt to discourage identification. I'm sorry that the department cannot provide any more facts at this time. We anticipated having more information by now. But we don't. Thank you, everyone."

Toni leapt from her seat. "What about any other identifying characteristics? Any broken bones?"

Without a response or even a glance, the sheriff stepped away quickly and walked through the back door of the conference room.

Hmm . . . no mention of their pursuing that avenue? I'll have to smile very nicely to that officer on the way out. At least she gave me something of a head's up. And the colonel's name.

After a sweet grin and nod of gratitude to the long-lashed woman behind the desk, Toni continued out of the building and into the bright sunlight. But she didn't feel enlightened at all and wasn't sure she even wanted to report to Mike. She needed to get her belongings out of her hotel room in Lutz, now thirty minutes east and in the wrong direction. Home turned out to be her new destination for the day. And that was forty-five minutes southwest.

What next? I can think in the car. At least Bubbles will be happy I'm home early. We'll chat about this situation over dinner.

She raced up to her hotel room, packed and grabbed her new wardrobe treasures she had purchased at the mall. After loading her car, she pointed it toward the Suncoast Parkway. Toni placed her cell phone in its dashboard cradle, and then tuned on her car radio for rock and roll music, a brain relaxer for her. The highway traffic moved at a good pace, so she settled in for serious contemplation.

Who was this person? My intuition keeps pulling back to a definite link to Seminole. Could I know this person? Worse, could I know the killer? The person could have just been visiting Seminole from Land O'Lakes or elsewhere. But how the hell did that badge get left near the body? Was it planted? Or did it actually fall out of someone's pocket—or purse?

A familiar phone tune and lighted name signaled a call from Peggy. Toni turned down the volume knob on the radio. The phone automatically picked up the call, and her earpiece was already attached in case a call came in. "What's going on? Did something happen at your Brownie Troop extravaganza?"

"No. All the little urchins are fine. The house still stands, and it's in one piece. The troop behaved well, I must say. I was impressed."

"Good. So?"

"The mugs—"

"Oh no!" Toni cut Peggy off in midsentence realizing the shipment had been delivered late in the day. Toni had forgotten about getting them to the bank. In fact, she'd forgotten about them altogether after the event was cancelled.

"Relax, I got you covered. I left my umbrella at the office last night, so when I went back today, the mugs were waiting at our door. They're safely inside. You can take them over to the bank on Monday."

"Great. Thanks, Peg. But I haven't heard from Emily and I've sent her a gazillion texts."

"She'll surface. No new victims here. Are you getting what you need up there, oh body sleuther?"

"Actually, no. I went to the Sheriff's press conference this morning and they can't I.D. the body. Burned to a crisp no less—and get this—nothing about dental records. In fact, the teeth were smashed. He wouldn't comment on anything else helpful about the body or the I. D."

"That's weird. But do the authorities usually say everything about an ongoing investigation?"

"No. You're right. I'd hoped for more. But I did get to that cool Wiregrass Mall last night. Got a new outfit. I'll wear it on Monday unless I have to confront bank execs or pitch a new client. Any ideas for a new client? This bank fiasco is killing our cash flow."

"They'll be back. It's just a temporary setback. Do you think Emily was fired?"

"I wish I knew. Ray was non-committal. He only said she went to corporate."

"We'll find out soon enough. Got to run. The kids are here in the car."

"So that's the squealing in the background. Torturing them again?"

"Not to worry. But they did destroy everything on your desk."

"Amusing. See you on Monday. Thanks."

"Be safe, Toni."

Toni pushed the end-call button on her phone, but thoughts in her inquisitive mind picked up speed. As did her drive back to Seminole.

Chapter Fourteen

Safely home, Toni unlocked the door to her condo. She surveyed the living room landscape for Bubbles. Up popped two tan ears linked by wide brown eyes and a tiny pink nose.

"Hey, kiddo," Toni said. "Miss me?"

A string of loud meows sounded more like a royal reprimand for abandonment than a warm welcome back.

"Okay, okay. I get it, Bubbles. Come here and I'll get you a treat. You know, sleuthing's hard work. A battle with a burned body makes this job even harder. It's not a job, but you know what I mean. Come here, kitty. We girls need to talk."

The cat took the treat from Toni's hand and purred in response to serious behind-the-ears scratching. Toni liked to converse with her cat. She believed Bubbles appreciated the sound of her voice. And the exercise in feline affection provided them both with time for mental digestion of information.

"I have to call Mike. I told him I would report what I found out. Problem is I discovered nothing new. But wait 'til you see my new outfit."

Not that you would have an opinion. Just look at me with those big, brown eyes, and I'll feel okay about everything—well, not quite everything.

Toni decided to try on the clothes and allow her brain time to assess her next few moves. First, she'd join Plait Gym. She believed that the membership card at the scene was some type of clue. But what? More about that piece of evidence needed to be uncovered.

Heck, I could use a little exercise for stress relief. The gym might be a good idea just for fun . . . if it turns out to be what I'd call fun.

Next, she would check in with Mike. She needed all the feedback she could get, even if he didn't exude enthusiasm for her endeavor.

Damn, I can't get to the bank until Monday to find out about Emily.

She slid into her new indigo floral-print skinny jeans. *WOW. These'll turn Mike's head.* Next, she pulled the dark blue, wide-sleeved top over her head. She turned around and examined herself in front of a full-length mirror.

With a glance at the cat behind her, she asked, "Bubbles, are you proud of me?"
The feline examined her with a lack of expression that only a cat could pull off.

"Yeah, I know. Stunning." *A girl has to get a mental boost from somewhere, might as well be my clothes and my cat.*

Toni changed back into her regular blue jeans and headed for the door. She checked her phone, which rested on the table beside her handbag. No messages. Four o'clock. Bolstered by her fashionista pretend-model session (even if the audience included a mere ball of fur), she hit speed-dial for Mike.

"I happen to have one day to relax, and here's your flagrant face all over my phone screen." Mike's temperament pleased Toni. She knew that tone—an attempt to sound like a tough guy.

"This is exactly why I called. Can't have you become a slacker in one weekend."

"Right. Where are you now? I suppose you think you're an investigative reporter again."

"But of course. Once a reporter, always a reporter." She held back a chuckle while she paused.

"I do believe you are confused, Madame. That's a Marine."

"Anyway," she continued ignoring Mike's words of wisdom. "I did go to the Sheriff's press conference in Pasco this morning. The deputy who gave the report did a great job with absolutely nothing in several empty sentences."

"What do you mean nothing?"

"Mike, the body they found was burned without recognition. And, get this, the teeth had been smashed. Sounds like anger to me."

"You don't say?"

"You knew that, didn't you?" Her unenthused tone reflected her increased sense of frustration.

"Yup. Alan sent over the press release that the sheriff issued. I saw the email a little while ago on my home computer."

"Of course you did, slacker you've become."

She heard Mike's muffled chuckle but had no response. For once, she stood quietly, eyes focused on the floor.

"You sound a bit down," Mike empathized. "Look, if you're free for dinner, I can buy, as usual. Your food budget must be nil these days with the bank out of your financial picture."

What? Is this a date from the I-swear-off-all-dates Michael?

"Mike Milner. Wonders never cease. Are you asking me out?"

"Look, ad exec, don't push it. By the way, let me rephrase. I know you're never *free*. A bit high-maintenance if you ask me."

"Cute. Well, worth every penny for sure." She smiled back at his photo on her phone. "Yes, I am *available*. First, I have an errand to run. Where should I meet you?"

"Why don't you text me when you get home? I'll pick you up. See, I can even be a gentleman, at times."

"The royal treatment? I'm impressed, and I don't impress easily. Give me a couple of hours. I'll be in touch."

"Fine. Bye," he said and was gone. Toni could hear Mike's smile in his parting words.

Finally, a date. Dinner with Mike is just the pick-me-up I need. Maybe he can help me figure out how to save Emily and the bank as a client.

***

After she hung up, Toni bid Bubbles farewell and headed for Plait Gym just a mile from her condo. Saturday exercise enthusiasts included cyclists, torso crunchers and weight lifters—with activity all around the gym, on almost every machine. She walked directly up to the front counter and greeted the twenty-something, muscular gentleman behind it.

"Hi. Can I help you?" he inquired.

"Yes, I'd like more information about a membership. And can I have someone take me on a tour of the facility today. I've never belonged to a gym."

"Sure thing," he stated. He pulled out a brochure and other papers, explaining the different membership levels and fees.

"I just want the basic membership," Toni indicated. "And if this isn't right for me, I can cancel?" *Or if I find a killer. Whichever comes first.*

"Sure. It's a month-to-month deal after the annual fee."

Toni signed the papers and handed over the first payment. *Investment in my investigation. Of course, it's logical rationalization.*

The muscular man called over his shoulder. "Hey Joey. Have a few minutes for a tour?"

Joey turned. "Yeah. Be right there."

As Toni waited for Joey—another man of pronounced muscular physique—to finish with a customer, she glanced around the large, neon-yellow and blue room. *Darn. No one I know. Man, I guess I'm not in the physically-fit circle.*

"Hi. I'm Joey." The voice jolted Toni out of her momentary sleuther-want-to-be room-gazing.

"Toni Jasper," she affirmed, returning the handshake. *This guy is strong.*

"So, first time here?"

Toni nodded. "Yes. It's time I got more exercise. Can you explain these machines? They look pretty complicated."

"Actually, they're easier than they look," he replied as they started walking around the gym. "See, instructions are here on the side of each machine. Just be sure to adjust the weight and do about twenty reps each time."

"Reps?"

"Repetition of each movement. You can always ask for information at the desk, too."

"Great." Toni sighed, relieved about that.

I might actually have to come here every day to watch for a suspicious person or persons. Of course, it could be someone I know from the chamber or . . . well, I'm here now.

"I had hoped to see someone I knew so I could have a buddy. Do the same people come each day? I mean, I can ask my friends if they belong, but I just want to start out with a supporter. Someone to keep me on track."

"Yeah, people get into a routine. And that's a good idea. When do you think you'll be here during the week?"

"My schedule varies. I'm in business for myself, so when fires happen, I have to put them out."

"Fires?"

"Problems with clients." *At least I'm not the only one with unique lingo.*

"Oh right. The best thing is to ask around, as you said. Then maybe with a different workout time each day, you'll see someone you know."

"You don't have a membership list?" *Probably won't share, but heck, I can play dumb and inquire.*

"Nope. That's all private. Just hang around often. I bet you'll find some friends before you know it."

Joey continued to go over the basics of most of the machines. He reassured Toni that she should be patient with her progress, come as often as she could, but establish a routine.

I'll be here, buddy, but routine is not my priority. I'll be exercising my powers of observation.

Chapter Fifteen

Toni hoped that her gym experience would present a new perspective on Seminole's residents. She felt eager to come back in fashionable workout clothes.

Okay. What do I have in good workout clothes? Note to self: better check my closet.

After one more stop at supermarket for human and cat necessities, Toni found herself unloading groceries and texting Mike. "Be there in thirty," flashed a return text. Toni headed for her closet to don the snazziest possible "Mike outfit," brushed her hair and smoothed on lipstick.

In twenty-nine minutes, Toni stood by the window, waiting. Mike pulled up in his gleaming white Jeep exactly on time. She watched him step out, and then opened her condo door, key in hand, ready to go.

"You look lovely, Toni," Mike whispered as if seeing her in an entirely new way.

"Thanks, handsome." Toni looked into his eyes and smiled. She slid into the vehicle with Mike closing the door after her.

"So where're we going?" Toni asked, eyes shining in Mike's direction.

"Oh, I thought all your hard work deserves an appropriate reward. How about The Beach Grill?"

Wow, this IS a date. "Fantastic. I love that place."

"Good, but it's just because you're working hard at your agency, not because I approve of your meddling in police business."

"What meddling? That word sounds so—"

"Intrusive?"

"Did Alan tell you to divert my attention or something?"

"No. Alan and I do not discuss you—hard as that is to believe."

"Yeah, right."

I know better. You guys don't want me meddling. Just as you said.

"We just don't want you to get hurt in any way," Mike stated.

"Well, I appreciate that. My cash flow will recover. I just can't figure out *what* is going on at that bank? Even the corporate execs seem to be acting weird."

"That's not what I meant, Toni."

"Huh?"

"I mean physically hurt. If the murder in Land O'Lakes is related to someone here in Seminole, then you shouldn't be poking around. Leave that to the police and FBI."

Toni turned a serious face toward Mike.

Holy crap. Do my suspicions have merit? Are the authorities linking that body in Pasco to someone living here? But what about the bank robbery—or could it be an inside job? I'll think about it later. We're here and I'm starved.

Luckily, a table on the deck was available. Toni loved the intimate spot on the Intracoastal Waterway, especially with a little chill in the air and the restaurant's elegant, tall heaters hovering over them, like warm air hugs. She glanced at the menu, but her mind flashed back to the murder-Plait Gym link.

"Know what you want, Toni?" She thought he acted way too cool to be genuinely concerned about her safety.

"Yeah, I want to know what's going on."

"We're ordering dinner."

"No, you know what I mean. Do the police believe there is some type of link? I mean, could I be onto something?"

"They don't know. I'm just saying to be cautious."

"What about the bank robbery? Is that connected? I mean that FBI guy wanted to put Chloe and her pals in the loony bin."

"The FBI is conducting its own investigation with the bank thing. I don't know exactly what they're doing. For some reason, they don't report to me."

"Amazing." Toni managed a small smirk. "I'll focus on food. For now."

"Alleluia," Mike stated flatly. "Does this mean we can order before sun-up?"

"Mr. Milner, with all your snide remarks, I just can't imagine why I agreed to eat with you tonight."

"Because you're hungry, too. And I'm great company." Toni saw the twinkle in Mike's eye. "Here comes our waiter."

After ordering her favorite of coconut-crusted shrimp, Toni looked on as Mike selected the six-ounce filet mignon, medium-rare.

"Could I actually be in some type of danger?"

"Maybe not," he reassured her. "But I did make a substantial investment in your career over the years. Now I'm just looking out for the future of our community's advertising."

"But—"

"Toni. Do we have to talk about the alleged case all night? Can't we just have a nice evening?"

"Okay. I get it. Enough already. So . . . how's that Harry at his job?"

Toni allowed herself to engage in conversation about others at the paper and in the community, just like she and Mike had done when she worked at the paper. She almost forgot about her client concerns and self-imposed investigative duties. After a splendid meal and several hearty laughs, Toni found herself less stressed.

Mike drove her home and walked her to the door. He took her hands, leaned down and gently placed a kiss on her cheek. "Good night, Jasper. Thanks for a fun evening."

Elated and barely feeling her feet, Toni uttered, "Yeah. It was terrific."

She stood, planted on her front step with her eyes fixed on Mike's Jeep as it turned the corner and sped down the street.

Toni slowly pivoted and went inside the condo. She turned the dead bolt and secured the chain on her front door. Just to be safe, she also toured each room, making sure that all windows were locked as well.

Chapter Sixteen

Toni didn't even need her alarm clock. She bolted out of bed with a sweep of her feet around the cat that had warmed them all night. Bubbles held firm at the end of the bed as if she had cat-claw roots extending into the mattress. The cloud-nine effect from Mike's brief, cheek-focused kiss still lingered in her mind. Then reality hit.

Sunday. I have to figure something out today—a new lead for the case. Okay, alleged case. I am investigating no matter what anyone says to the contrary.

Toni dressed before having breakfast concurrently with her cat. She went to the living room and made her list for the day. The cat jumped on the couch beside her, ready for her morning attention. Pulling the animal onto her lap, she stroked the cat's silky fur while she analyzed the day ahead.

"I guess I could go to the gym," she told the cat. "Then again, I can get started on the next Pine Oak Place newsletter. Getting ahead will give me more time to prowl, right kitty?" Toni hugged the cat as she chuckled to herself.

"That's it, kitty. Office first, then Plait. The Sunday afternoon group should be interesting. I wonder if we'll have the working crowd who can't get there during the week. Muscle Joey told me that the gym is busiest on weekdays from five to seven. I'll put that on my calendar. Geez, Bubbles, I better get there today so I don't look like a fool on those machines during the week."

She gently moved the cat to another couch cushion. After a slight jog to her closet, Toni packed a small athletic bag with workout clothes. She figured that she could change at the office. Then, she penciled down "gym locker lock" on her to-do list—just in case she needed to change at Plait one day.

***

An eerie loneliness hung over Toni as she opened her office door in the quiet building. Usually, she liked solitude that allowed her brain to focus on work. But today, something seemed different. Concentration proved to be more difficult. Did Mike's cheek peck strike that much of a new note? Or did the case leave her sixth sense gnawing with uncertainty? The question was: uncertainty of what? What did her gut feeling convey?

Maybe I'll add Alan to my Monday investigative duties. Could I be in danger? What the hell motivated Mike to mention that?

She rose from her desk and walked back to double check the lock on the office door. From the window behind her desk, she could see that her car stood alone in the parking lot, the solitary signal that one person demonstrated the need to work on a Sunday. Finally at ease, Toni pulled the Pine Oak file and returned to her computer.

After several hours of penned notes and typed paragraphs, she sat back with contentment. She made a note on the client's job list summary sheet, asking Peggy to proofread the newsletter's text. Then Toni sat back to relax for a minute.

I guess it's gym time. I can get a snack at their juice bar. Time to change. Why didn't I just wear those workout clothes to begin with?

The cell phone resting on her desk began its cheerful dance song announcing an incoming call. Mike's photo popped up on the screen.

"Hey." She chirped with glee.

"Where are you?"

"I'm at work. Thought I'd get a jump on the week. After all, I had my little sojourn in Pasco County. Back to the grindstone."

"Come to the newspaper. Now."

"What? Why?"

"Ray Edwards from PinCo Bank is missing. His house burned down early this morning. The arson squad is on the scene."

"Oh my gosh Ray?" Toni stood up without realizing her action.

Mike asked, "You there, Jasper?"

"Yeah, yeah."

"Then get the hell over here. Five minutes. Got it?"

"Sure. But why do you need me? I'm just wrapping up. Give me about twenty minutes. I want to check on a few other jobs."

"Leave it. Just get in that damn little car of yours and get your ass over here. NOW. Do you understand?"

"Mike, you're scaring me."

"Good. Drive cautiously but get here. I want you in front of my desk ASAP."

"I'm on my way."

Toni realized that her hand shook as she locked her office door. She examined the hallway before she ventured down it. Then she surveyed the parking lot before she locked the building's outside door. With one of her keys protruding from her thumb and first finger for safety, she jogged across the lot. Almost all in one motion, Toni disarmed the car alarm, hopped into the vehicle and hit the door lock. A few minutes later, she stood in front of Mike's desk, eyeing him warily.

He motioned for her to sit down.

"Can I get you anything? Water? Coffee?"

"A bottle of water would be good." When Mike returned with the chilled bottle, she continued, "You frightened me. What the hell happened and why the alarming dictate for me to get here pronto?"

"Ray's house exploded. And Ray is not just missing. He's presumed dead. As I said, the arson squad is investigating. And the police are calling it murder."

"But why?"

"That's what needs to be determined. Alan will be here soon. He wants to know what you found out. And since no one's heard from Emily, he's worried about any person connected to this situation."

"What situation? You mean the robbery and the body?"

"If a true connection exists. We don't know. But you were one of the last people to see Ray alive—at least according to the one teller they were able to contact on a Sunday."

Toni pondered the distressful information. She considered Ray a friend. He'd annoyed her at times, but he'd treated Chloe well. He'd been on her good-guy list.

"What do we do now?"

"Hey snoopy, we wait for Alan." Mike stared at Toni. She knew that serious stare.

Chapter Seventeen

Tension engulfed Alan Dietz's face. The tightness in his broad shoulders reflected the enormity of his concern. He pulled a chair over from another desk and straddled it, arms up on the chair back, eyes glued on Toni.

"Toni, we have information you and Ray Edwards had a meeting on Friday afternoon." Suddenly, Alan's formal tone sent a chill down her spine. She felt the hair on her arms stand up in alarm.

"I wouldn't call it a meeting."

"What would you call it?" he probed.

"I just dropped in on him to find out about Emily."

"Why do you want to know about Emily Phillips?" His direct manner sent shivers up Toni's body, leaving tense muscles in their wake.

"Alan, you know the bank's one of my clients. I had a big event planned for tomorrow, that open house. The bank robbery—sorry, *alleged* robbery or incident or whatever—forced the bank to cancel it. I stand to lose money if they don't reschedule. I had hoped to find out where Emily was so I could speak with her. She usually communicates well, but I haven't heard a thing from her since I saw her on Thursday. Besides, I'm concerned about her safety."

"Who said it *was* a bank robbery? And why are you concerned about her safety?"

"What is this? An interrogation?"

"No. But I need to know what Ray told you. The bank manager is missing, and now he's presumed dead."

Toni felt a lump in the pit of her stomach. Her lips wouldn't move. She felt frozen to the metal desk chair.

Presumed dead? Again that phrase. I can't believe it.

"I asked Ray if he knew how I could get in touch with Emily."

"What did he say about her?"

"Ray said that Emily was at the corporate office."

"Did he confirm that the bank had been robbed?"

"No." *He didn't say it was robbed, but I still believe Chloe and Walter.*

"Then who did?"

Toni thought for a minute. But Alan's stare unnerved her. "My friends at Pine Oak Place," she muttered.

"What friends? Do they have proof that the bank was robbed?"

"A couple of the folks told me items were missing from their safe deposit boxes. They don't have proof—not really. But they know what they put in their safe deposit boxes and when they put them there."

"Look, Toni. These are unfounded rumors that need to be stopped. The FBI will find out what happened to those folks' items, if anything."

"But Alan—"

"Toni. What else did Ray tell you on Friday?"

The young ad exec sighed in resignation. She'd have to plead the sapphire ring and bond theft case another time.

"After he told me that Emily had gone over to the corporate office, he said to 'Let it go.' But I couldn't let it go because it was so odd for the corporate office to cancel the event. Emily should have sent us the information. And she's usually prompt to confirm our appointments and meetings. In fact, she had texted me twice on Thursday morning to be sure I got the press release into the paper. So I thought it was totally out of character for her to avoid us on Friday."

"Who's *us*?"

"Peggy, my associate, and me."

"And that's it? Did Ray use wording that seemed unusual for him?"

"No . . . oh yeah, when I initially asked about both Emily and the robbery—" Toni winced at Alan's expression of exasperation, but continued, "You asked, Alan. Ray told me that he didn't know what was going on. And I asked him to clarify if he 'didn't know about the robbery or about Emily?' He replied: 'I'm not sure exactly.' Then I left. That's it."

Alan continued jotting notes. Then he glared directly into Toni's eyes.

"That's it for now. Just be careful. The bank teller we spoke with today told me Ray appeared to be nervous after you left. Are you sure that he didn't seem worried or overly concerned?"

"Of course, he seemed worried. As I disclosed, he told me he didn't know what was going on. Doesn't that imply that the bank's activities were not run-of-the-mill or normal for a bank? Which, for a financial institution, should result in a great deal of concern for one of the vice presidents?"

"Maybe. But we need to find out what those activities were and what Ray knew, and if he became involved somehow."

"No," Toni said. "Ray would not be *involved,* as you put it." Even Toni surprised herself at her rapid-fire defense of the man.

"No what? Just because he seemed like a nice guy? Is that what you mean?"

"Ray and I had our differences. But I can't imagine a dishonest bone in his body."

"You mean what was his body. The explosion resulted in a big fire."

Toni turned to a block of human ice. She had a hard time processing the situation.

Who would do that? What the hell is going on?

"Just let me know if you get any pertinent information," the investigator continued.

"Yeah, sure." Toni muttered her response.

Alan stood and replaced the chair behind the adjoining desk, then turned to shake Mike's hand. "Thanks, Mike."

Mike nodded as Alan pivoted and walked away.

Toni, still sitting in her chair, watched them. But she couldn't move. She kept trying to think how the situation made any sense. First Emily goes missing. Now Ray is gone.

The auto recording in her brain played "what the hell is going on?" over and over.

Chapter Eighteen

For a few moments, Toni and Mike faced each other in silent disbelief, spellbound by the horror of the situation rocking their normally-serene community.

Toni's inquisitiveness surfaced. She had to ask. "Are they sure Ray was in the house when it . . . exploded?"

"CSI found a partial denture. Oddly, though, they found it just inside the structure, not far from the back door."

"A partial? Did it belong to Ray? I mean, I never talked with him about his dental work."

"They called his dentist, Dr. Raphael. It's in his records. He had a partial. But you know, what's kind of weird is that most of the structure and its contents were all but obliterated. Yet the partial looked pretty much intact."

Toni pondered this piece of evidence. "That is weird. Of course, it was an explosion. Who can explain what happens? When you called me at the office, you said the arson squad had already been called in. Why do they consider arson as a possibility? Who the hell would want to hurt Ray and his house?"

"The police on the scene smelled gas. They also saw what they believed to be burn patterns, which suggest that it was arson. That's all I know. And the only news I can report in the paper is that there's no evidence of any kind of utility failure. They don't want the neighbors in a panic because they read that a gas leak might have caused the blow up."

"Right. The scare wouldn't be good. But arson, Mike? Does it sound like the work of a pro or an amateur—especially with proof—if those areas do turn out to be burn patterns?"

"I know. I don't want to think about hit men—or women . . . ." Mike stopped to nod toward Toni. ". . . here in our little Seminole. But I'm inclined to think you might have a point about the bank being robbed. I just don't get why only a few items were missing. It seems, at this point, only two safe deposit boxes were compromised."

"How do *you* know only two boxes allegedly had contents taken? Milner, are you holding out on me? You talked to that FBI guy, didn't you? Come on. Give."

Mike sat up in his chair and with solemn expression declared, "Ms. Jasper, the insinuation of 'holding out' implies that you, madam snoopy, actually have a need-to-know."

"Oh crap. You know I'm concerned about . . . well . . . this whole case. Even the FBI guy drove me nuts the way he talked to Chloe. He was so rude, and I need to have information for Chloe and Walter at Pine Oak. Though I understand the FBI has a job to do."

Toni stopped to give Mike a look of utter exasperation, then inquired, "So no other valuables have been reported as *allegedly* gone? Just Chloe's ring and Walter's bonds?"

"That's it. Of course, all the snow birds aren't back yet from their summertime trips up north."

"Right." Toni's brain began to pick up speed, in recovery after the arresting shock of Ray's death. She considered the two people who were robbed.

"Mike, Chloe told me she doesn't go into her box for jewels on a regular basis, only before the holidays. Walter and his wife aren't normally here in September. They came back early this year and went to check on their bonds. Do you think the bank will find that other items are not in their boxes when more residents return from the north?"

"Maybe. I don't know," he answered with raised eyebrows.

"How could anyone get into those boxes?" Toni whispered, with a need to verbalize her question. She looked out the window past Mike's shoulder. After a few minutes, her eyes widened as she turned toward Mike, and at the same time, her hands slapped the front of the desk.

"Damn."

"Whoa, Jasper." He said slowly as if to ward off a vicious animal. "Did you have some type of revelation?"

"Holy shit," she shouted. "A couple of years ago, I moved my account to PinCo and opened a safe deposit box at the same time. Lo and behold, a few months later, I got a call from the assistant manager they had back then. She told me that the teller who set up my safe deposit box did not rekey that box's lock. So, they had to give me a new key. The teller who called me in also asked me to check the contents. I went in and accounted for all items. The sign-in logs didn't show anyone else besides me signing into that box. After she gave me a new key, she had me double check my code and hand print for the safe's entry. I had a busy schedule that day, and since all seemed fine, I just didn't think about it until now."

"So? Your code remained the same. Unless you changed your hand in some mysterious way or someone has your exact palm and fingerprints . . . what are you getting at?"

"Mike, I stood in the teller line a few months ago when I saw someone struggle to get into the safe. I figured he forgot his code. Emily came out and bypassed the system with a master key. She asked him to reset his code. At the time, I thought she was helpful because the guy had been through a rough time."

"Again Jasper. So? She didn't go into the safe with him. And how did you know the guy had been through a rough time if you were just eavesdropping?"

"Mike, the guy happened to be Emily's brother-in-law, Jesse Morton. You know. He had been married to Jon Phillips' sister, Debra. What if some of the other boxes were not rekeyed and Emily knew it. I mean, did Jesse have his own box? Or are he and Emily engaged in some type of small heist? She disappeared after Thursday's *alleged* robbery. "

Mike's expression became taut. Toni knew his years as a foreign correspondent meant puzzle-solving at the highest level. She believed he might comprehend her robbery theory. She hoped the recent development of events struck him as pieces of a still-somewhat-disjointed puzzle. Though sensing his hesitation, Toni could see that Mike was intrigued.

"They've all known each other for years—Emily, Jon, Jesse and Debra" Toni said. "I think they all grew up here. But Jesse and Debra moved away when Debra got a great job offer in Orlando."

Mike's expression didn't change. But Toni wanted to keep Mike on her fast track while she had his attention. "However, Emily told me Jesse became so depressed after his wife left him that he moved back here to be closer to Jon and Emily. It seemed kind of weird to me when I first heard it. I mean, who would want to live close to your ex-wife's brother and his wife after a divorce? Wouldn't that association make a person more depressed?"

"Maybe the Phillips' wanted to help them get back together. You know we don't always get the whole story."

"Yeah, but somewhere I heard that Jesse and even Jon hadn't had any communication with Debra in months. Do you think that, in some way, she blamed both of them for her failed marriage?"

Mike sighed. "I don't know, Jasper. Rumors. Where are the facts? At one time, you were a half-decent reporter."

"I'm still a good reporter. This case, though—"

"Even if you are, I mean were, a good reporter, you're not on *this* case. *Understood?*" His voice became stern, his brow furrowed. "As Alan said, you're on the record as the last person to speak with Ray. I don't want anything *even close* to bad happening to you. If Ray's house explosion was arson, maybe some plot *is* underway at that bank."

Toni felt touched. Her cheeks flushed as she imagined a genuine kiss from Mike, not a simple cheek peck. The warmth of his lips against her check did have great merit . . . for a start. She possessed strong feelings for Mike. Did she love him? She gazed into his mesmerizing, deep-blue eyes with a romantic fantasy close to an out-of-body experience.

"Hey." Mike's voice landed on her ears like a solid note of security. "Want to grab some lunch?

"Um . . . I planned to go to the gym this afternoon."

"You belong to a gym?" Toni didn't utter a sound, merely glanced sheepishly in his direction with no direct eye contact. Mike continued, "Oh no, let me guess. Plait. Are you crazy? What the hell am I going to do with you?"

Toni's muscles tightened as if she had been cast in stone, attached to the chair. She felt busted, guilty as charged.

But I didn't do anything wrong. I'm right. I can feel it.

"Mike, I—"

"Okay. Heaven help me. I don't suppose they have any good food at your *gym*?"

Toni managed a half-smile. She felt the tension begin to flow away from her shoulders. "You've no idea what *good* is. But you don't have any workout clothes with you, do you? That get-up is banned on the treadmill."

"This turn of events has squashed my fashion sense for the day," he smirked, yielding to the situation. "We can stop at my place on the way. I actually own workout clothes. Come on. First, we'll leave your car at your condo. I'll follow you, just in case."

"In case of what?"

"In case of this *case*, you ex-reporter-snooper. Now let's get to that gym of yours, Jasper, before I lose my nerve."

Chapter Nineteen

With people home for the weekend, Toni had to park her car a few doors away from her condo. Mike waited for her in a guest-designated space.

"Let's go," Toni said as she clicked the seatbelt. Eager to get to the gym, she anticipated recognizing someone.

I know I'm not supposed to be "on the case," but I feel safe with Mike along. Besides, a good reporter's job is to seek the truth. So I'm not really a reporter. I do have an editor with me. That counts. We'll help crack this case.

The pair approached the front desk. Toni pulled out her membership tag and the young muscle man behind the counter swiped her in. "Hi. Have a good workout."

Toni smiled at him. "I have a guest with me today. He wants to try out some of the equipment. Is that okay?"

"Sure. Hi there." The young man turned his attention toward Mike and extended his brawny arm for a firm handshake. "I need a couple of forms filled out for our records. Step over here if you will." He placed a couple of papers on the counter and handed Mike a pen.

While Mike etched his name and other information on the required forms, Toni stepped around the counter. She scanned the workout machines and mats. Equipment blocked some of the exercisers' faces.

So far, no one suspicious. There's my neighbor. I didn't know he worked out. Oh wow! Sue Anderson. No wonder she lost weight. When did she join? I have to talk with her. I'm glad she wants to get in shape since her rat-of-a-husband's out of the picture. What?

Toni's perusal of the facility halted when she caught sight of Jesse Morton.

Damn. He and Sue are in a conversation. Sue put her hand on his shoulder. How do they know each other? This, I've got to check out. Jesse can't be the boyfriend that Paul alluded to.

"Ready to prove your workout ability, Jasper?" Mike stood beside her, peering down with a smile of triumphant confidence.

"Don't be so sure of yourself, Milner. How long has it been since you set foot in a real gym?"

"I do run five miles three or four times a week. That counts."

"Yeah. Maybe. Look there's Sue. Let's go and say hi first."

"Are we here to socialize or work out? I get it. You're intimidated already. My mental powers are reaching out and—"

"Your what?" Toni interrupted. "Delusional are we? Come on. We can't ignore her. We need to be friendly."

"But *we* haven't got all day."

"Right. Football season."

Sue saw the pair approach and jumped with excitement. "Hi, Toni! Mike! Do you guys know Jesse?" She gestured toward him. Mike and Toni reached out and shook Jesse's hand in turn.

Jesse nodded toward each of them.

"Toni Jasper," Sue said, "she used to work with me at the paper, and Mike Milner, our editor and publisher. Now Toni has her own ad agency, so I don't get to see her as much."

"I've seen you at chamber meetings, Jesse," Toni said. "Glad we finally get to meet. So both of you are members? I didn't know you worked out here, Sue."

"Actually, Jesse got me to join. About time for me to get in shape," she responded.

"So how do you two know each other?" Toni's mind went into probe gear.

"We bumped into each other in Publix. Literally. I'm such a klutz."

"No you're not," Jesse quickly jumped in with an amorous glance her way. "Fate prevailed. I came to the aid of my damsel in distress."

"Anyway," Sue continued, while she sent a smile toward Jesse, "we started talking. And that was it."

"It?" Toni echoed.

Sue looked at Toni as if she landed from another planet. "Jesse asked me out. A gym membership makes sense. We can work out together. And I never thought I'd like exercising like this."

"Right . . . ." Toni's voice—and her thoughts—began to drift into suspicion mode.

"So why are you two here? Of course, you both look super." Sue looked back and forth from Toni to Mike.

"I'm a member," Toni spurted with strained confidence. "I convinced slacker guy here to come and see what this gym is like."

Sue addressed Mike. "You're not a slacker, whatever Toni says. I see you running sometimes if I'm on my way to work early. Just don't laugh at me if you see me limp around the office because I overdid it on the treadmill."

"Not to worry, Sue. I've had my share of pulled muscles. Look, guys, nice to see you. But we have to go." Mike's eyes motioned toward Toni. "Lots of work to do with this one." Toni's hand flew at Mike's arm, delivering a back-handed reprimand.

Toni led Mike over to what she called the tummy cruncher located in a corner of the facility. She believed a bit of privacy was required to share her suspicions.

"First, adjust the seat and the weight," she instructed. After Mike became comfortable on the machine, she sat on the other identical one. "Don't you think that's odd," she asked in between crunches.

"Odd? What do you mean? I like this machine."

"No, Sue with a man like Jesse. He's *the* Jesse Morton. Married to Jon Phillips's sister. He doesn't seem like her type."

"Are we here to exercise our bodies or *your* half-baked, nosy ideas?"

"I've noticed Jesse at several chamber functions. He's a computer programmer—a tech guy. But he's an extravert, too. He talks with the other people and doesn't just sit in a corner. And Sue is reserved."

"Good for them. Opposites attract."

"I get it. But something about that man seems off."

"You haven't had a conversation with him. Just examined him from across the room. And now you're about to judge him? I'm glad you don't watch my every move from afar."

"And who says I don't?" This time, her eyes rolled toward him.

"What's your basis for this assessment? They're two decent humans at a gym."

"But Jesse hasn't been divorced that long. Emily is the one who told me his wife left him."

"Emily? From the bank? What's she got to do with this?"

"Jesse's her brother-in-law. You know that."

"Ooh." Mike's long, drawn-out syllable had Toni straining her neck to see him around her machine's side.

"And here he is at Plait," Toni said.

"A lot of people are here."

"No one has heard from Emily since Friday—actually Thursday. She could be in big trouble. But Jesse doesn't seem to have a care in the world. He gawked at Sue as if she was the only woman on Earth. You would think he'd be worried about his former sister-in-law. And what happened to that concern for his ex-wife? He only moved here a year ago—upset about his wife leaving him. These events don't add up, Mike."

"Those two and their affairs, pun intended, are none of your business, Jasper."

"What if," Toni continued as if oblivious to Mike's pushback and feeble attempt at humor, "Emily is out of touch because she's embarrassed by what happened with the vault and the bigwigs' cancellation of her event? Or she knows what really happened in the vault?"

"Toni." Mike rose from the machine and stood squarely in front of her, with a pointed stare into her eyes.

"I'm crunching." Her lips strained in pretend effort while her body bent with the machine. She let the subject drop.

After an hour of machine reps and treadmill jogs, the two headed out to Mike's car. Toni agreed to eat at the new burger place in spite of the menu being, as she put it, "counter-intuitive to the whole fitness hour."

Mike chuckled. "I'm sure they have items even for picky eaters like you."

"Hope so. Do you know what those burgers do to your arteries?"

"Now you're suspicious of burgers?"

"Not suspicious. They've been tried and convicted."

Chapter Twenty

The quick lunch turned into an extended afternoon of conversation and laughter. Toni felt relaxed and relieved to have a little time without worry. She almost forgot her client retention concerns and shady character assumptions.

When Mike stopped his car in front of her condo, he leaned over and gave her cheek a kiss. But this time, he took her hands in his.

"Nice day, Toni. I enjoyed being with you." he stated with sincerity, as his eyes met hers. "I especially appreciated your winded efforts on the treadmill," he added with an attempt to hold back a grin.

"Touché. Thanks for tagging along. Maybe we'll do it again. I liked having you along—even if you considered yourself my watchdog. See, nothing happened. All's fine."

"Maybe."

"Maybe what? You'll come and exercise with me or I need a watchdog? Not that I object to either one?"

"Maybe for both. The treadmill's good, but I like my run—early hours outside in this nice weather. And maybe you should still watch your back. Just to be safe."

"I will. Thanks. See ya," she called as she shut the car door.

Once inside her condo with the deadbolt secure, Toni checked her phone. She'd put it on silent when she got to the gym and hadn't given it another consideration.

That's a first. I never forget to look at my phone. Ah Milner. I think I'm even more hooked on you. I even missed a couple of calls.

Peggy had left the first message. She had some ideas to promote the agency and drum up new business. When would Toni be in on Monday? The next message came from Chloe. She wanted to close out her safe deposit box and asked if Toni could drive her to the bank first thing in the morning. Toni dialed Chloe's number first.

"Hi Chloe. It's Toni. I just got your message. Sure, I'll be happy to take you to the bank tomorrow. What time?"

"Oh, Toni. Thank you for calling back. Can we go about ten o'clock? I've been so worried about the safe deposit and my jewels. I've decided to move them here to the Pine Oak vault. I thought the bank would be safer, but now I just want my magnificent jewelry close to me after the robbery and poor Ray's death. Wasn't it awful? I can't believe his house exploded. That's what they said on the news. Is it true? Do you know what really happened to my Ray?"

Chloe sounded distraught, and Toni could empathize. Several serious incidents had occurred that directly impacted Chloe. In a short time, her sedate world had been disrupted. Chloe tried to exude a tough exterior. However, Toni knew the façade included a need to prove herself on her own. After many years of marriage, Chloe now swam in uncharted waters.

Toni also realized she happened to be free most of the day since the bank's open house was no longer on her Monday schedule.

I guess I'm destined to be at the bank anyway. Maybe Emily will be in by then. Or at least I can find out more about her whereabouts.

"Sure, Chloe, I'll pick you up at ten. We'll head right over to PinCo. Are you sure that you don't want to move your valuables to another bank?"

"No, I just want my gorgeous gems here. I don't know what to do about my investments. I had such confidence in Ray. I don't know what to do." Her voice trailed off into silence. Toni didn't say a word. Chloe continued, "Since my husband died, I counted on Ray. I think I'll just get my items out of that vault for now. I'll consider what else to do later."

"Good idea, Chloe. We can interview other bankers another day."

"Will you help me with that, too? I do so trust you, Toni. I trusted Ray, and now I don't know . . . ."

Toni felt for Chloe. A discussion about the explosion didn't seem appropriate. The woman's "I don't knows" multiplied by the paragraph. She sounded lonely and vulnerable. At Pine Oak Place, she circulated at the parties and events with her head held high. But

Toni knew Chloe had no true close friends. She had to be Chloe's best friend, and Toni always stood by her pals, especially BFFs.

"I'll see you in the morning. We can talk then. Get some sleep."

"Thank you. I'll be ready. Brutus and I will wait for you in the lobby."

"Brutus?"

"Why yes. He's coming with me. If that FBI agent is back, this time I'll definitely sic my ferocious beast on him."

"I believe Agent Nelson is gone, at least for now. But I'll be happy to give both you and Brutus a ride to the bank. Bye, Chloe."

"Goodbye." After Chloe hung up, Toni wondered what had become of the FBI's investigation, if anything.

Next, Peggy needed a call back. As Toni's associate, Peggy often functioned in the role of boss. At the least, she took command to steer the day-to-day activities and keep clients under control.

"Hi Peg."

"Good, you caught me. We're about to go for pizza. Want to join us?"

"No. Thanks though. I just got home. Tomorrow, let's talk about new business. I'm eager to hear your ideas. First, I have to take Chloe to the bank. Maybe I'll even find out about Emily. I haven't seen any new emails from her or the bank execs. Have you?"

"Not a peep. I did see the news about Ray. Can you believe it? We don't live too far from him. They've confirmed it couldn't have been a gas leak. Still, we're a little unnerved."

"Don't worry. The police are positive no gas leak occurred. Rest assured."

"And how are you so certain?"

"Well—"

"Well?" Peggy echoed. "What then? Look, Toni, I know you. Did you meet with Alan?"

"He and Mike had a conference. They both insisted that I be there."

"Insisted you be a part of their conference? Now, that's a twist. Explain it all tomorrow. What time will you be in?"

"Probably around lunch time. I can grab a couple of sandwiches. I'll text you when I'm close to find out what you want. Okay?"

"Fine. You're still the business owner. It would be nice of you to show up."

"Peggy. What kind of comment is that? My bank visits are critical to check on our investment. The bank has to pay for those mugs and perhaps the caterer's fee. I'm not getting stuck with those invoices."

"Fine, again. I'll have my plan mapped out when you get in. Meanwhile, I'll hold down the fort."

"You can proof the copy I wrote today. It's in the Pine Oak folder. I got a jump on their next newsletter. See, I'm at work when you least suspect it."

"At work on Sunday? I guess you've redeemed yourself. I'm impressed. Good luck. Hopefully, we get a check from the bank soon. Say hi to Chloe for me."

"Will do. Enjoy your pizza mess." Toni imagined Peggy's two kids with little red, tomato-sauce faces.

"We always do."

Toni hung up and suddenly felt somewhat lonely in her condo. Silence. Where was Bubbles? The cat should have appeared by now.

She saw movement from the dark top of the stairs even though she hadn't switched on any lights yet. From the shadows, her cat stepped forward, stretched and yawned after a long day's nap.

"What are you? Sleeping beauty?" Toni loved the gracefulness of the cat and admired the fur-clad animal padding her way down the plush carpeted steps. "Come here. Time to cuddle. What's on TV, Bubbles?"

But Toni found it difficult to focus on any show after such a delightful day with Mike.

I miss him. Does he miss me? Wonder what reason I can conjure up for a visit to the newspaper tomorrow? Mike's always there. Maybe I should start jogging.

Chapter Twenty-One

The alarm blared. Toni reached out and slammed the button on top of the clock. She had company in bed. Bubbles huddled close to her head, intent on waking her bedmate with a stare. The cat had learned that when staring failed, a lick on the face with a rough tongue always worked. Her purring questioned when fresh food would fill her dish. Leftover dry morsels did not meet the sophisticated feline's fine dining requirements.

"Oh, kitty. You're so picky. I'm getting up. Let's go down to the kitchen." Toni stroked the cat's head and then swung her feet onto the soft carpet.

It's a serious bank-business day, she thought as she headed back upstairs to her closet after breakfast with Bubbles. Toni donned a steel-gray pantsuit accented by a crisp, red collared blouse. Her silver hoop earrings, inset with Australian crystals, added polish to her executive appearance. She examined herself in the full-length mirror. *Nice. Just what I want for today's image.*

"Bye, Bubbles," Toni called as she grabbed her keys and locked the front door.

The digital car clock showed exactly ten o'clock when Toni pulled into the circular driveway of Pine Oak Place. She spotted Chloe's animated wave as the woman reached to pull little Brutus' leash so she could pick him up. With Chloe buckled in the front seat and Brutus secured in her arms, they were off to accomplish their bank-vault-extraction task.

A mid-month Monday morning at PinCo Bank normally proved uneventful. Then again, the bank's activities over the last few days had been anything but uneventful. And on this Monday, the bank's lobby boasted more customers than Toni had expected to see.

She recognized the teller who had had evasive answers to her questions on Friday. She squinted to see the young woman's name. Penny Parker. *Okay, I'll get something out of her this time.*

"Let's get all the items out of your box first," Toni suggested as she walked with Chloe to the vault door and stood silently at her side while Chloe pushed her code buttons and pressed her palm on the glass to release the vault door.

"Come on," Chloe said as she opened the steel entry. Once in the small room, Chloe aimed her key at her specific, numbered lock and pulled out the metal box. Toni grabbed the box to transfer it to a small desk. After she sat down, Chloe began to examine the contents.

"Is everything there?" Toni asked with trepidation.

"Yes. Of course, my treasured *genuine* sapphire ring is missing, but all the other pieces are still here. Oh, I so love that ring. Do you think I'll ever see it again?"

"I don't know. I can keep asking the police investigator. Maybe the FBI didn't give up." Toni felt like a hypocrite.

Oh great. I've provided a small glimmer of hope for Chloe. And yet, is the FBI doing anything? I want her to be optimistic, but something is wrong here. Only one ring missing with all these other valuables still in place?

"Toni, hold my purse open please. At least all of these gems are coming with me."

One-by-one, Chloe handed pearl necklaces, sparkling gem-embellished bracelets, semi-precious stone rings in velvet boxes, and ornate diamond earrings in small pouches over to the open purse. With this duty complete, Chloe lifted the safe deposit box back into its appointed slot. She left the door to the box open and kept the key in her hand to give back to the bank.

"Let's go talk to the teller about closing this out." Toni put her arm around Chloe as they walked out of the vault.

By the time they emerged, teller Penny had no customers at her window. "Penny," Toni called to her. "Can you help us, please?"

The teller smiled and nodded. "Sure. Come right over."

Penny's evasiveness during their previous conversation about Emily's possible departure from the bank was not evident. This time, her demeanor was one of total customer satisfaction.

Funny switch from just a couple of days earlier. Was something already resolved with Emily? I have to find out.

"Young woman," Chloe began authoritatively, "I want to close my safe deposit box. I've removed my belongings from it. So here is the key."

"I can help you with that. Can I have your name please?" The eager expression of the teller demonstrated her naïveté, or at least masked any concern about the troubled bank situation.

Chloe raised her head in astonishment. "Why, I'm Chloe Ford. I was robbed last week."

"I'm very sorry, Mrs. Ford. I'm sure the bank is doing all it can. Let me pull up your record."

Penny turned to her monitor and typed. Toni noticed that she avoided eye contact with Chloe while she tapped away at the keyboard. The teller had yet to look at Toni.

Chloe signed a form to officially close out her safe deposit box. "Thank you, my dear," Chloe said with a formality uniquely her own.

"Penny," Toni began. "Has Emily come back to work? Will she be here today? I see her office is vacant and her desk is cleared off."

"No. We were told earlier that Emily will be on leave for a while and may not come back. I don't know who will replace her, but I'm relieved to move on. I think a new manager will be appointed soon. We heard that corporate may hire someone from outside the bank."

Suddenly startled by a small but intent growl, Toni looked down near her feet. She observed Brutus in firm stance with head turned up, his eyes focused on the customer in front of the adjacent window. Toni's eyes circled up to see none other than Jesse Morton. His head swung in their direction as he took a side step.

"Jesse," Toni said. "Here we are. Twice in two days."

"Oh hi, Toni," Jesse replied in a flat tone. "Is that your dog? What's its problem?"

Before Toni could respond, loud retorts came from tiny Brutus. His Shih Tzu barking had taken on over-achiever status. Customers throughout the lobby stopped to gawk at such loud noises emanating from the diminutive, furry creature. The beast, as Chloe had called the dog, exhibited his best beastly manner. Chloe had to rein in the leash to prevent the dog from taking a leap toward the man's shin.

"Brutus. Stop," Chloe chastised. "What's the matter with you?"

"Hey, lady," Jesse addressed Chloe, "what the hell did you bring that thing into the bank for? Obviously, it can't behave."

"*Obviously*," Chloe echoed with emphasis, chin held high and leash held firm, "Brutus does not like you. And my dog behaves very well, I might add."

"Yeah, it wanted to take a bite out of me. That's not very well mannered. Just keep that leash secure."

Jesse turned away to finish his banking.

"Here you go, Mr. Morton," the teller told him. "Just sign on this line and you're all set. We're sorry to lose you."

Toni and Chloe headed for the exit. By Chloe's uncharacteristic rapid gait, Toni figured she'd been embarrassed by Brutus's outburst. Toni had never seen the dog act that way. In fact, she tried to recollect when she'd even heard the animal bark. But something about Jesse Morton made the dog angry or scared—or both.

"Hey, Chloe. Are we in a race? Hold up a bit. I can tell Brutus doesn't like that man. But can you have a seat for a few minutes please? I need to speak with him."

"Him? That awful person? He upset my Brutus and me."

"I understand. The confrontation was weird. But I know him from the chamber. I have to ask him a question. Okay?"

"Hmm." Chloe's narrowed eyes indicated her disapproval. "I'll be right here. Don't be long."

"Thanks. And Brutus," Toni lectured the dog. "Keep it down."

Brutus positioned himself close to Chloe's feet. He raised his large brown eyes and gave Toni a Shih Tzu-look of triumph.

Toni rotated to catch sight of Jesse speedily heading for the door. "Jesse," she called. "Wait a minute."

The man practically screeched to a halt and snapped his head around. "What now?" he barked.

"I just want to apologize for my friend's dog. Brutus is usually quite the charmer."

"Right. That's hard to believe."

"I want to ask you a question. I know Emily not just from banking here. She's also a client of my ad agency. I know the bank's had some serious . . . well, disruptions lately. So I'm concerned about her. She's usually a good communicator, but no one at my firm has heard from her since Thursday. I want to be sure she's okay."

Toni hoped her words came across with utmost sincerity. She didn't want Jesse to consider her tactic one of snooping, as Mike would call it.

"She's fine. Just needed some time off, you know. I may see her so I'll tell her you asked."

"Excellent. That would be great." Toni visibly sighed in relief. "Can you ask her to call me please? She has my number in her phone."

Toni smiled and extended her hand toward Jesse. The man maintained a serious expression, but after hesitation, shook her hand. Then without a word, he resumed his long strides out the front door.

Toni headed back to the seating area to get Chloe and Brutus.

"A most unpleasant man." Chloe's strong opinion caught Toni off-guard.

"Why Chloe Ford. How can you say that?" Toni asked. "Just because he and Brutus didn't exactly hit it off."

"Brutus is a good judge of character. My dog has never let me down. I think that fellow is up to no good." Chloe's laser focus in the direction of Jesse's departure left Toni with an uneasy feeling.

What was going on? Did he just close his account? The teller said the bank was sorry to lose him. Why'd he take his money out? He can't be leaving town. He's dating Sue. Or I think he is? She thinks he is. I better pay a visit to Sue to get some answers.

***

Toni escorted Chloe to the front desk of Pine Oak Place. "Hello, Mrs. Ford." The attentive receptionist greeted Chloe with a pleasant smile. "How can I help you today?"

"I want to put some items in my little vault for safekeeping."

"Absolutely. Just come this way." The receptionist looked down at Brutus. "Hi there, little fellow. What's your dog's name, Mrs. Ford?"

"He's Brutus. My protector," Chloe affirmed.

"How lucky for you." The receptionist maintained her automatic smile, fixed like her short, pixie hairdo, as she led Chloe on a brief walk to the residents' security room.

If only she knew Brutus' vicious side, Toni thought. "I'll wait out here, Chloe," she called.

Toni ambled over to the marketing director's office, but Bob Wolfe was not behind his desk. She circled the lobby and peeked into the dining room, but the man was not in view.

Too bad. I want to get him to sign off on this month's newsletter. I'll call him later to set up a meeting. Better make sure Peggy doesn't have any changes or suggestions. If we edit it fast, we can get done early. More time to snoop, as Mike calls it.

Chloe and her receptionist escort returned to the lobby.

"All set?" Toni asked.

"Yes. I feel better now. Or as good as I can feel. Do you want to hang around for lunch? We can talk about this year's fashion show."

"Thank you, but I can't. I have to get to the office. Want me to walk you back to your apartment?"

"No. Brutus and I will take our stroll in the garden. We need to enjoy this lovely weather."

"Good idea. I'll check with you soon." Toni and Chloe hugged before heading in opposite directions.

Since the bank errand had gone faster than Toni anticipated, she had an hour or so before meeting with Peggy. The fact that Jesse Morton had closed his bank account tugged at her thoughts.

What if he's only taking Sue out because he needs something from her? But what? Brutus could be right. I'm going to pry—not that Mike will approve. But who's going to tell him?

Toni started her car and took off in the direction of the newspaper. She knew that she could slip into the advertising department without anyone in the newsroom spotting her.

Sue won't be at lunch yet. I can find out more about Jesse Morton. Oh man, avoiding Mike. I can't believe I'm doing this. Maybe I'll head over to his office after I talk with Sue. He'll think I stopped in to see him.

Maybe there are new developments on the bank heist and the FBI, Ray's death, or the gruesome Land O'Lakes body. Besides, I have to see how Mike survived his first workout at the gym. Wonder if he feels sore? He runs a few days a week. Hmm . . . I'll just have to watch those leg muscles . . . .

Chapter Twenty-Two

The Retail Advertising Department had a ghost-town aura at this time of day. Desks were left cluttered as if to validate that a neat work area meant a rep's poor dedication. Thus disorder became the sign of advertising's practical organized mess, mirroring the chaotic activity of success.

Most of the sales representatives were out in the field soliciting new contract signatures or ad copy approval. Some of their secretaries hovered around the coffee machine, gainfully—or not— biding their time until lunch.

As an inside sales rep, Sue Anderson appeared affixed to her desk. Toni knew that Sue was delighted to have a position where she could stay inside, have customers come to her and avoid the horrid humidity of Florida summers.

"Hi, Sue," Toni called.

Sue looked up from her proofreading task. "Hey, Toni. Come and have a seat. You look very distinguished in that suit. How can I help? The bank's not planning another open house yet, is it?"

"No such luck. In fact, I'm not even sure where Emily is. However, I ran into Jesse this morning at the bank and asked him about Emily. He said she's fine, just needed some time off. But since she's my client and my friend, I want to get in touch with her. Jesse said he'd have her call me. I know he's busy, so I thought I'd see if you heard from anyone at the bank."

"Not a word. Their corporate ads are handled by Cliff, who doesn't usually confide in me about client details."

"Yeah, you're my rep, not the bank's. I am eager to know if Emily's okay. This whole situation is pretty unnerving."

Sue nodded. "True, but the FBI is investigating the rumors about a robbery, right?"

"Rumors?" Toni responded with dramatic upscale tone. "Is that what people are saying?"

"That's what I have heard. Don't shoot the messenger here."

"Sorry. I appreciate your information. But the residents at Pine Oak Place who have missing bank vault items are not senile. In fact, Chloe Ford, a good friend of mine, discovered the theft in the first place. I helped her plan the fundraiser fashion show for the hospital. She's one incredibly sharp lady."

"I went to that event last year and really enjoyed it."

"Terrific. We can use another capable person on our committee. How about it? We have a great time selecting the clothes, getting the models and even sampling some of the food we choose."

"I don't know, Toni. It sounds like fun, but with work, kids and now Jesse, I'm swamped."

Toni smiled inwardly and seized the opportune moment that justified more inquiry into the Jesse situation.

"Mike and I thought you made a nice couple when we talked at Plait. How long have you guys been going out?"

"Not long. A couple of weeks. But, Toni, he's so good to me. I can't believe it. It's almost too good to be true. Me and a distinguished, successful man like Jesse. And he's good with the kids. They're warming up to him." Sue's business-formal expression melted into an adoring fantasy gaze.

Oh great. Now what can I say? She's head-over-heels for this man. Brutus probably knows best. That pooch sensed something amiss about Jesse, but what?

"Yeah, Jesse's quite a catch," Toni said with as much enthusiasm as she could muster. "I guess he does pretty well with his computer business."

"He's a programmer—quite talented. And he's picked up some terrific clients. Since he moved back here, he's worked hard to build his business, and it's paid off."

Sue's effervescence helped Toni to sound a bit more upbeat. "Excellent. I'm a little confused though. When I saw him at the bank this morning, he was withdrawing all of his funds. Is he changing banks? I'm just curious if it's because of Emily being fired or something?"

Toni attempted to establish casual eye-contact with Sue while making a mental note of her emotional reaction. The woman's wide eyes almost spoke for themselves.

"I see," Sue said.

Okay, that revelation struck a note. Toni waited, hoping she appeared calm while on guard for what Sue might say next. But Sue just seemed frozen in mind and in body.

Finally, Toni had to comment. "Maybe he's mad at the bank."

"What?" With a jolt, Sue thawed from her reverie. "PinCo is one of his clients, Toni. I don't understand. He bragged about how thrilled he was to land them. I presumed everything—at least for him—was going well."

Sue's face reflected sad disbelief, and Toni felt her stomach turn at the idea of another man hurting this nice, unassuming woman.

"Look, Sue. I shouldn't have pried," Toni fibbed, "but I'm just trying to find out where Emily is and figure out the truth about the alleged bank theft. I bet Jesse has a perfectly good reason to withdraw his funds. He may have gotten an even better client." Toni smiled back at the immobile Sue.

Good grief. I hope she's breathing because my CPR's out of date.

"Maybe . . ." Sue's voice trailed off as Toni rose to leave her suspended in contemplation.

***

Mike's desk held fewer papers than the desks in the Advertising Department, but the appreciation for disorganized mess made its presence known, nonetheless. The editor, himself, was nowhere to be seen. Harry, on the other hand, hovered over the area, apparently looking for something.

"Hi, Harry," Toni said in a low voice after stealthily approaching.

"Hey." Harry straightened in surprise. "What are you doing here, Toni?"

"Good question. Isn't this Mike's domain?"

"Right. I need a phone number. He copied it for me earlier, but I lost it somehow."

And that's a surprise, Toni thought sardonically. "Can you just tell the boss I was in to see him? I have some news he might find intriguing. Okay?"

"News?" asked the assistant editor. "I'd be happy to tell him what the news is."

I bet you would. "Thanks, but I need to speak with Mike. Look, you're busy. I'll write him a note."

Toni left her memo on Mike's chair, considering, at least, it wouldn't be buried in the array of white paper jumble disguising the color of the brown desk.

I guess I'd better get my own work done before Peggy has a fit. Or . . . oh my geez, why didn't I think of this before? I can just find out where Emily lives and pay her a friendly visit. I have a little time. I'm done with this 'I don't know anything' excuse from bank tellers and waiting for Jesse to tell her to call—if he ever will.

Toni extricated her cell phone from the side pocket of her purse and tapped the Internet icon. In a moment, she had Jon and Emily Phillips' address from public records and was proud of what she called her "super-sleuth Internet ability."

Onward to get some information from at least one suspect in this caper. If she's home.

Chapter Twenty-Three

Toni presumed she was destined for good fortune. The driver in the car ahead of her punched in the code, and the gate to the prestigious collection of luxury homes slowly opened its welcoming arm. Gratefully, Toni steered her car right behind and into the land seemingly forbidden to non-code-holders.

On high volume, the cell phone's voice directed her to turn right at the third street. And, Toni realized, there it was on the curve of the cul-de-sac. Emily's much-bragged-about stunning house.

With a three-car garage flanking one side and lush greenery adding its living presence to the other side, the home's columned portico stood in a majestic yet inviting manner. Though the grass needed trimming and edging, the home appeared grand. Toni stepped along the pavered drive and walkway leading to the double, etched-glass front doors. She rang the doorbell and stood motionless, attempting to hear any noise from within.

Debating for a few minutes about whether to ring the bell again or leave, she heard footsteps shuffling toward her from beyond the glass. A man's face appeared between etchings. Jon Phillips. Or a not-so-pleasant-looking appearance of the man she had met.

"Hi, Jon. It's Toni Jasper. Remember me? Is Emily home?"

The grayish, pained countenance did not speak. Toni shivered as she peered back.

"Are you okay? Are you home sick today? You look exhausted, to say the least."

"Yeah," the mask of illness emitted, "haven't been feeling well. I don't know where Emily is. She's away, trying to figure out who may be framing her for the bank theft."

"I see. Sorry to hear you're sick. Geez, you look terrible. Can I get you anything?"

"No. I need to sleep. Waiting for tests from the clinic where I work."

"Okay. Well . . . if Emily should call, can you please have her get in touch with me? I want to help. Emily's my client and my friend."

"Sure." Jon's face floated back into the darkness of the foyer. Toni turned to go.

That was nonproductive to say nothing of strange. Man, he looked awful. He can't be contagious through the door. I'm in the fresh air. Wonder why none of their windows are open? This is the best September weather we've had—nice and breezy, and kind of cool.

Even stranger is Emily leaving him alone in this big house. Where the hell would she need to go? What could be so damning from the bank that she'd leave her sick hubby to fend for himself? Unless she was in on the robbery.

Toni passed the well-manicured lawns and steered out of the exit gate that opened in reactive smoothness as she approached. Back on the road to her office, mental wheels turned in her head with incessant speed.

Where IS Emily? Will she come back if she's guilty? But leaving her sick husband in his condition? Even if he just got sick, why in God's name wouldn't she come back to help. The man embodied death warmed over. I have to talk to Mike—to someone. Good lord, the newsletter deadline. Maybe Peggy can inject a shred of sanity into this situation.

***

After picking up Peggy's order and her own salad, Toni pulled into her favorite parking spot directly in front of her office building door. Her phone rang as she grabbed the bag of food.

Before she could utter a sound, she heard, "Toni, don't say anything. This is Ray."

"What?" Toni's shrill response echoed her more-than-surprised expression. "Who is this? Don't pull some sick joke on me. I—"

"Wait, Toni. I *am* Ray Edwards, Chloe's personal banker, advisor at the bank. I told you to 'let it go' the last two times we talked in my office. Remember?"

Toni sat in stunned silence. Finally, she managed to move her lips.

"Good God. Ray. You aren't dead?" Toni's incredulous voice in no way masked the bizarre absurdity of the question. Toni's brain and body both halted.

"No. I am more alive than ever. And now I'm ready to talk with you. But I didn't want you to get hurt. So I couldn't say anything on Friday. I figured that the bank execs needed to figure it out. However, after what's happened, I have to trust someone. Knowing you, I figured you hadn't left well enough alone."

"There's no 'well enough' in this whole deal. Where are you? And why are you hiding?"

"No location—not yet. I have to stay where I am. Since I'm still in danger, it's better if you don't know. My house explosion wasn't an accident. I'm too careful, and I took good care of that property. I would never have left the stove on. And I don't smoke. Besides, the neighborhood isn't very old. It was developed about ten years ago when I bought the house. So a gas or any type of incendiary leak is far-fetched."

"What are you saying?"

"I was murdered."

No. Two murders on my brain in less than a week? Holy crapola.

"Toni, are you still there?" Ray's tone became intense.

"Yes. I'm here. What do you want me to do?"

"Just listen." Ray's voice was steady and determined. "The morning of the explosion, Emily and her brother-in-law, Jesse, came to see me. They wanted to talk about the hypothetical robbery. Jesse did the programming for the bank's computers, or so he said. I never saw an actual invoice to the bank for his work. His office is in downtown Tampa, but one day, he probed me for information about this branch. I wasn't sure what he was getting at. Furthermore, I never let on that I saw both of them in the bank after hours when the alarm should have been on and the vault's master door should have been closed."

Toni injected, "You saw them?"

"Yeah, but that doesn't mean anything. What looked suspicious was that I saw Jesse's car parked a block away. If he was on bank time, why would he park so far away?"

"So they were up to something?" Toni's gut feeling was screaming foul play, especially with regard to Jesse. But Emily?

"Nothing I can prove. And Thursday afternoon, Emily maintained that the retirees were just absentminded. She wasn't happy the FBI was brought in for what she called 'dumb people.'"

"She called your customers dumb? That's not like Emily." Toni never heard Emily be rude to the customers. Just the opposite. She was friendly, even if a bit aloof.

"Anyway, when they came to my house," Ray continued, "Jesse went to get glasses of water from the kitchen. On their way out, Emily took the glasses back to the kitchen. A few minutes later, I smelled gas. Of course, I ran to the kitchen. Just inside the door, I saw a small lit candle. That's when I jumped out of the back door and rolled into the little gully near the bushes. I knew I was lucky to be alive. So I threw my partial denture back in afterwards so it would look like I was killed."

Toni sat in her car, holding her keys and phone, yet not feeling a thing.

"Toni?"

"I'm here," she said. "You believe Jesse and Emily tried to kill you?"

"Yes. They must have assumed I know more than I do. You have to talk to the police. Have them look more closely into Emily's financials and Jesse's business. Just don't tell them I'm alive."

"What? So how do I know this? Some psychic dream? You have to come forward and let them protect you."

No answer from the other end of the phone. Toni didn't know what to say. She sat and waited.

Ray finally answered, "Not yet, Toni. Soon. I promise." The line went silent.

Chapter Twenty-Four

For several minutes, Toni gazed down at the noiseless phone in her hand. Her head and hand felt numb. Her body remained motionless. But her ruminations galloped on.

Ray. Alive. Not murdered? This can't be a joke. The voice seemed convinced of the murder attempt. If it was Ray . . . but the voice sounded like Ray. Yeah. He did tell me to "let it go" when I left his office. Where the hell is he? Emily? Jesse . . . he is such a creep. Shit. I have to talk with Alan. But Peggy?

The fact that her business had been almost neglected the past few days jolted Toni out of her Ray reverie. Her vision refocused on the building's door waiting for her a few feet beyond the car's bumper. In a flash, she'd formulated a plan for the rest of her day.

Toni grabbed the food and leaped out of her vehicle. She pulled the building door handle, flung the door wide open and bounded up to the second story. Halfway down the hallway, she noticed light flowing from beyond her office door. Peggy would be hungry.

"Ah. The prodigal owner arriveth and bearing lunch, no less," Peggy teased. Then she observed the expression on Toni's face. "Hey, you look like you just saw a ghost."

"No. Heard one."

"What?"

Toni put the packages on Peggy's desk. Then she flopped down in the gray, upholstered chair across the room, which angled—in good design sense—toward Peggy's desk. Toni considered how to begin the tale of risen Ray. She hung her head as if analyzing each carpet fiber on the floor beneath her feet.

How can I phrase this? Oh heck, it'll be a shock no matter how I put it.

"What's going on?" Peggy inquired after the prolonged silence got to her.

Looking up at Peggy, Toni said, "Ray is alive."

"What." Peggy sounded forceful. She leaned forward and landed on her elbows. "Are you okay?"

"Yeah, I think so. I can't believe it."

"Neither can I. Did you get any rest this weekend, Toni?"

"What?"

"I mean you've been on this quest for justice, and well, you do have a vivid imagination. But voices—"

"Peggy. I'm *not* nuts. He just called me. I *know* it was him. Sounded like him. And he reminded me of words that he used on Friday when I saw him at the bank."

"But on the news, they said the body was his."

"Body? They never said 'body' per se. And what do they know? They found a modicum of evidence and called it a day. Accidental explosion? Bullshit. Ray told me Emily and Jesse visited him at his house right before it blew up. And I believe him. So I've got to talk with Alan."

"What do Emily and Jesse have to do with the explosion?"

"Maybe everything. And don't tell anyone. Ray has to stay in hiding."

"What?"

"Don't tell anyone—"

"I heard you, Toni. Why on holy earth would Emily and Jesse be trying to kill Ray? That *is* what you're saying, right?"

"I guess so. That's what he said. Meanwhile, do you need me to do anything here?"

"You mean in your own advertising agency? Now why the hell would I?"

"I know, I know. Geez, Peg. I appreciate you holding down the fort. Did you see the copy I wrote for the Pine Oak newsletter? I did accomplish something."

"Yes. I saw that. Looked good to me. Just a few typos. Maybe I'll award you one of our leftover Brownie troop baking night points."

"Very funny."

"Okay. I know you're under a lot of stress. Not to worry. I can organize the photos and add the cut lines. We're way ahead of schedule due to our friendly bank fiasco. Oh, forgot to tell you. PinCo's corporate accounting called. Since the mugs didn't have dates on them, they can use them for other events. So they'll pay our invoice. The accountant is checking about the caterer's cancellation fee. Nice of them, huh?"

"Damn right. I wasn't eating that cost. Good. Did the accountant say when?"

"No, but it's in the payable queue." Peggy took a forceful bite out of her sandwich while Toni stabbed her lettuce adorned with tuna. And then gulped down the sustenance as fast as she could.

"Okay. Check with Brad and see how the hospital project is going. Have we heard back from the cable company or that doctors' group about our proposals?"

"Nope. *We* have not heard about the proposals. I'll touch base with everyone."

"Peggy," Toni sighed, "despite your diminished sense of humor, you're the best. Thanks. Text me when they all come to their senses and sign the agreements. One more thing. See what you can find out about Jesse Morton's company. He works out of downtown Tampa, I believe. Gotta go."

Toni discarded her salad bowl and grabbed a bottle of water she'd gotten with her order.

"I will. Listen, be careful."

"Okay. See ya," Toni called over her shoulder as she jogged down the hall.

Once belted in her car, Toni pulled out her cell phone and punched in the police station number. "Detective Alan Dietz, please."

A faceless voice responded, "I'm sorry, he's in a meeting. Can I take a message?"

Toni thought for a moment while she gritted her teeth. "Yes. Please have him call Toni Jasper as soon as he can. I need to speak with him regarding a very important matter."

"Okay, ma'am. Is the number that you're calling from the one he should use?"

"Yes. It's my cell phone. Please tell him I need to speak with him as soon as possible. It's critical. I must talk with him—only him."

"I understand, ma'am. Is there anything else?"

Toni was tempted to shout, "Look you idiot. Nothing else matters." But she held her tongue and stated, "No. But the situation is urgent. I need to speak with Detective Dietz."

"I'll see to it the detective gets the message."

Toni considered her next move. She didn't want to talk with Mike before explaining the development to Alan.

Hell, how long can Alan's meeting be? I'm going to sit in his office and wait. Just let them try to throw me out.

Chapter Twenty-Five

Alan's desk clutter would have been right at home in the newspaper building. Another organized mess, Toni observed.

As Toni perused the disorder, two words caught her attention in the pile of papers. Debra Morton. She didn't expect to see that name, especially on Alan's desk.

What the hell? What's Jesse's ex-wife's name doing there? Is she back in town? Holy crap. What about Sue? Oh no. Does Alan consider Jesse a suspect? But how could he already? Ray told me I had to go to the police for him and specify Jesse's involvement. Did Debra call Alan about Jesse, too, or did Alan call Debra? And how did he know where to find her?

"Messing with my stuff?" The gruff Alan Dietz query startled Toni as he approached with noiseless footsteps.

"Alan. Good grief. You want to give me a heart attack?"

"Will that get you out of my desk?" he asked.

"You're a riot. Listen, I need to talk with you. Can we go somewhere private? Please?" she begged.

"You look a bit frightened. I didn't know I had that effect."

Toni shook her head. "No. Something else. Big."

"The conference room is open."

Alan led Toni across the room past officers busily conversing on their phones or punching reports into their computers. Once inside the room, Toni plopped into a chair at the end of the expansive conference table. Alan stood as he looked down at Toni, indicating a short conversation on his part.

"Ray's alive."

Toni looked up at Alan with a grave almost chilling expression, one that Alan had never seen on the vibrant, smartass ad exec's face. He pulled out a chair and lowered his large frame into the seat.

"What the hell, Toni? Are you on drugs? The report is in. Ray was in that fire. That partial was definitely his."

"I know."

"*What?* You know? And how in blazes *do you know*?"

"No, I wasn't there. Ray called me today. He's in hiding but told me the whole story. I recognized his voice, and he repeated words he used when I was in his office on Friday. And yes—it was his partial. He threw it back into the burning house before he escaped."

Alan sat straight up. His piercing stare bore into Toni's blue-green worried eyes. After a few seconds, he commanded, "Wait here. I need a pad for your statement. Let me have your phone."

Minutes later, Toni penned her account of the mysterious phone call from the perceived-to-be-alive Ray Edwards. She made certain that her words were specific and her handwriting decipherable. She owned this case now, despite warnings and reprimands from Alan and just about everyone else in her life.

At least Bubbles has supported my efforts all along. Thank God for feline companionship.

"Okay, listen up, Ms. Jasper," Alan began in an official law enforcement tone, "you need to report back to me if you get any more communication from Mr. Edwards. Do you understand?"

"Yes, Detective. I came here right away, didn't I? I've told you all along I can help."

"No, no, no." Alan rose from his seat in a sudden rush to exude lawful superiority over the young, eager but former reporter. He began to pace as if in a physical way to demonstrate his mental anguish of how to get through to this human epitome of obstinacy.

"This is where you back off. Police are trained to handle dangerous situations. You are not a trained investigator, or a reporter anymore, or anything else that entitles you to probe into this criminal matter. Run your business, Toni, and let us do our job."

"Our job? Does that mean the FBI is still on the case?"

Maybe there's hope for Chloe and the Pine Oak gang.

Alan ignored the questions and continued to review the words written on the stiff yellow pad. "Now, let me clarify this statement.

So Ray—or someone who sounded like Ray—called you out of the blue."

"Yes. Ray himself called me."

Oblivious to the interjection, Alan continued, "And he claimed that Mrs. Phillips and Mr. Morton came to visit him on Friday evening, opened the gas on Mr. Edwards' stove but without a flame, then left a lighted candle in the kitchen, thereby causing the explosion and subsequent fire which demolished Mr. Edwards' home. Are those the facts, Toni?"

"Correct, Alan. And furthermore, what the hell is Debra Morton's name doing on your desk? Did she contact you? Is her ex-husband considered dangerous?"

"Lord, help me. Did you hear anything I just said? I don't know about Mr. Morton or even what you now claim in your statement. We've got the word of a risen-from-the dead man, over the phone, no less. Why in God's name won't Ray Edwards come in to the police station—if he is alive?"

The detective's face began to flush. Toni saw his anger percolate. But she knew he was in good health, so she figured he could stand a little heat from her.

"Alan, calm down. I asked him the same question. He said it's better if certain people—mentioned in my statement—did not know he's alive. He only trusts you and me."

"All right, all right. You're sure you didn't have a three-martini lunch?"

"Alan. Would I make this up?"

"Okay. I'll see what I can find out about Mrs. Phillips' and Mr. Morton's pasts. Emily's been at the bank a few years, but Jesse Morton—how long was he married to Emily's husband's sister?"

"I'm not sure. But he came back here about a year ago. I saw him at chamber meetings, but I didn't speak to him much until lately."

"You spoke with him?"

"I ran into him at the gym over the weekend. Then again at the bank this morning."

"Why'd you talk to him at the gym?"

"I spotted my friend from the paper, Sue Anderson, and went over to say hi. Jesse Morton was with her. I don't want Sue to get hurt so I was alarmed she was with him. Sue's been through an abusive marriage and a rough divorce. And something about Jesse gives me the creeps. Can't put my finger on it. But if his ex is back in town, well, fishy, is an understatement. So, is Debra in town?"

Alan stopped his striding back and forth, and glared down at Toni. "Did you breathe at all during that diatribe? Look, Toni, I appreciate your concern for others. I do. And I know your tenacity is what helped you do well at the paper. But you have to back off this time."

Toni sighed. "Alan, this bank fiasco is costing my agency a lot of money. I'm pissed no one will own up to what actually happened there, why they cancelled the open house and where in God's name Emily is. I even went to her house, and she wasn't there."

"Maybe she didn't want to talk. She could've ignored the doorbell."

"No, her husband was home sick. Man, he looked like death warmed over. There's another creepy situation. He works for a medical clinic. Who knows what he contracted? And yeah, he told me that Emily was—and I quote, 'trying to figure out who may be framing her for the bank theft.' What'd you make of that?"

Alan shook his head. "Maybe he's on drugs. Who knows? I'm not considering the delusions of a sick guy. We're done here. I've got to do my job. How about you go back to your agency job?"

Toni followed the detective out of the conference room and reminded him that she wanted to help. When he closed the door to his office, she took the hint and headed for the parking lot. She buckled her seatbelt and pondered where to get more information.

Ah: PinCo owes me an explanation. Even if they think they don't, they do. I'll save the account if I have to barge in on the regional VP himself.

Chapter Twenty-Six

Go figure, Toni thought, *my best suit day and I have to dodge this deluge.* She steered through puddles surrounding PinCo Bank's regional headquarters. The stately brick building stood fortress-like against the early fall Florida downpour, creating small moats along rows of parked cars. After she pulled her purse strap over her head and across her body, she grabbed her umbrella and navigated opening it while closing the car door at the same time.

Come hell or high water, Toni was determined to see Carl Johnson, the bank's regional vice president. She watched the elevator floor lights head toward first floor as she considered her approach with the man. Once inside the compartment, she confidently pushed the button for seven and waited for the door to open.

A few steps from the elevator, a secretary sat hunched over her keyboard. Behind her, the financial institution's regional vice president's office door was open. Toni felt lucky.

"Hi Nicole." Toni extended her hand after reading the woman's name plate on the front edge of the desk. I need to have a quick word with Mr. Johnson. I guess no one's going out in this rain." Toni smiled as she stepped around the desk.

"Wait," Nicole barked. "Do you have an appointment?"

"No, not today. But with the urgency of the matter, I believe Mr. Johnson will appreciate my visit." Toni projected her voice to assure it carried well into the huge office.

The gray-haired executive could see Toni and called from his inner sanctum, "Nicole?"

"Yes, Mr. Johnson," the secretary replied.

"Let her in. I know who she is."

The mid-fifties, medium-build man in a tailored black suit stood up, remained behind his desk and smoothed his bright blue silk tie into place.

"You're the advertising woman Emily Phillips was working with."

"Hello, sir. Toni Jasper," Toni said extending her hand across the large mahogany desk. "Yes, I do have the pleasure of working with Emily. Of course, I'm here because I'm concerned about her."

"You needn't be. She'll survive, I imagine."

"What do you mean survive? I know the episode with the bank vault was serious, but don't you think Emily and I should set another date for the open house event? I mean, you do want to reassure your customers so they have confidence in your bank."

"Ms. Jasper, the contrived open house was never authorized. Our executive team had no knowledge of the plans. Add to that the complaints of the customers against Mrs. Phillips. Well, she is no longer affiliated with this institution. She may never get another job in finance."

Toni was stunned. "What do you mean the open house at the branch was never authorized? Emily and I had several meetings about it. She showed me papers from the legal department approving the press release. My business values your bank as a client, sir. I need to know what's going on here." Toni stood in front of the desk, but found herself sinking into the plush beige carpet.

"Do you want to sit down?" The man all but ordered her to do so, motioning toward the seats facing his desk. "You look a bit pale."

Toni shifted her weight and sank into the deep blue, stylish wingback chair.

"It seems we've both been duped. Mrs. Phillips had no authority to arrange an event of any type at her branch. And we've discovered no such validation from anyone in legal. I'm aware your firm incurred expenses relating to several hundred coffee mugs and a caterer's fee. I've signed off on payment of both invoices. I respect the finances of small entrepreneurs such as you, Ms. Jasper. I'm glad I did since you're diligent enough to be here. Apparently, you were not in on the con to bilk the bank out of any funds."

"No, sir, I most assuredly was not. I was assisting Emily and your bank in good faith, as I do with all my clients. I just can't believe Emily would 'bilk the bank' as you put it."

"We're conducting our own investigation. It seems funds and other . . . dealings have gone unaccounted for. Hopefully, we'll find clerical errors. But for the moment, we had to let Mrs. Phillips go. As I said, she is no longer employed with us."

Toni was uncharacteristically at a loss for words. She mulled the situation over in her mind as she stared into the gentleman's hazel eyes. Then she looked away to consider the next step. The word "rekeyed" caught her attention, as it was stamped atop several documents fanned out on the expansive mahogany desk. Toni was proud that her ability to read upside down documents was still a valuable skill.

"Are you working with the FBI?" she asked.

"If you're referring to the *alleged* bank vault theft, I cannot comment on the FBI or anything else pertaining to it."

"Why does everyone have 'alleged' on the brain as if it never happened? I realize you don't know the people involved, but they aren't a bunch of senile old fools." Toni stopped as she saw the tightening of the executive's lips.

"Ms. Jasper—" he said in a resolute, deep voice.

"Mr. Johnson, they're your valued customers," she jumped in with a resolve of her own, "and some of them have great personal wealth. *And* their minds are as sharp as yours, sir."

The man leaned back in his chair and managed a hint of a smile.

That was a close one. Okay, I need to be sure he's on my side. He relaxed a bit. Progress here. But I don't want to seem too anxious. Sit straight. Confidence.

After hesitation and a sigh, Carl Johnson continued, "All of the evidence is not in, Toni. Therefore, I am not at liberty to make any comment. I have to report to my higher-ups first."

Ah, my first name. Got him. "Of course. And I want to help. I always do my best and go the extra mile for my agency's clients. Can I tell you what I have learned so far? Those Pine Oak Place residents are pretty good friends of mine. They talk to me."

Carl sighed. "I guess it wouldn't hurt. Go ahead."

After an hour with the regional VP, Toni had provided a step-by-step account of Chloe's traumatic tale of woe and Walter's vanished bonds. She dubbed Carl her new BFE or "best friend exec." By the time Toni headed out of the majestic building, she was pleased to have gained another ally.

It's me, cat and regional VP against those doubters. And now, alleluia, no rain.

Carl Johnson wanted her to keep him informed. All PinCo higher-ups were attentive to the situation, so he realized that the more he knew from her perspective at the ground level, the better.

Time for a pow-wow with Mike, a formidable doubter who needed to understand her perspective. *This time, I've got developments to share. He'll need to listen and work with me.*

Chapter Twenty-Seven

The crisp melody of her cell phone ringtone broke the fast gait of ideas racing through Toni's mind.

"Hi Peggy." she responded as she buckled her seatbelt.

"Hey, how'd it go with Alan? What's he going to do about Ray?"

"Sh. Remember, you don't know about Ray."

"Right. What'll he do?"

"Okay, he took my statement. I think he believes me. You know Alan. When it gets official, he has to be very methodical. He told me he's the one to handle dangerous jobs, and of course, warned me to stay out. But you won't believe what I saw on his desk. Some memo or something with Debra Morton's name on it. You know, Jesse's ex-wife. I tried to find out if she was back in town. However, official Alan wouldn't budge. Oh, I forgot to tell you that Mike and I ran into Jesse at the gym yesterday. He was with Sue from the paper. Man, was I surprised when—"

"Wait, you and Mike at the gym? What gym? And when did this start? Come on, Toni. You can't hold out on me."

"I didn't mean to. I got a little distracted after that phone call from Ray. Mike called because he was worried about me after the explosion, especially when he found out I was working alone at the office. I met with him and Alan at the paper. Afterwards, I kind of talked Mike into going with me to the gym."

"Gym? Don't tell me. Plait."

"How perceptive. When I came back from the press conference in New Port Richey Saturday, I thought I needed a relevant place to check for suspects."

Toni waited for a response. But Peggy was silent.

"Toni." Finally, her voice came through the phone. "I'll run the agency. You obviously are a hopeless snoop or incessant investigative reporter or some such animal. Go and get it out of your bloodstream."

"Peggy, don't be mad. I have good news about the bank, or it could be good news."

"We're jumping from gym to bank?"

"Sure. I met with Carl Johnson, the regional VP, and he's fired Emily. But—the good news part—he's paying both the mug and the caterer's invoices. And he wants me to keep him up-to-date on the vault theft from our perspective."

"What's this *'our'* perspective? I don't have a perspective. That's your jurisdiction."

"Hey, the more I can communicate with that guy, the better our chances of getting the bank's business again It sure beats stomping the pavement for another good client when the bank could be a great client. I still want to know what's up with Emily. She hasn't emailed or anything, right?"

"Right. Not a thing. But Brad called. He'll bring the new billboard draft in whenever you'll be here. Something about loitering in the lobby last time?"

"I was a little late. Brad's cool. I like his work. I'll call him and set it up. Anything else need attention today?"

"Nothing urgent. Newsletter delivery for Pine Oak is scheduled for tomorrow. The mail house knows the newsletters are coming. Meredith dropped off a few file samples. They look amazing. We got exceptional photos this time. And Wolfie should contact us today regarding any mailing list changes."

"Why do you call him Wolfie? The guy's pretty nice and efficient. And he pays quickly."

"Right. Efficient doesn't mean personality plus."

"Come on. Not everyone can be as dynamic as we are."

They both laughed, and Toni thanked her dedicated pal. Then she sent a text to Brad letting him know she was free for the rest of the day before putting her phone in its designated purse pocket. A few seconds later, she'd just started her car when Brad responded. So she peeked at the screen.

111

"How about four o'clock, your office?" A little over thirty minutes away.

She replied that he was pretty quick and four o'clock would be fine.

***

The office was empty. Peggy had gone home to her hubby and young Brownie troopers. Since Brad would be there any minute, Toni looked around for an easy, quick task. She picked up the office job list and took it to her desk for review. She heard footsteps in the hall. Toni glanced at the door, expecting the imaginative Brad to appear. But the door knob didn't turn. She sat stiffly in her chair, aware of tension starting to crunch muscles in her back.

Damn, my pepper spray is across the room in my purse. It's nothing to be alarmed about. Other offices on this floor get visitors. Well . . . not many.

She rotated in her seat to survey the parking lot. Only a few cars were there. Not one of them was Brad's old compact car. Still nothing from the hallway.

Alan and Mike, they've got me panicked to the point that I dredge up spooky notions. I better get my purse and that pepper spray, just in case.

Halfway across the room, Toni saw the door knob turn. Then the door swung open.

"Hi there. You're here this time."

Brad stepped inside the room, tucking his phone into his pocket with one hand while toting a large, black leather portfolio in the other.

Toni's surge of relief almost had her leaping across the room to hug the artist.

"Hi!" she shouted as her shoulders relaxed and she exhaled. "Thanks for coming in. Let's see what you've got."

.

Chapter Twenty-Eight

The image of the foyer behind Jon's creepy face popped into her mind. There was a hole in the wall, maybe where a sconce should've been? Electrical wires dangled from it. On a whim, Toni pulled up the satellite imaging on her computer screen. Punching in the Phillips' address, she zoomed in for a crisp, bird's-eye view of their "dream house."

Funny. Pool in the back of the house has boards across it. The cage would keep neighborhood kids out. Emily and Jon don't have any little ones. Wonder if the real estate site still has the listing from a couple of years ago?

The real estate listing, marked "off the market," was accessible along with historic photos. Interior photos may have been historic, but to Toni, they looked more like horrific. Light fixtures were absent, wires hung from ceilings and walls, some bathroom counters were gone, and the pool was covered in a makeshift wood lattice.

That's some dream house. Emily did say it was big, and they negotiated a super deal. Wonder what "deal" meant? That darn pool cover. Looks like the same decrepit thing from the satellite images.

Toni's gut feeling or "super snoop intuition"—as she had called it when Mike assigned difficult investigations to her back in her reporter days—was grumbling. She knew better than to ignore it.

Good thing Mike and Alan aren't here now because neither one would approve of this research or my next move. What they don't know won't hurt them.

She left the material for her upcoming fundraiser fashion show scattered on her desk. After all, she remembered, organized mess was in style these days. She locked her office door and bounded down the stairwell.

Exercise. I guess I could go back to Plait to see who shows up for their Monday routine . . . maybe later. I need to check out another environment first. In this case, maybe more than just the criminal will return to the scene of the crime.

She gripped the wheel of her car and roared out of the parking lot. Toni knew Ray's address—or former address. Maybe he'd be lurking around to see who might show up.

Just five minutes from her office, she turned into a narrow street and parked a block away from Ray's burned-out former abode. A couple of young teens passed her on their bikes, gawking at the charred house.

Crime scene tape covered the doors and windows as if a large yellow marker had slashed across the gaping black holes. The slashes only increased the eeriness level. Toni did her own gawking up and down the street. After an hour of patient stake-out sitting, Toni accelerated for a slow patrol around the block.

After a couple of tours de Ray, she decided to head home. Not much was going on there. No investigators, no Ray, nothing suspicious. She needed to get out of her "business-formal" pantsuit and blouse, anyway. And Bubbles would be howling for her dinner.

*****

The cat's ears stood firmly at attention but her tiny jaws opened and closed as loud meows filled the room. Toni barely made it inside the front door when she saw and heard Bubbles express her feline opinion. The cat's stare posed the rhetoric questioned, "Where have you been?" Not that the cat cared.

"Okay, Bubbles. I can hear you missed me. Have you been busy today? I can tell you're hungry? What's been going on?"

Toni hugged the champagne-colored fur body, and Bubbles purred decisively in response. Their love-fest was a daily ritual that occurred upon Toni's return from a day at work—or anywhere. They reassured each other that somehow, all was right with the world—at least for those few minutes.

Bubbles' evening repast was placed in her bowl along with an extra treat, which meant her owner was in a good mood. The charity fashion show production was underway, the physicians' group would be happy with the billboard for their Grand Opening— fortunately still on schedule, and she had her new regional VP ally at the bank. Maybe hope floated for some of those pending accounts.

Toni ran up the steps of her two-story condo to change. With her pantsuit off and jeans ready to step into, she heard her cell phone sing to her from the floor below.

Darn, who's calling now? I should've brought that phone upstairs.

After hopping into each leg of fabric, Toni charged down the stairs.

"Hey Mom. You're back." Toni hadn't expected to see her mother's number. Emma Jasper, on vacation in Vermont, had left firm instructions of "don't bother me with small stuff."

"I got back a day early. Some crisis with a survey for my real estate closing on Friday. My buyer called me, worried that the title company isn't following through. Anyway, what the hell happened here? I just picked up the paper, and the residents in one section of Bardmoor are demanding to know the cause of an explosion. What explosion? And which section? I have a couple of listings in the neighborhood. Isn't that where Peggy lives?"

"Slow down, Mom. Did you have a good time? Are you rested?" Toni paused, hoping to decelerate the conversation.

"Yes. I had a great time. The food was amazing. But my rest is in question until you give me some answers. What happened? And I know you know. You must have some information from Mike."

"Okay. First, PinCo Bank—or at least the branch I'm working with—had a breach. Some items were taken from their vault. Remember Chloe from the fashion show?"

"Yes. But stick to the subject."

"I am, Mom. Chloe was the first to discover an item missing. Her sapphire ring wasn't in her safe deposit box."

"Maybe she put it in a drawer at home."

"Mom, let me finish. Chloe's on top of things, especially her treasured jewels. And her husband gave her that ring. There's no way she'd misplace it. Then the branch manager, Emily, disappeared."

"Disappeared? What do you mean disappeared?"

Toni sighed. Her mother's third degree was worse than Alan and Mike could ever be, even if rolled into one person. Toni continued to reveal the details about the case. Her mother seemed particularly worried about the explosion of Ray's house and her own listings in the same area. Toni tried to reassure her.

"The neighborhood's not in danger," Toni said, though her mother had the patience of a hawk ready to snatch its prey. And Toni felt like the prey. "Ray lived in the older section. Aren't your listings in the new gated area?"

"Yeah, they are. Good. I'll touch base with my clients in the morning. Just keep me informed, Toni. Listings like I have don't come along often. So I have to keep my sellers happy."

"Yes, Mother." Emma Jasper's dictates were not taken lightly by Toni. Her mother had a memory like the best artificial intelligence available.

Then Toni had an idea to get more information for her quest.

"Hey, can you do me a favor please?" she asked. "Can you look up this address and tell me what it sold for a couple of years ago?"

She gave her mother Jon and Emily Phillips' address. Since Emma could search the Multiple Listing Service for the house's history, she was just the source for this part of the investigation.

"And one more thing," Toni continued, "find out about their mortgage, too. I have a hunch it might shed light on Emily being fired from the bank. Just don't tell anyone why you're searching."

"Sure, no problem. But why does it matter to you? You still have the bank as a client, right?"

"I'm working on it. That open house—scheduled for today— never happened. But I met with the regional vice president, and he said Emily was suspected of other wrongdoings. I'd like to give her the benefit of the doubt, but in reality, I have to save the account first. I think I made a good impression with the VP At least he'll pay for the mugs we ordered. Don't repeat any of this, Mom. Emily's husband told me that she's trying to find out who's framing her. But I can't get in touch with her to hear her side of the story. Obviously, it's complicated."

"Sounds like it. So much secrecy. It seems like you're on one of those investigative articles like Mike used to assign. For now, I'd better unpack. I'll call you when I have that price and mortgage information. Love you."

116

"Thanks. Love you, too."

Okay, the mortgage info will help. Something about that house and Jon bugs me. If Emily was so proud of it, why did it look like a disaster, at least from the front door vantage point? The yard looked good. But that pool. They couldn't even swim in it.

Five-thirty. Just enough time to run by the newspaper and share my Ray news with Mike. Unless he already knows. He never did call me. Wonder if Harry threw away my note? Or Mike is, again, one step ahead of me on this case. But I only told Alan and Peggy.

Chapter Twenty-Nine

Toni banged on the newspaper office's locked front door. The new person from classified cautiously approached. Then she recognized Toni as a frequent visitor and let her in.

Mike was leaning over the keyboard and staring at the computer screen in traditional editor form, reviewing photos and cut lines in press proofs. His eyes moved from screen to Toni, yet his body remained in position.

"What now, Jasper?"

Toni smiled. "I can see I'm not interrupting you. Pretending to work, huh?"

"Not funny. I need to finish so I can sign off these last pages and they can go to press. Just sit down and try not to make a nuisance of yourself."

Toni remembered well the last-minute photos and additions that often kept the newsroom and press operators on edge. She sat in the chair next to Mike's desk and pulled out her phone. One text: "Don't go by the house again, Toni. I saw you there. It's not safe." The phone number was unavailable. *Damn. Ray was there.*

Toni's heart practically jumped into her throat. She glanced up at Mike, still engrossed in his editorial duty. Evidently, he and Alan hadn't talked, or Mike wasn't commenting—yet.

After what seemed like forever, Mike sat back and announced, "There. Off to the presses." He turned to face Toni and continued, "Now, to what honor do I owe this visit? Whoa. That's some serious face. What happened?" Mike's concerned expression brought him one hundred and eighty degrees from editor to friend.

"I take it that you haven't talked to Alan today? Or got my note?" Toni asked.

Mike leaned forward, his eyes fixed on hers. "No and yes. I was going to call you after the deadline. Should I have spoken with Alan?"

"No. I had a meeting with him, and the news I had for him was strange. Ray *is* alive. He, himself, called me today."

Mike's face didn't move a muscle. Toni knew his expressionless façade had aided Mike with many dangerous assignments. She vowed not to be affected. After all, she knew the Mike beneath the façade.

"I know it was him—not some jokester," she continued. "He revealed specifics about our last meeting that only he would know."

"Wait a minute," Mike said, "is Alan buying this?"

"I believe he is. He took my statement. Then, I went by Emily Phillips' house. Jon was there, and he looked sick as a dog. But no Emily. Jon told me Emily was off trying to prove she was framed."

"Framed," Mike echoed staring into Toni's eyes.

"Yeah, but I met with the bank's regional vice president as well. He fired her. And just now, a text told me not to go back to Ray's house. It has to be from Ray. He must have seen me when I drove around the block this afternoon."

"What did Alan say when you mentioned that you drove around a crime scene?"

"I didn't exactly *mention* that part to Alan. I drove around after I met with him."

Mike's facial lines softened as he leaned back in his black, faux-leather arm chair and sighed. "Jasper, what are we going to do with you?"

"We?" Now it was Toni's turn to echo.

"Didn't Alan tell you to leave the detective work to him? I bet he did. And did you listen? Of course not. You are impossible, Toni Jasper."

"I get it. So what's next?"

"Ack!" Mike threw up his hands and ran all ten digits through his wavy hair.

"Mike, I have to follow my instincts. And they're in scream-mode indicating that something—actually several things—aren't what they seem. And one more key point, I have reason to believe Jesse Morton's wife, Debra, is back in town."

"Are you done?" Mike asked emphatically as if to assure Toni that she was, indeed, done.

"Yes. That's about all I've uncovered today."

"Uncovered?" Mike screeched with eyebrows arched and palms firmly planted on his desk. "Just listen to yourself. Do your words sound like those of an *advertising agency owner*? And have you given one iota of consideration to your own safety, let alone the well-being of other people involved?"

They remained silent in a contemplative standoff for a few seconds, eyes locked. Then Mike turned and reached for the off button on his monitor.

"Let's go," he said as if he and Toni were on a mission to some predetermined destination.

"Go where?" Toni stood as if on cue.

"Your place. Got anything to eat, Jasper? Or does your snooping preclude buying groceries? I mean, when do you have time to stock up on life's basic necessities?"

Toni glared back. "I have food, just not the kind you like."

"In that case, I'll suffer if I have to. On second thought, maybe we should stop by the grocery store to be on the safe side."

"Safe? What I consume is always safe and even healthy."

"Hmm. That healthy consumption is the worst. Got any hot dogs or chips? Don't worry, Jasper. I know the answer. Come on. I'll follow you, and we *are* stopping at the store. I have to keep my stamina up to deal with your unassigned investigative tactics."

Chapter Thirty

With groceries on the counter, Toni and Mike began to prepare their meal. Bubbles circled below, sniffing every stitch of Mike's sneakers. Mike moved cautiously, not wanting to tread on the feline's toes and incur the wrath of their owner.

"That's it, Jasper. I did my part," he announced. "You cook. I'll play with your cat. Darn, forgot cheese. I like cheese on my dogs."

"Amazing, Milner. I actually have pepper jack in the fridge, unless that's too tangy for a tough guy like you."

"Funny. And good alliteration."

Mike plunked down in the corner of the living room sectional, lifting the cat onto his lap. With the great-room design of the condo's lower floor, Toni was still in view.

"So Bubbles," Mike commanded the cat, "tell me everything your human mistress has been up to. I want every detail. Leave nothing out."

The purring response left everything to question.

A few minutes later, Toni had their food ready. A walnut-colored dining table boasted enough room for four small adults or two very hungry ones. Toni stood next to it and smiled at her two favorite beings.

"Either spoil my cat or eat, Milner," she said.

"Tough choice. Sorry, Bubbles, you lose, dogs win."

Mike loaded his bun-clad hot dogs with all available condiments, and Toni lined her dogs with mustard. They both dug into the coleslaw. Then, Mike lifted his beer bottle.

"Toast, Toni," he proclaimed, "to fewer investigations and more advertisements."

Toni clanked his bottle. "On the other hand, to solving serious Seminole mysteries."

Mike took a long swig and exhaled with exasperation. "More alliteration. That's what happens to a mind divided. Especially when the investigation is a compromise to the creative nature of your ad business."

"No compromise. I just want to get my client back. I need their revenue to balance off the slow-to-commit other clients. Besides, we don't want the Pine Oak residents to wonder what bank they can trust or Ray to live in fear . . . wherever he's living."

Mike gave Toni a resigned gaze. "If truth be told, Alan did call me. He told me you gave a statement about Ray. Forensics hasn't turned up any evidence of Ray's remains, other than that partial. So what you told Alan about Ray having tossed it back into the burning house makes sense. The location where the forensics team found it was pretty close to the door. If Ray had it in his mouth at the time of the fire, then other human remains would have been close by."

"Good. Someone believes us."

"Us?"

"Ray and me. Look, he and I've had our differences, but he's a good guy. I'm happy he's alive."

"Does he actually believe Emily and Jesse tried to kill him? That gas and candle story is a bit far-fetched, though plausible to start a fire. Maybe they just wanted to scare him. But that's crazy. A blast would be inevitable."

"And why? What're they up to? Maybe Emily conveniently forgot to rekey a few safe deposit locks when new renters came along? Remember, I told you I saw Emily letting Jesse into the vault with a master key. I think Ray knows something about those safe deposit thefts, and that's why they're after him. Or they believe he knows. But something about that hand I.D. entry bothers me."

"Okay, you, Alan and the FBI—trust me, I hate the fact that I'm verbalizing this—are thinking along the same lines. The FBI doesn't want to spook whoever's involved, so they're not releasing the details."

"That lack of news got my mother all over my case today."

"Your mother? She's not in Vermont?"

"Came home early for some real estate snag. She wanted to know what caused the explosion. She's got some listings in

Bardmoor, but they're in the new gated section, so I calmed her down. But I did ask her to look up the sales history on the Phillips' house. The place is pretty weird. The pool has a gruesome wood lattice cover over it. As persnickety as Emily is, I expected the place to be exquisite."

"How do you know about the pool?"

"I could see it through the front door when I was talking to Jon. That guy looked awful. He works for a health clinic, too. You'd think he'd get some meds."

"Maybe he did. Or maybe living with Emily has taken its toll."

"Mike." Toni gasped. They couldn't help but chuckle. "Yeah, she is a bit of a prima donna. Still, she's a client and a friend."

"Friend? From what I see at the chamber lunches, Emily has acquaintances, not friends. No one rushes to sit at her table. I admit I felt sorry for her one day and sat down next to her. That rock on her finger could do some serious damage. Does it look real to you?"

"She claims it's real," Toni said. "Who knows? Emily just wants everyone to see her success. She grew up in a very poor family. Now she believes she deserves the best for all her hard work."

"Where'd she grow up? Do you know for a fact that her family was poor?"

"Well, no. I didn't research her. I have a lot to do."

Mike stretched his neck toward Toni. "So prioritize and stick to your agency."

"You sucked me into that one, Milner. I *am sticking* to my business. These tangents I'm diligently pursuing have integral impacts on my success."

Toni took another swig of water before she made another remark she'd regret. She didn't want Mike to be mad at her. He was, she hoped, one of her fans. She even liked his being protective.

"I realize the bank is a key client for your success this year," Mike said, "and they seem to be back to normal. But Ray won't come forward, Emily's missing and who knows when the situation will be straightened out. So what business will they give you? And when?"

"I had a good meeting today with the regional vice president. I believe he'll think about the open house again. At least, he seemed conducive to my ideas."

"You *were* busy today."

"You bet. And I'm glad the FBI is investigating the bank robbery. Is that Agent Nelson still the one on our case?"

"Maybe. What's this *our* case? You, Madam Jasper, have *no* case. However, the attempt on Ray's life was a tipping point. They don't know how it's connected, but they now believe too many coincidences are tied to that bank."

"About time. Does this mean I can reassure my Pine Oak Place friends that they'll get some justice?"

"No, no. Not yet. The less everyone knows, the better at this point. We need evidence. I assume you remember that word?"

"Yes." Toni scowled.

"In fact," Mike continued, "the FBI would like to speak with Emily. And Jesse Morton is on their watch list. They brought him in for questioning since he managed some of the bank's technology. He's convinced his wife lives near Orlando. After a bad marriage break up, she wrote a note stating that she never wanted to talk to him. But he'd asked her to let him know she was okay, so she sent a few postcards. Alan saw the postcards."

"Is Debra Morton in town? Has the FBI contacted her for questioning? I saw her name on Alan's desk. Maybe she has incriminating evidence about Jesse? Do you know where she is?"

"Yes. I do know where she is," Mike said. He then hesitated. "This won't come out in the news. Debra had a broken arm as a young child. The doctor put a pin in it, and for some reason, he didn't take it out."

"So? Did she come back to see a doctor?"

"Toni, as smart as you are, you can be a little dense."

"Dense?" Toni was beginning to get frustrated with Mike's evasiveness.

"As we know, Debra didn't move here with Jesse last year. But she did visit for a week or so and got a visitor card for Plait. The number on the card they found in Land O'Lakes was legible—just barely. It was linked to her. But a pin in the left arm of the burned corpse led authorities to confirm her as the victim. The killer thought he or she was being so ingenious by smashing the teeth. But, whoever it was didn't know Debra once had a small fracture in her left radius bone."

"Oh no." Toni was momentarily speechless. "The crime does relate back to Seminole. Does Jesse know his ex-wife was murdered?"

"I imagine by now he does. He's no longer next of kin. But Jon Phillips has been informed. Alan doesn't know what Jon told Jesse, especially since Jon's so sick."

"Wow," Toni whispered. She considered the whole scenario for a few minutes while Mike cleared the table.

"How do you know this? Alan? He shared this, but won't let you print it?"

"I'm a newsman, Toni. I kept after him, especially about the body. But the situation is pretty sensitive and it's an ongoing investigation, so I agreed to hold off on any release. Honestly, he's worried about you and, as Alan put it, your damn nosiness. Ironically, haven't you noticed undercover police following you?"

"What?"

"Enough. Come here."

Mike took Toni's hand and led her to the L-shaped couch that seemed like open arms of comfort. He pulled her down next to him, wrapping his long arms around her in a more-than-friendship caress. She laid her head on his shoulder. Toni understood the gravity and possible danger that orbited somewhere between a bank, a fitness center and a body in another county. For tonight, though, she knew she was safe. Being in Mike's arms felt right. Especially when Bubbles jumped up beside them.

Chapter Thirty-One

Toni was laid out on the living room couch, covered with a white crocheted blanket. The sensation of a sandpaper tongue on her forehead brought her to consciousness. Crouched just above her head, Bubbles stared at her human companion, breathed into her pal's face, and mewed concern. Not that cat's action was itself unusual. The furry pseudo-alarm clock possessed an array of techniques designed to get her owner out of the deepest reverie. Toni forced her tired body into a sitting position.

"Geez, Bubbles," she whispered.

Midnight. I must have fallen asleep after dinner. Some good company for Mike. I'm on a quest for romance and managed to doze off.

Toni pulled the crocheted throw onto her lap to fold it and toss it into the corner of the sectional. Her keys were on the coffee table in front of her and not in their usual spot atop the three-drawer accent table by the entrance to her condo. A note was tucked beneath. The more she read, the more she smiled:

"Hi Toni, glad you got some rest and ceased being a pest even if for a few hours. I borrowed your keys and made a duplicate of the house key so I could lock your deadbolt. Besides, I may need to rescue you in the future . . . it'd be nice not to have to break down the door. Love, Mike P.S. When you get up, please go to your real job. Please."

Toni stared at the short letter as if she had never seen anything like it. And she hadn't—not from Mike—which meant that she hadn't smiled nonstop like this in a long time.

Love, Mike. The two-word close echoed in her brain. Did he love her? Did she truly love him?

"Come on, kitty," she commanded as she ascended the carpeted stairs to her bedroom. "Might as well claim your half in the middle of the bed, as usual."

***

By eight-thirty, Toni was on the go. She steered her car onto Seminole Boulevard toward her office.

Won't Peggy be surprised to see me bright and early?

Toni made a fresh pot of coffee and familiarized herself with the latest changes on the current job list. The final version of the physicians' group billboard art, which she'd scanned and sent for approval the previous evening, should be on their manager's desk by now. Toni decided to peruse her emails before a call to confirm.

"Lord almighty. Shut the front door." Peggy stood in the doorway, her jaw dropping in its best display of disbelief.

"And a good morning to you, sunshine." Toni responded. "I even made coffee, so be nice."

"Good. I spent most of the night with my daughter and her math problems. How did we ever learn that stuff? I can't even figure out any memory hooks for her."

"Wow."

"I know. Math—"

"No. That new manager over at the physicians' group sent a go-ahead for the billboard. And he only got the artwork this morning. Good. I'll call Brad."

Toni dialed the phone and hit the speaker button. She listened to it ring while updating the job list and starting a note to alert Zoe at the billboard company. After she received the art file, the rep would get it on the production list right away.

"Hi Toni."

"Hey, Brad. Your billboard design got final approval already. I was afraid that they'd make another change. This new manager gets things done. How good is that? I've already alerted Zoe to watch for the file you're sending. Email your invoice to me, okay?"

"Sure thing. I have time today to begin that fashion show for you and Chloe. I came up with an idea last night. If you want to see it, I can come by later, like after lunch . . . maybe one or so? Will that work?"

"Sure. I'm excited to see it. I'll call Chloe. What about if we meet over at Pine Oak Place?"

"Sounds like a plan. Text me to confirm."

"Will do. Please get that billboard file over to the Zoe right away."

"I'm on it as we speak."

"Excellent. See you later. Thanks."

"My pleasure. Bye."

Toni sent her quick note to Zoe. In the note, she asked the rep to confirm when she had received Brad's art file. Then she pushed the phone icon and scrolled to Chloe's number.

"Hi Chloe, glad I caught you," Toni said.

"Caught me? Why, Toni, do I need catching?"

"I can hear you're in the right mood to see some prospective ads for this year's fashion show. I've enlisted a terrific artist to design the materials. Can we come by about one o'clock?"

"An artist? We don't have the budget for any professionals other than you, dear."

"I know. I'm the *free* professional. But don't worry. My agency will cover the cost. Besides, it'll be worth it. The guy's talented. His name is Ed Bradbury, but he goes by Brad. He'll make the materials polished and first-rate."

"Alright. I'll trust your judgment. One o'clock will be fine. I'll meet you in the dining room."

"Good. I already told Brad he's now a member of our committee. Of course, we'll have Peggy, too. And I hope to recruit a friend of mine from the ad department at the paper."

"Oh my. Our little committee is growing to a large group."

"Only five people counting you and me. We'll need the help this year, especially on fashion show day. I have people at the chamber asking me about it already. This year, I'm confident we'll have a bigger attendance and raise a lot more money."

"I hope you're right, dear."

"Chloe, when did you start doubting me?" Toni's question brought no immediate response.

"I'm not." Chloe stated with a sigh. "My fellow victims have been prodding me to find out what the police are doing to find the bank thieves. Do you have any information?"

"I wish I did. However, I believe the FBI hasn't given up. I'll see if I can get an update before I come over."

"We'd appreciate that. You don't want me to sic Walter on you again."

"No. Not Walter," Toni said in her best fearful tone.

Toni could hear Chloe chuckle. *Good. That helped to brighten her spirits. Better text Brad and let him know we're on.*

Toni updated Peggy about this year's fashion show. Then she sent a few more follow-up emails and made calls from the "to-do" list left on her desk a few days earlier.

With an hour-and-a-half available to figure out what she could tell Chloe, Toni realized she'd better think fast. She hit Mike's number, eager to hear his voice.

"Mike Milner," came the formal response after just one ring. Toni smiled. Mike's phone demeanor was always executive-sounding.

"So formal? After all we went through with those hot dogs at my place?" Toni struggled to keep her voice level sounding concerned. She had to put her hand over the phone so Mike wouldn't detect a little laugh.

"You again," he said.

"Hey," she continued, "I'm starved. How about if I bring lunch to your office? I can run by that new café and be at the paper in twenty."

"It's always food with you. Did you get any real work done yet today?"

"Amazingly I did. Must have been the good night's sleep on the couch. Thanks for the cover, by the way. And don't let my house key get into the wrong hands."

"Nah, I'll put it in the bank vault."

"Mike. Has anyone ever told you what a smartass you are?"

"Actually, many have done just that."

"Okay, the café's fine for lunch," Mike said. "Get me hot pastrami with cheese on rye, potato salad and a Coke. If they ask about sauerkraut, tell them no."

"Will do. Remember, sauerkraut is a vegetable."

"Exactly."

"But you ate coleslaw last night."

"That's different. Thanks. And don't forget the napkins."

"I would never forget such an important item."

She heard the connection end. Though hunger started the call, Toni now found herself starved for time with Mike. She craved his presence even after their busy weekend. Toni grabbed her purse and a fresh legal pad.

Toni walked by Peggy's desk, "I'm off to lunch with Mike, and then a fashion show meeting with Chloe. I'm excited because Brad will be there to show Chloe his designs for the show. Don't you think his work gets better with each job?"

"Yes. He was a good discovery. And he's punctual. Reliable, too, which is more than I can say for—"

"I get it. I was here all morning. Even went through that to-do list which was, for some reason, conspicuous on my chair. Didn't want me to miss it, did you?"

"I knew you'd see it. However, you've been leaping before looking a lot these days. And speaking of a big leap, Mike . . . again . . . for lunch?"

"No. I'm having a salad."

Peggy's expression didn't change. "He doesn't expect you to be funny, does he?"

"Absolutely." Toni couldn't control the grin sliding across her face.

"Come on. I heard you say 'thanks for the cover.' And something about your 'house key in the wrong hands.' Those words are not business. And I, of all people, have a need to know."

Toni thought about the evening. "No one can fault you for your hearing, Peg, or your editorial details. Mike came over for dinner last night. But I fell asleep early and he had to lock up. He's such a nice guy. He didn't want to wake me."

Toni's gaze had been on some point in outer space. Then her eyes focused on Peggy, who was shaking her head while her lips divided her face with a wide smile.

"What? He *is* a nice guy." Toni heard herself sound defensive. "I've got to go. I'll deal with you later."

As she rushed down the hall, she heard Peggy call, "Sure. I know you. This one is bad." Toni couldn't contain her cheerfulness. *Maybe Peggy's right. This one does feel good.*

Chapter Thirty-Two

The pastrami aroma wafted from the brown bag in Toni's right hand. Her left hand clutched a clear plastic bowl of romaine topped with tuna salad while a drink holder dangled from two fingers.

"Hi." Mike's tender tone pleased Toni. It wasn't his usual newsroom-and-I'm-in-charge voice. "Let's take the interview room. No one's scheduled, and I don't want a mess on my desk."

"Ha." Toni couldn't contain herself. "On that desk? Who would notice?"

Once in the conference room, Mike closed the door. He extended his long arms around her shoulders and gave her a gentle squeeze.

"Thanks for lunch, Jasper. How come you were never this nice when you actually worked here?"

"You were the boss then," she proclaimed.

"Right. In those days, you almost listened to me."

"Your order's correct, isn't it?" Toni and Mike dug into their lunches.

"That it is," he stated before taking a large first bite.

Toni watched Mike down most of his sandwich while she stabbed chunks of tuna and recognized she was, indeed, famished.

"I'm on my way to meet with Chloe Ford to start the charity fashion show plan. My Ed Bradbury will be doing the ads and the program, so they'll look super this year."

"They looked pretty good last year," Mike said.

"Thanks," Toni felt proud Mike remembered. "But this year, I'm confident we'll have a much bigger turn-out, maybe even some TV coverage. I want everything perfect."

"Give the ads to Sue. I'll see what free space I can dredge up for your cause."

"Good. And put the date on your calendar." Toni ignored Mike's instant expression of dread. "So . . . just in case she asks me, what should I tell Chloe about the FBI and the bank robbery?"

"Don't say a word."

"But the FBI's still involved."

"All I know is that the authorities, all of them, don't want certain facts revealed. No statement's been released about how Debra Morton was identified. And who knows what, in reality, happened at that bank? Look Toni, the facts aren't verified. We can't speculate."

"I know, I know."

"Stick to fashion and ads and leave everything else out of the picture for now."

Mike studied her. She noticed that his stare wasn't as intense as usual. The softness around his eyes sent caring signals.

"I want you to be safe," he said. "That's all."

"I appreciate that." She eyeballed Mike and found it hard to pull away from the hazel-green pools beneath two eyebrows, narrowed in apparent concern. "Fine," she continued, "I'll divert the conversation if I have to."

"Excellent. Now you're listening. I think." Mike shot a tenuous glance before consuming a forkful of potato salad. "Even Alan isn't positive what's going on. And, Ray has not surfaced. I trust you haven't gotten another call?"

"No. Nothing since that text when I was here."

Mike nodded. "Emily Phillips is still missing. I know Alan questioned her husband as to her whereabouts because she disappeared so quickly after the bank incident. He now has Jesse on his radar as a person of interest in the death of his wife. That's all I know. And more than anyone else *should* know."

Toni studied the remains of her meal. "*Bank incident?* I certainly don't want to use those words at Pine Oak Place." Her pleading expression reflected her concern for her Pine Oak pals. "Mike, these retirees can't be ignored."

"I don't believe they are. Alan and the FBI are just being cautious."

"Cautious," she repeated. "Like hell they are. Nobody's even followed up with those folks. I'll figure something out."

Toni shoved her bowl in the garbage and departed with a display of exasperation, her brain wrestling for an appropriate answer to Chloe's inevitable query.

Incident? Jesse on radar? Even Brutus could tell that something was up with that guy. Now I have all of ten minutes to think of some response for Chloe and her cohorts.

***

Toni pulled into the Pine Oak Place parking lot behind a striking, new red Jeep. She was surprised when Brad stepped out.

"Brad," she called as she chirped the lock for her car "Did you get a new vehicle?"

"Yeah. It's last year's model but hardly any miles on it," he replied with enthusiasm. "I've been saving up for a while. My clunker was almost nine years old. I was ready for new wheels, to say the least. Do you like it?"

"Heck yeah. It's gorgeous. And it suits you. Wow, that tan interior is pretty. No wonder I didn't see your car in my parking lot the other day."

"Right. No more jalopies for business," he said.

"Come on. I can't wait for you and Chloe to meet. She's a pistol. Believe me. She knows what she wants, too."

"Now I'm nervous."

"Don't be. She'll love you. I guarantee it."

Brad stopped in his tracks. "Just a sec. I want to be sure my cell phone's off. I hate when it rings and I'm with a client."

"Do you always do this? Stop before going into a meeting?"

"I do my best to remember and check my phone."

"Did you stop in the hallway outside of my office door yesterday?"

"Uh . . . yeah. I did. I got a text message so I remembered to put it on mute."

Toni's was relieved. *And I was spooked for nothing.*

***

134

Chloe was seated close to the middle of the nearly-deserted dining room. Brutus' head, with ears at attention, popped up from another chair. Chloe waved as Toni and Brad approached.

"Hi Chloe. This is Ed Bradbury, the artist I told you about." Toni took a step back as Brad bowed slightly and shook Chloe's hand.

"Please call me Brad."

"Okay, Brad. Do you two want any coffee or peach cobbler? We have *the* best desserts, not that *I* need any of them," Chloe snickered.

"I'm fine. Thank you," Brad said shaking his head as he sat.

"Chloe, I asked Brad to do the creative for the ads and the program because I believe we can take our event up a notch. We did well last year, but a bigger audience is critical. Our ad campaign will also promote donations from those who can't attend. So they have to be eye-catching and pop off the newspaper page. I think we can get at least one of the TV stations to help with the publicity   more than just a mention on the community event list."

With a head tilt in Brad's direction, Chloe said, "Let's have it, young man."

As Toni expected, Brad and Chloe seemed to hit it off immediately. Brad was a gracious gentleman to Chloe's—as Toni saw—just being Chloe. Toni was thrilled when her BFF loved the new theme of *Operation Runway with Benefits* and the subtitle, "Fun, Fashion and Food for the Children's Hospital." The art featured a modern, vibrant design composed of fashion images surrounded by pertinent wording, including the theme and the date in a shadow-frame. The coordinating program was gorgeous, as confirmed by Chloe's gleeful comments and radiant persona.

"Why Toni," Chloe decreed, "I must say you were correct. This young man does exceptional work."

"Thank you, ma'am." Brad looked happy with the outcome.

"Oh please, call me Chloe. We're in this together now. No formalities among committee members. That's the rule."

Brad beamed. "I like the rule, Chloe. And I'm happy to be on the team. That children's hospital is a wonderful organization."

"Outstanding. Let's get this show on the road," Chloe ordered.

"Will do," Toni said. "Brad, are those 'Save the Date' ads ready for production?"

"Yes. I can email the file today."

"Okay, great. First, though, can you stop by the paper and speak with Sue Anderson in Retail Advertising? She needs to know the ads are in the works. When she gets the email and logs them in, she'll send them to Mike for placement."

"No problem. Glad to do it."

"Once the ads are in Mike's realm, my job is to beg and grovel for the best spots possible. Of course, the paper's space is given pro bono, so I do my best. But Mike's a supporter of the event. He's generous when he can be."

Chloe interjected, "Mike? Isn't he the editor? The one who's supposed to make sure news gets in print? I haven't seen any news about our theft. You promised an update, Toni."

"Yes, well . . . I only know the FBI is still on the case. But the authorities can't release anything yet." Toni cringed. She knew that weak explanation wouldn't carry any weight with a sharp mind like Chloe's.

"The FBI? You mean that rude agent? Humph."

Toni faced Brad, "Remember the bank trouble last Thursday?"

He answered, "The paper said a breach occurred, but I didn't see many specifics."

"The bank vault was broken into. One of the items stolen was Chloe's beautiful and expensive sapphire ring."

"Yes. My husband gave me that ring. I wouldn't misplace it," Chloe said. "The FBI man thinks I'm nuts."

"Agent Nelson knows you're quite competent." Toni reached out and touched the retiree's arm.

"Like hell he does," the woman retorted. "Well, team, Brutus and I need to have our stroll in the garden." Chloe stood and reached for the dog's leash. In Brad's direction she emphasized, "That means we need to take our walk. I just don't want to use a mundane term like 'walk.' Thank you for your creativity, Brad. Welcome aboard. Toni, I'll speak with you soon."

Close to their parked cars, Brad said, "Thanks. I'm glad you asked me to work on this event with you. Chloe's a hoot. It'll be fun."

"Yeah, she's a character. And quite a smart lady. I feel terrible about her ring being stolen."

"That's weird. How could someone get into the bank vault, especially a safe deposit box?"

"The big question indeed."

Brad shook his head. "For now, let's get these ads in. I'll go and meet Sue right away."

"Perfect. Thanks Brad."

In her car, Toni sat and checked her messages and email, but her mind wandered.

How did someone get past a double-secured entry? And maybe it's the key to everything. Not only how did someone get into the bank vault, but also how did the culprit manage to open a safe deposit box? Jesse Morton did tech work for the bank. But Debra Morton? Her murder can't be a coincidence, or can it?

And where is Ray? Maybe if I creep around his old neighborhood he'll text me again. I'm sure I'm not in danger. Am I? I wonder if Mike was kidding about that undercover officer.

Toni turned around to see beside and in back of the car, her eyes focused on bushes and as many parked cars as she could see. No one lurked inside any of them. Not a soul.

Of course, undercover people are supposed to blend in. So are the bad guys. Time to question Alan.

Chapter Thirty-Three

Toni steered out of her parking spot and stopped at a red light on Eighth Avenue. With a peek in the mirror to check her hair, she noticed a black SUV pulling out of the Pine Oak lot.

Funny. I didn't see anyone come out of the Pine Oak Place entrance and go toward a car. But I talked with Brad and scanned my phone. Still, no one was walking out of the building.

Toni stayed in her car after she turned into the police station lot. Not one vehicle arrived after her. *I must be imagining things. Okay, Alan, I need to know the truth.*

Alan Dietz leaned back in his overstuffed chair, supported by a sturdy wall and balanced by size-twelves crossed on his desk. His polished but worn shoes stood out to the fashionista.

"Alan," she announced.

"Oh no," came his expressionless reply without a twitch of a muscle or raise of an eyelid.

"I demand an answer. Is an undercover officer assigned to follow me?"

"It's a comfort to know Mike can't keep a damn secret. We've got eyes on a number of people. Don't think you're special."

"But what kind of danger can I be in? I don't know anything."

"Your involvement with Emily Phillips and Ray Edwards puts you at risk. You may have pertinent facts and not even realize it."

"Have you found Emily or Ray?"

"Working on it. This case is an ongoing investigation. You know I can't tell you anything."

"Which case? The murder? Or the bank robbery?"

"Toni." Alan's voice boomed and his eyes opened to the size of quarters.

"Not one law enforcement person has followed up with my friends at Pine Oak Place since that unpleasant Agent Nelson practically lambasted Chloe Ford on Thursday. Don't you consider it odd that Jesse handled the bank's technology, he was married to Emily's sister-in-law and his wife was found murdered? I mean—"

"Stop. This discussion is over. Goodbye. Your doggedness is, well, a pain. Believe me. I'm well aware of all the people involved."

"Thank you, Detective," Toni stated in a firm voice, "I believe I'm getting through to you."

Toni turned on her almond-tone bootie's chunky heel and marched out of the building. Onward to her next conquest—of what she wasn't sure. Her gut feeling was acting up more than ever.

Five days and this investigation's going nowhere. Going to Ray's house again to see what's happened since yesterday. Probably nada. Who knows? Maybe those little rascals on their bikes will be in survey mode. If school's out for the day, I can question the kids.

She pointed her car toward Ray's street. When she arrived, no child or adult was visible either on a bike or on foot. It seemed deserted. The yellow tape on Ray's house was intact, as if a permanent forbidding fixture. Toni parked behind a sleek, white vehicle to get a clear view up and down the street. The scene in her rear-view mirror was a portrait of quiet suburbia. No human arrived or left for over an hour. Finally, she realized it was a waste of time.

The text chime from her phone grabbed her attention. Brad's name was displayed in the corner of the screen.

The text read: "Toni, first ads at the paper. Met Sue. Nice person. Have to say she wore a large, sapphire ring. Caught my attention. Said it was gift from her boyfriend. Thought you should know."

Toni sat, mesmerized by the tiny letters on the blue background. She couldn't move a muscle, but her mind raced.

Sue? Sapphire ring? From Jesse? Good God. Did I tell Alan about Sue's involvement with Jesse? Does she have an undercover cop assigned to her? She may be the one who's in true danger. I can't talk to her, though. Or can I? But what if she's involved? No, it's Sue. On the other hand, many crooks aren't what they seem to be.

Toni wrote her reply, "Thanks," and pushed send. The little words jumped from the message bar onto the cell's screen. She scrolled down to Sue's number. *Wouldn't hurt,* she thought.

"Sue Anderson, Retail Advertising. How can I help you?"

"Hi Sue. So you met my artist, Ed Bradbury."

"Yeah. He was here a little while ago. What a nice guy! Efficient, too. He already sent ads in for the Children's Fashion Show. I'll get them up to Mike before I leave. Anything else, Toni? I'm on my way to the gym to beat the after-work crowd."

"Uh, no. That's it. Are you meeting Jesse there?"

"That's the plan. Listen, if you need something, just email me, and I'll get right on it in the morning. Okay?"

"Yeah. Have fun."

"Bye." Sue hung up in a split second. The silent phone lay cradled in Toni's palm.

The gym. If Jesse gave her that ring, how'd he get it? Did Emily give it to him?

Maybe Sue likes sapphires and Jesse bought her one. Brad doesn't know what the missing ring looks like. Still, a bit fishy to me. I'm not going to sleep if I don't investigate. Right. I'm not an investigator. Damn wrong.

After only a few seconds' deliberation, Toni's finger pressed Mike's number. "Mike. Don't you need more time on that treadmill?"

"Now you're an exercise freak? But the way you left after lunch, I figured you're mad at me."

"No. I can't be mad at you. Just frustrated. A little exercise will be good for me. Don't you agree?"

Toni could hear Mike's sigh. "I need to go home and get changed."

"Good. Meet you at Plait."

"What time? It's almost four now."

"I don't want to lose momentum. Can you be there by four-thirty?"

"Lucky for you, it's a slow day here. Fine. Don't be late. I'll need one of those guest passes. And they need a somewhat sane member to vouch for me."

That guest pass. Someone at Plait might have seen Debra. A fight between her and Jesse? Oh my God. What did that man do to his wife?

Toni raced to get home. She needed to change clothes, too, and leave dinner for her cat. Bubbles was persnickety about feeding time. Furthermore, she had to think through the ring situation before she got to the gym.

What if Jesse does show up? He can't know that I suspect him. Or could he?

Toni made a quick turn and then came to a sudden stop in her driveway. She ran to her front door, unlocked it and stepped inside. She then stopped dead in her tracks. Bubbles sat in straight and statuesque form just a few feet inside of the foyer.

"Good grief, Bubbles. You startled me."

"Meow." One short sound loaded with expression. The human was home early. Perhaps a nap was disturbed. Or maybe the furry critter was hungry.

Toni sprinted up the steps to change. Then she jogged down and headed for the kitchen. She checked the cat's food and water. The cat followed, in watchful mode.

"Good kitty, but all you get is dry food. I have a crime to solve," Toni said as she poured the crisp morsels into the small dish labeled "Feed me." Out the door , Toni jumped into her car and zoomed off "to investigate a case that was not supposed to be her case."

Chapter Thirty-Four

Mike relaxed against the front counter of the gym. But his head turned in a slow, studied fashion from one area to the next as though he was screening the place for something—or someone.

Toni snuck up beside him. "You're goin' down today, Milner."

Mike turned just enough to give Toni a firm, one-arm hug.

"Confidence only goes so far, Jasper," he said with a sly grin. "I've got the pass already. Joey here remembered you."

"Good. Where should we start?"

"You choose. I'm here to follow."

"Right," she laughed. "Humility won't help. Either you've got it or you don't. So, let the best woman win."

"Or man. I can't believe I'm actually here without undue pressure."

"No pressure, you say? Let's start with the treadmill. That's your specialty. Running."

They walked to the back where treadmills and stationary bikes lined the walls. Toni figured it would be the best vantage point to observe Sue and Jesse. They found two side-by-side treadmills and hopped on.

Mike assessed her lookout tactic for a few minutes. "Who do you expect to find, Toni?"

"Oh I don't know. Maybe someone we know." Toni knew she was a horrible fibber.

"Like Sue or Jesse from the paper?"

"Why Michael Milner . . . there she is." Toni spotted Sue sitting at the table just outside of the snack bar.

Damn. Maybe we should have stayed closer. Just in case. Poor Sue. She doesn't realize what danger she could be in. But I don't want to spook Jesse.

Mike followed her gaze. "She's alone," he commented.

"Yeah, but she told me she planned to meet Jesse." Toni turned see Mike's look of moderate disapproval. He had stepped off of the treadmill still gripping the handle.

"Toni—"

"Okay, okay. I sent my artist, Brad, to meet Sue today and tell her that the charity ads were coming. He texted me that she was wearing a large sapphire ring. It sounded like Chloe's stolen ring. Doesn't that seem coincidental?"

Mike remained motionless and stared at Toni. She could tell his mental wheels were turning. Though she wanted him to think about the situation, she had to plead her case.

"It's a good theory, Mike. And we should be worried about Sue."

"For what reason?" he asserted after a few pensive seconds. "It's in the hands of the law right now, who, by the way, chewed me out today."

"What?" Toni kept her eyes on Sue while she talked with Mike.

"Alan phoned after your outburst in his office. He thinks that I shouldn't even speak to you, especially about an on-going investigation. What did he call you? Oh yeah: a pain."

"It wasn't an outburst," she protested. "I needed clarification."

Mike put one foot on the edge of the treadmill and leaned on his knee. "Do you want to go and see what Sue has to say?"

"Great idea. See, you can't take the pressure."

"I can take plenty of pressure," he said.

By the time they had traversed the floor, Sue's seat was empty. Both Mike's and Toni's eyes moved in rapid fire around the machines. Toni took a few sidesteps toward the front door.

"There." She pointed toward the center of the parking lot.

From behind the facility's doors, they watched Sue in a physical struggle alongside an SUV, and then she was yanked in before it drove away. By the time they moved outside, the vehicle had disappeared around a corner.

"Call the police!" Toni's excited voice sent the front desk attendant flying for the phone. "Oh my God, Mike. Did you get the license?"

"No, damn it. Too far away. Shit. Now, maybe this is our case."

The police were on their way, but Mike told Toni he needed to take action.

"Stay put. Do you hear me?" Mike ordered. He retrieved his cell phone from the locker room. In what seemed like seconds, he was beside Toni again.

"Who're you calling?"

"Alan. I need to redeem myself with him. This time, I'll be the one having the outburst. Where's the undercover?"

Mike's expression exhibited more angst than Toni had ever seen from him. She stood still, but questions bounced around her brain.

Was that Jesse's vehicle? Why would he kidnap Sue? Shouldn't he just get the hell out of town? Where does he live? Oh God. I hope he doesn't take her out of Pinellas County.

The deputy from the Sheriff's Department approached and interrupted Toni's suppositions.

"What did you see?" he inquired as he pulled open a small notebook.

Mike and Toni explained what they'd witnessed. He thanked them and proceeded to gather other statements. Outside, the CSI unit combed the parking lot for possible evidence.

"This is awful," Toni said.

Mike turned toward her. But his eyes looked past her. She glanced over her shoulder as FBI Agent George Nelson strode toward them.

Mike extended his hand. "Hello, Agent Nelson." He looked toward Toni. "You remember Toni Jasper."

Toni knew darn well the federal investigator remembered her.

"Hello, Ms. Jasper." The agent's acknowledgement sounded flat.

Toni took her turn. "Agent Nelson, you got here quickly."

"Apparently, Ms. Anderson was kidnapped. Didn't you witness her being dragged into a vehicle? Other witnesses stated she was pulled in against her will."

"Yes. Mike and I both saw that."

Toni shuddered as she pictured Sue's struggle. *If it was Jesse, maybe Brutus is a type of "people whisperer,"* she thought.

"So you'll follow up?" Toni asked.

He nodded. "Yes."

"What if I told you she's dating a person of interest concerning the bank robbery? Jesse Morton. He could've been the driver. But I don't know what kind of car he drives."

"Actually, that is why I'm involved."

"Good." Toni said.

"We know where Mr. Morton lives. Is there anything you want to add to what you saw tonight?" The agent's pen was perched above a small notebook, ready to write.

"I'm afraid not. I know he has an office in downtown Tampa, too. But . . ." Toni found herself on the verge of tears. She struggled to compose herself, the enormity overwhelming.

Mike and the agent looked down at her. Neither one had a comment until Mike finally asked, "Can we leave now, Agent Nelson? I believe we've told you and the deputy all we know."

"Sure. Just be available in case we need you."

"I'm not going anywhere," Toni assured him, "at least not until my friend is found. And I hope it'll be soon."

I'm not leaving the county until Sue's safe.

Agent Nelsen nodded and shook their hands.

"Come on, I'll take you to dinner," Mike said as he took her hand and led her away.

Where do you want to eat?" she asked.

"In these clothes? Who'll let us in?"

***

A Chinese restaurant was close by. Toni agreed that the food would be good, quick and contain veggies. Still shaken from the shock of the evening, they ordered and sat in silence.

Finally Mike spoke. "I'm glad Agent Nelson got there fast."

"Yeah. He's okay. I mean, he is FBI. He needs to move fast to find Sue."

They stared out the window. Toni prided herself on her ability to plan—to know the next step and where to go. But after tonight's events, a curve ball seemed to land smack in the middle of her strategy.

"Look, Toni." Mike's voice was tender as he pulled her hands into his. Toni's heart pounded at his touch, yet his affectionate tone had a calming effect. "Let the FBI and Alan do their job. They'll pull in other officers if they need to. They'll find her soon. There's nothing you or I can do but be ready when Sue's found."

"I know. I wish I'd warned her."

"Of what? How could you know? And we don't even know Jesse was in the car."

"Who else could it be?"

Neither one had an answer. When their number was called, Mike jumped up to get the order. They decided to stay and eat in the small restaurant. Since people were in and out to pick up their food, no one could truly listen in on their conversation. They tried to assess the reason Sue went out to the parking lot. If Jesse stole the sapphire ring and Sue was indeed wearing it, had she told him about Brad's comments?

By the end of the meal, many unanswered questions stayed unanswered, but Mike seemed revved up. *Challenge was his middle name, too,* Toni thought. But her lack of appetite didn't do the food justice. The situation was too personal now, and her friend didn't deserve this. Toni's half-full trapezoid boxes of leftovers would rest in her refrigerator until tomorrow.

Chapter Thirty-Five

"Lock your door." Mike insisted. He had followed Toni home and then walked her to the door.

"I will. And I'll run around and check the other door and all windows. Trust me," she said, "Watch for my wave from the front window when I'm done."

"Deal," he said as he planted a firm kiss on her cheek before hugging her. The warmth of his arms comforted Toni, at least for a few minutes.

She clicked the deadbolt. Toni then called for Bubbles as she dashed from room to room on the first floor, double checked the back door and bounded up the steps.

Two minutes later, she waved at Mike who had held patient vigil in his car. She observed with regret as the car's taillights disappeared around the corner. She needed him now. A quiet loneliness surrounded her. Finally, the stillness was broken.

"Meow."

"There you are, you little rascal. I've been calling you." The cat yawned in the wide and blatant expression of a nap well-enjoyed. "I see you had a good snooze. Come here. We need cuddle time. At least, I need it. I'm worried about my friend."

They curled up on the couch. Toni stroked and the body of fur purred approval. The tender moment was broken when a loud ringtone emanated from Toni's purse.

"Who's calling at this hour?" she asked the cat.

She maneuvered under and away from an "I'm-not-budging-an-inch" feline. The phone's screen identified her mom as the caller. *Oh yeah. She probably has info on Emily's house.*

"Hi Mom," Toni answered.

"Are you okay? I just saw on the news that a woman from the paper was kidnapped. Did you hear about it? Do you know her? Are you being cautious? Who knows what's going on in this community?"

"Mom. One question at a time. Yes. Yes. And definitely yes." For a second, Toni pondered if her success as an investigative and inquisitive reporter was an inherited trait, not a nurtured skill.

"I'm worried about you all alone over there."

"You live alone, Mom." Toni rolled her eyes. How come her mother never saw the actual truth? Do all mothers have a clouded vision of reality when it comes to their children?

"That's different." Her mom's voice brought Toni back to current reality. "Now, do you know the woman—"

"Sue Anderson." Toni inhaled deeply and exhaled slowly. This conversation required stamina. "I worked with Sue when I was at the paper, and now she's my ad rep. I was at Plait when it happened."

"What? At the fitness center? Are you all right?"

"Mom, I believe I covered the 'all-right' question. I'm fine. And the condo's totally locked up. I was with Mike at the gym when Sue was taken."

Better leave the witness part out . . . a convenient omission for both of their blood pressures.

"Oh no. You can come and stay here if you want." Toni appreciated her mother's offer but couldn't see the need for a mom sleepover.

"I'm fine. Besides I have to take care of Bubbles. She won't let me move out."

Silence. Okay. Lame joke. Mom didn't even snicker.

"Do the police have any leads? I know you, Toni. If Sue's a colleague, then you must be asking questions."

Okay, she's right. I want to solve the crime. But for now, better stick to Alan's official wording.

"It's not my case. The police and FBI are on it. Besides, I need to run my business. I have clients to attend to." Toni realized her fibs now rolled off her tongue.

"Yes. You should focus on your agency. If you believe you'll be okay, then stay there. Just call me tomorrow."

Toni knew if she didn't call, her mother would take the initiative. *No need to make a note about that,* she thought.

Getting back to business, Emma Jasper reverted to Realtor mode. "I have that information you wanted about the Morton home," she said.

Whew. Off the hook for a drawn-out inquest. At least for now.

"Great. Let me get some paper." Toni dug deeper into her handbag and unearthed her notepad and a pen. "I'm ready."

"Jon and Emily Morton got a marvelous deal. The house was a bank-owned property. They paid three hundred thousand cash two years ago. Homes in their neighborhood sold for a lot more then. And now, well, one sold last week for over four hundred and twenty. I'd say it was a very good investment. What are you looking for?"

"I'm not sure, but something's fishy. Emily told me she came from a poor family. I'd like to believe her, but three hundred thousand is a big chunk of cash for a young couple. And in two years, I don't think they've fixed it up much. At least not from what I saw from the front door and satellite images."

"Satellite images?" Toni heard Emma's skeptical tone.

"Yeah, a good viewpoint of the property. We needed to figure out some other unknowns."

Uh oh. Shouldn't have mentioned the "we" word. And satellite images. Focus, Toni.

"We? Who's we?" Emma was on the offensive. Toni knew she had to free herself from the current line of questions. Her mother was a worry expert. And this was shaky worry-launch territory.

"Oh Peggy and I. We were just curious and brainstorming about Emily being fired."

"I see. Well, Peggy has good ideas. Why don't you get a good night's sleep? The situation will be clearer in the morning. I'm sure you can save the bank's account. I mean, you go out of your way for your clients."

"Thanks. Always the optimist."

"I believe in you. And I'm glad I could help. This one was easy. Now if you can send me a referral—"

"I've got your cards. Good night, Mom. Love you."

"Bye. Love you, too."

Cash? Three hundred thousand? On a bank manager's salary? And Jon's a med tech. Wonder where all the cash came from?

Maybe Mike can find out. I'm not sure he meant it when he said this is our case now. But a friend's kidnapping? Oh yeah. He'll be on the case. I know Mike. And I wish he was here.

Toni turned on the local TV station to see if they had any update on the kidnapping, then she headed to the kitchen for an ice cream sandwich. Comfort food was in order. Bubbles slurped in rapid pink tongue repetition from her dish labeled "Water me." A few minutes later, breaking news flashed on the TV.

"Now for an update on tonight's kidnapping from the Seminole Plait parking lot. Police have identified the vehicle used in the abduction. The SUV had been stolen an hour earlier. It was found abandoned on the top floor of the Seminole City Center parking garage."

Enough of that. Toni grabbed the remote and hit the off button. *Damn. Who would do such a thing, especially in a public area? Risky. Or desperate.*

The chime of her phone broke her train of analysis.

"Hey. I stayed put if that's what you want to know," she told Mike. Then she hit the speakerphone button to handle what was left of her ice cream.

"Maybe I just called to say hi. What's that sound? Are you eating?"

"That sound is a chocolate treat. Required stress management. And I'm still in my condo. Don't worry. I'm being a good girl . . . so far."

"Right. It's the 'so far' that keeps me on edge. You *are* aware that Sue's abduction is *not* truly our case?"

"Oh sure."

"Jasper. You're never a good liar."

"It wasn't an actual lie. Just a bent fib or something." Toni wriggled in her seat. If her mother knew her, then Mike had her down pat. She finished eating, a good excuse not to say the wrong thing.

Mike's sighed, a frequent sound these days. "At least you're still safe. I'm just worried about you."

Oh good. No more reprimands from him tonight.

"I appreciate it and the torture endurance at Plait. Listen, did you see the news?"

"Yeah. Stolen then abandoned SUV."

"So the kidnapping *was* spur-of-the-moment. The SUV was stolen only an hour before. Sue told me at four o'clock she was on her way to the gym. She left work early. Brad had been there earlier. Maybe she'd told Jesse about Brad admiring her sapphire ring."

"Toni." She knew what a firm verbalization of her name meant.

Toni was undaunted. "We're talking about Sue. And Jesse as her boyfriend is a little suspicious. Why would an extravert like him latch onto an introvert like Sue? Even Chloe Ford's dog didn't like him. Almost bit him at the bank."

"Chloe Ford's dog? I remember that mutt. Small thing, isn't it? Hardly a big threat. And opposites do attract. I don't mean the dog."

"Hey, animals sense people."

"Are you drinking, Toni? Maybe those leftover hot dogs have poisoned whatever logic used to reside in your brain."

Toni had to stop and laugh. "See what I mean about processed food."

"Oh man. I walked right into that one."

"Yes you did. Didn't need any help at all." Toni was pleased with herself. *Score one for the Jasper.*

"Look," Mike said, "I'm turning in early so I can get to the paper first thing in case any new developments come in overnight. Sleep well."

"Thanks for calling. Bubbles and I are headed for bed, too."

Bubbles and I in bed? Ach. What kind of comment was that? Man. I sound like quite a romantic catch. Me and the cat. A package deal. Oh well. I should say a prayer for Sue. She does seem genuine, not a criminal. I hope Jesse didn't hurt to her. She deserves better.

True to their usual routine, Toni her furry bedmate headed up to the loft bedroom. After settling under the covers, Toni turned to the cat for a final conversation.

"Mike was right, Bubbles. We need a good rest to tackle tomorrow. Hopefully, the FBI will have Sue back by morning. There's no way I can help, even if I wanted to, right? I mean, this isn't my case. Or so I'm told."

Curled contently in the middle of the bed, the champagne-toned cat purred in agreement, as usual.

Chapter Thirty-Six

The local TV news station blared, but no new developments surfaced for Sue Anderson's whereabouts. Since it had been over fifteen hours, Toni was beyond worried. She was frustrated. And she was determined to find the missing link between the robbery and the murder . . . and now Sue's kidnapping.

Toni sat in her dining room, a flow chart of events in front of her flanked by a coffee mug and small yogurt. The initial event was Chloe's revelation of the theft. Then again, *was* it?

Carl Johnson said Emily had taken money, or as Carl put it, "bilked the bank." But how, and for how long? Maybe he wasn't as he appears? Did he use Emily as a scapegoat for his own thievery?

He said that Emily planned an unauthorized event for her branch. What was the purpose of the open house? The crowd would only draw attention to that location. Was that the point? A crowd? So Emily could nail the V. P.? But how would she do it? Or Ray? No. I can't believe he's involved.

And Sue? Did Jesse give her Chloe's ring? How did he get it out of the vault? Emily? She did have those master keys to get into the vault. Some keys may not have been rekeyed. Ray implicated Jesse and Emily in his home's explosion. Now I'm getting somewhere. Maybe. Where the heck does Jon fit? I can't believe he's a crook.

On the verge of a headache, Toni reached for the pain reliever. This day called for relief before it even began.

Toni glanced at her no-care-in-the-world cat seated with perfect feline posture at the end of the kitchen. After finishing her coffee, she swooped up the cat for their morning goodbye. The human stroked. The cat purred. They had the routine down pat.

"Look here, Bubbles. I've left a chart of suspicious events and characters on the table. I know you'll jump up there even though you're not allowed. Please solve the mystery. Just don't chew on the corners. Okay?"

The furry-body was the epitome of relaxation. The cat's half-closed eyes indicated content and not the deep deduction requested. Nevertheless, the feline purred to acknowledge her owner's instructions. For all they meant.

"Naptime already?" Toni asked seeing the cat's weary eyes. "Fine, be that way. I'll still expect your total analysis by this evening."

Toni set the cat down on the couch and headed for her office. *One of us has to get some work done*, she thought.

***

"Hi, Peggy."

Toni's trusted assistant stopped typing and turned with a look of near panic.

"Good God," Peggy blurted, "Sue was kidnapped. It's all over the news."

"I know. I was there. Mike, too."

"You and Mike? There? Oh yeah, now you're a gym body."

"Sounds like you're a genuine supporter of my new endeavor, Peg. Ah, coffee smells good. Thanks."

"I imagine you didn't sleep much. But what happened? My kids are getting creeped out about a kidnapping in our small town. They say this is big city stuff."

"Tell 'em they're fine." Toni poured coffee while conjuring the best way to alleviate Peggy's fears. She knew Peggy was probably the one creeped out. And, Toni figured, her kids were just annoyed at any new restrictions.

Toni clutched her mug, "Bubbles and I had an important conference this morning about the case. And her task today, unless she chews up half of the papers on the table, is to solve it."

"The case? Which case? Robbery? Murder? Kidnapping?"

Toni said, "Or all related?"

"So Alan has leads? What does Mike know?"

"Hold on. Mike doesn't know any more than I do. And I'm the last of Alan's confidants. But I can tell you that the annoying FBI fellow was there last night—the one who drove Chloe nuts."

Peggy just stared at Toni. However, Toni didn't want to speculate on any other facts. Alan and Mike were her audience for theories and suppositions.

A cell phone ring pulled her attention from the computer. She dug into her purse for the small device. Brad's number.

"Hi Brad."

"Toni, I worried about Sue all night. Do you have any news?"

"No. I'm afraid all I know is what I saw on TV."

"Nothing new has been reported in the paper or on TV the last couple of hours. If you hear anything, can you let me know?"

"Sure. How thoughtful, Brad."

"I want everyone to be safe. Be careful, Toni."

"I will. I usually am."

"Good. Talk with you later."

No sooner had Toni hung up with Brad than her phone chimed again.

"Chloe. Hi." Toni wanted to sound upbeat for her BFF. She mustered as much positivity as she could.

"Oh this is terrible. I need to speak with you—in person. How soon can you get here?"

"You sound upset. Do you feel okay?"

"It's not my health. Oh please. Come. I don't know who else to talk to."

"I'm at the office. I'll be there in a few minutes. Where will you be?

"Up in my unit."

Toni's gut instinct was jolted. She could feel her chest tighten and her hands tingle.

As she jerked open the office door, she said, "Something's happened to Chloe, and she needs me. When I know more, I'll check in."

"Wha—" Toni didn't hear the rest of Peggy's sentence. Her mind was focused on Chloe as she sailed down the steps and flew to her car.

Chapter Thirty-Seven

In record time, Toni was on the second floor of the Pine Oak Place independent living facility. She knocked on the door and waited with heightened anxiety.

Lucky Alan wasn't out and about to catch me speeding. He might not have been as lenient this time.

Chloe's face was lined with worry. She turned after opening the door and plopped down on her Victorian upholstered love seat. Toni sat on the cushion next to her. Loyal Brutus rested near a leg of the couch with his head on his paws.

"Look." Chloe pointed to a childishly scribbled note, obviously printed in haste with a bold, black marker. It lay in the middle of Chloe's solid cherry Queen Anne table. Next to it, there was an envelope with the words "Chloe Ford" neatly written. Apprehensive, Toni pinched a corner of the letter and held it up.

The verbiage read, "Look you bitch. Your ring is gone. Let it go. And don't go to the police again or your friends die."

Toni was at a loss. Who would threaten this kind, generous woman? A couple of names stood out. More importantly, who the hell would *need* to send this note? Someone guilty? Panicked?

"Chloe, our Seminole detective, Alan Dietz, and the FBI need to see this note. I promise they'll protect everyone. No one will know you shared this letter."

"I can't. What if something happens to . . . to anyone? Especially to you? Good gracious, I couldn't live with myself."

Chloe's face fell into her hands. Toni moved closer and put her arm around the distraught woman to calm her down. But Toni's investigative instinct and deductive brain cells raced in wild fury.

She hoped the note had fingerprints. Doubtful. But CSI might get a clue.

"Chloe," Toni began, "I need to take this paper with me. Do you have a plastic bag to put it in? I'll call Detective Dietz so he can have an officer or the FBI post surveillance at Pine Oak Place."

"A policeman? Or FBI? It'll draw attention. This wacko will know I went to the authorities. They said no police. They said they'd kill my friends."

"No. Everyone will be fine. The undercover officers are very good at their job. You may not even notice their presence. And you'll be fine. Trust me."

I still haven't seen hide nor hair of any undercover officer tailing me. And I'm on the lookout.

"I do trust you. But I don't know. I've never been threatened. I mean, what does this person expect me to do? I only want my ring back. I'm not vindictive."

"I'm glad of that, Chloe." Toni seized the moment to reassure her friend and lighten the tone, even if she couldn't uplift her spirits. "If you want to take it out on someone, those dinner rolls are hard as a rock. You could bombard the thief with them."

The senior citizen gave Toni a slap on the knee. "You're joking?"

"It'll be okay," Toni said with a penitent look. "And yes, your precious ring needs to be found."

Chloe dried her moist eyes. The tissue was spent, so Toni walked to the kitchen and brought back several more.

"I saw the news about the kidnapping," Chloe said. "Is it related? These things don't happen in Seminole. They said the woman works for the paper. Do you know her? Poor thing. I used to feel safe here. But now, I don't know what's happening."

"We *are* safe here. Just let me take this note. The police and FBI will be discreet. They'll get to the bottom of it and find out who sent it. It's the only solution."

Chloe stared into Toni's eyes as if she wanted to see through them to assess her intentions. "You're my best friend. I guess you're right. What would I do without you?"

"And you're my best friend fashionista. Who'd want to harm us?"

"Humph." Chloe walked to the kitchen, returned with a large baggie and held it open. Toni slowly lowered the note into the bag, maintaining a tight hold on the corner. She reached for the envelope.

"Wait," Chloe cried, "I've got tweezers. Let's be smart about this."

When the bag was complete with note and envelope, Toni hugged Chloe goodbye.

"I'll call you later," she promised.

"Good," Chloe said, "and be careful, Toni. Please."

Not that message again. I have to get this note to Alan quickly. Guess I'd better drive the speed limit, though.

***

Toni opted to drive right to the police station without calling Alan first. She figured he needed to see the evidence. When she arrived, Toni stood in the center of the squad room, not sure where to go. The detective wasn't in his office.

"Hi, is Detective Dietz in the building?" she asked the officer at a desk close by. He pointed behind her.

"And I was hoping it'd be a good day," came the distinctive Alan Dietz bellow as he marched toward her from the break room. "What now, Toni?"

Undaunted, Toni held up the bag. "A threat, Alan. Delivered to Pine Oak Place and sent to my friend, Chloe Ford."

Alan took the bag by the corner and examined the open note and envelope inside. He tilted his head toward his office for Toni to follow.

"When did she get this?" he asked as he sat behind the desk. Toni pulled a chair close.

"She said it was delivered this morning. The front desk receptionist saw it on the counter and contacted Chloe to come and get it. Fortunately, she waited to open it until she got back to her apartment. She's quite upset as you can imagine."

"So the delivery person was not seen?"

"I don't believe so. The front desk person said she found it there."

"Did you touch it? Or just Mrs. Ford?"

"I only held the top right corner. We used tweezers to get the envelope into the bag."

"Good."

"Thanks, Alan. Listen, my friend is beside herself. She didn't want me to bring this note in. She's afraid she'll be responsible if I get hurt—or anyone for that matter. And . . . I kind of mentioned you might have an undercover officer watch her and Pine Oak."

"What? Damn it. We're stretched thin as it is. And only I or the FBI can authorize resources. Not you." The man's angry expression softened. "I don't want the lady to have a heart attack either."

Alan stood up behind his desk.

"Anything else?" he asked.

"I—" Toni began.

"A rhetorical question. I don't need more trouble from you."

"Okay, okay. You have to admit this is important," Toni said.

"Yes. It is. I'll get the evidence to Agent Nelson and see what he can do about Mrs. Ford's safety. Just don't make any more promises. Got it?"

"Yes, sir."

"And be careful." Alan admonished as he rounded his desk to leave.

I am, she thought. Toni stayed in her seat for a moment. *Did everyone get the same "warn Toni" memo? Everyone except Mike, whom I haven't heard from.*

She pulled out her phone and punched his number. "Hi," she said.

"Ah, time for lunch and a call from you. How convenient," he teased.

"How about lunch in your interview room again?"

"What's wrong? You sound worried."

"You can hear worry in my voice?"

"Let's just say your tone is less bratty than normal."

"Marvelous. What should I pick up?" She began to fumble around in her purse for a pen. She saw a scratch pad within reach on Alan's desk.

"Don't. The Bistro delivers. Want Blackened Shrimp Salad again? Blue cheese on the side?"

"Sounds good. The food and your memory. I'll be there in a few minutes. I'm over at Alan's office."

"Alan's office?" Mike repeated.

"I'll explain in private. And don't worry. I'll be careful."

Chapter Thirty-Eight

Mike watched her approach from the door of the conference room.

"Hi," she muttered. Mike pulled her close and kissed her forehead.

Walled with windows, the private room provided an expansive view of the parking lot but was isolated from the rest of the office. One long, dark wooden table surrounded by eight padded chairs and a solitary framed painting of a lake dictated a business-only ambiance.

"You look awful," he began. She looked up in surprise. He added quickly, "I mean you look troubled. You always look nice, Toni. Very nice, in fact."

"Quick backpedal, Milner." She sat down at the table. "How long 'til the food gets here?"

"Hungry? Long day at the ad agency?"

"No. I mean, I was there. Yes, I know. Just where I should be. And I'm fine. Close the door please."

He sat beside her. "Is 'fine' the correct word?"

"Chloe Ford received a threatening letter," she began. "It stated in a nasty and direct manner, 'Look you bitch. Your ring is gone. Don't go to the police again or your friends die.' I can't believe some creep would rope Chloe into this mess. Of course, it was her ring. But Chloe?"

True to form, Mike's expressionless façade indicated objective concern and a readiness to listen. He leaned closer and said, "Go on."

Toni continued, "She didn't want me to take the note to Alan, but I convinced her that the police needed to know. Alan's taking it to the FBI, of course, but I can't imagine they'll find any fingerprints or clues."

Mike reached out to hold Toni's hands. "You did the right thing."

"I know. But I'm still concerned about Chloe. The woman's in her eighties. Who the hell would hurt her? Or send such a terrible letter?"

"Toni, it's not about Chloe. It's about the robbery. The police and FBI must be getting close."

"I get it. But I'm still pissed. What do you know that I don't?" Toni asked.

"Hey, secrecy is my business."

"Alan taped your mouth shut?"

"Only when it comes to you," he quipped.

They heard a knock on the door. Harry was there with the food.

"This came for you," he stated as he handed over the large paper bag.

"Thanks," Mike said. He closed the door to a motionless Harry.

Toni seized the chance to get a dig in on her perceived nemesis. "Hope you didn't smash his nose just then. You think he's eavesdropping?"

"Better not be," Mike answered.

Toni opened the door a couple of inches. No Harry. At least he was not in view. No one was. Most of the staff was either out for lunch or off to obtain a story.

"Any other suspects in my office?" Mike asked.

"I don't trust him. And I want to be careful. I've heard a lot of that today."

"A lot of what? Be careful? Who the hell would tell *you* that?"

Toni sneered at Mike as she chomped on a large bite of shrimp and lettuce.

"I'm pretty savvy and cautious," she uttered between bites.

"Pretty, I agree. Cautious . . . well. Alan's serious about you and the case," Mike stressed.

"Did I hear the word case?" Toni said with feigned enthusiasm.

"Okay smartass. Since Sue was kidnapped, it's a dangerous deal. And no one's figured out who killed Debra Morton. The ex-hubby is a person of interest. But he lives in Tampa, the Carrollwood area, so it's a bit of a challenge with police on the other side of the bay. And they don't have substantial evidence for his arrest. Keep in mind, this landscape's a lot different than it was for the stories I gave you."

"I get it. Still no clue as to Sue's whereabouts? Any clue at all? I haven't listened to the news since early this morning."

"Not that I am aware of," Mike said as he looked directly at Toni.

Toni studied Mike's eyes. His face was a mask of reserve. *Years of practice paid off,* she thought.

"Or not that you can tell me?" she asked between chews.

"Toni. The situation's taken an ugly turn. What was bad before is worse now. Please keep out of it. Don't you have enough to worry about?" Mike put his burger down and softly caressed her shoulder.

"I get it, again. I do. But Sue's my friend and colleague. I'm worried about her. And you're right. Peggy's begging me to get back to work full-time."

"Good. She's a very smart associate."

"And I have the fashion show to work on."

"Ugh. That again?" Mike wrinkled his nose. "I suppose you want me to fill my bank account so you can con me for a donation . . . which is stretching the word donation."

Toni shook her head. "Milner, if you're obnoxious, I'll get you *in* the show. Lucky for you, I'm in charge." she said with a haughty expression. "This year, I declare, we must have a male model. Though at the moment, I can't think what you're a model of."

"I'm a model newsman, Jasper. I know when to hold 'em and when to go to print." Mike smiled, proud that he may have won this round.

"Oh man. That's a stretch. I wish you'd print something to hold the Pine Oak residents at bay. I'm afraid I'll run into Walter again. He's a tough one. I'm surprised he wasn't some super interrogator in his past."

"Yes, he's got my phone number, too. I've only managed to avoid a couple of his calls."

Toni's cell phone beckoned from deep inside her purse. She reached inside, pulled the phone out. "It's my mom."

"Tell her I said hi."

"Hey Mom. What's up?"

"I want to make sure you're okay. I haven't heard anything about that kidnapped woman. Have they found her yet?"

"I'm fine. And no. No word on Sue. I hope they find her soon, too. I'm here with Mike for lunch. He says hi." Toni nodded at Mike.

"Tell Mike hello for me. Ask him when he'll print more about that house explosion?"

"Mom, Mike's doing his job. It's still an open case. Where are you? How about coffee? I haven't seen you since you got back."

"That'd be good. My next showing isn't until two. Can you be there soon?"

"Sure. See you in fifteen minutes. Love you." Toni hung up and tossed her plastic bowl into the garbage.

"I noticed you didn't mention your latest development," Mike commented.

"You mean Chloe's threat? She doesn't have a need to know. I don't want her to worry any more than she already does."

"Good." Mike pulled her close. They hugged in the privacy of the interview room. Toni felt protected. She hated to let go, but her mother was waiting.

Mike walked Toni to the front door of the building. He hugged her again as he whispered in her ear.

"Have a good time. And remember to be good for the rest of the day."

"I promise," she said. "I'm only having coffee with my mom. Then I'll go back to my own office, write some ad copy and be the ideal entrepreneur."

"Perfect." He kissed her cheek and pulled away, smiling as he stepped back into the lobby.

Chapter Thirty-Nine

Toni spotted her mother, Emma Jasper, seated by the window. Emma smiled in Toni's direction with a slight crane of her neck. The fresh-brewed smell pervaded the small, yet well-occupied café. An aroma Toni liked.

"Hi, Mom," Toni said as she hugged her mother before sliding onto the high chair on the opposite side of the round table. "Nice outfit. So no rest after your trip, huh? Did you have a good time? You look relaxed."

Obviously, her recent vacation in a luxurious New England bed and breakfast gave this overzealous Realtor the rest she needed. But she's back to her sweater-jacket and black slacks official work outfit. Nice hot pink blouse.

"Yes. Here, I got you a Mocha Latte."

"Thanks. I can use it."

"Vermont was marvelous. The scenery was fabulous though the trees hadn't turned yet. The weather was great. No rain."

"Get lots of pictures?" Toni asked.

"Oh yeah. I plan to organize them either tonight or tomorrow. I'll email you when they're online."

"I saw the inn's website. Looks like an old building."

"It is. Historic Victorian built in 1881, but now quite modern inside. That's half the reason I picked it. Only four bedroom too, which made it very peaceful. I slept well to say the least."

"No bothersome guests?"

"Nope. Everyone was great. And the French toast. Ah. To die for. The place even had a fire in the fireplace. The ambiance was so cozy, I hated to leave."

"Cool. Where was it? Burlington? What'd you see in town?"

"Plenty. The place is so cute. I walked to their Church Street Marketplace. I went in all of the shops—or almost all of them," she said with a grin, "then just around the corner, Lake Champlain was gorgeous. Speaking of shops, I got you a little gift."

"Nice." Toni opened the small box to find pewter petal earrings. "I love them. Thanks. They'll be perfect with my new outfit. I drove over to Tampa to those Shops at Wiregrass."

Emma asked, "Why in the world were you shopping over there? Mike didn't send you on a story, did he?"

"Uh, no. Not exactly. Well, not at all. I had a hunch I wanted to check out."

"Your hunches again?"

"Yeah, but Mom, this one tied in with PinCo and the robbery— or perceived robbery as the FBI calls it—so I had to go. Besides, you got a vacation. I needed a little weekend away."

So it wasn't quite a full weekend. Mom won't know if I skip a few little details.

"They still don't know what happened at the bank?" Emma asked.

"No. I'm not sure what the FBI's doing about it."

Emma stared at her daughter. "That's the bank you pitched for so long. What a shame."

"I know. No sooner did I get the manager, Emily, to sign a contract, and then this happened. That in itself is a bit weird."

"But you're not investigating? Come on. I know you," Emma said. Toni attempted to avoid her mother's stare. *She does know me. Damn.*

"Mother."

"Okay," Emma responded with hands up in acquiescence. "Tell me. What'd you hope to find in Tampa?"

"Maybe someone over there might know more about the bank."

"I see. Well, I'm glad it wasn't a wasted trip. Is Wiregrass that outdoor mall with the upscale shops?

"Yes. Don't worry, I know I'm on a tight budget, but the trip was worth it."

"I'm glad you had a good time. Now, how *is* Mike? Had lunch with him, huh?"

"He's great." Toni hoped her mother wouldn't make too much out of her automatic smile. "We actually went on a date Saturday night."

"In Tampa?"

"Actually, I came home early. Once I got my outfit, I was done. One night was enough for what I needed to find out."

"I see." Emma eyed her daughter with characteristic motherly-date approval. So what's next?"

"Mom. I'll report back if and when the relationship progresses. I won't push Mike. That date was a big step. I was kind of surprised when he asked me out."

Emma smiled. "Okay, I just like to keep up. I mean, you two have worked together for several years. And he'd be a great catch."

"Mother." Toni's look of exasperation triggered a guise of resignation from Emma.

They sipped their coffee in silence while Toni examined her new jewelry.

"I've got one more favor," Toni said to change the subject. "Is there any way for you to find out where Emily and Jon Phillips got the cash they used to buy their house?"

"No. That information's not public. And it's no one's business. But come to think of it, the Realtor who sold them the home is in my office. I remember her being relieved when that albatross sold. I hate to pry, though. Are you sure you need to know?"

"Yes. And this is totally confidential. The regional vice president at PinCo told me that Emily 'bilked the bank.' His words, not mine. Doesn't that language sound like she stole from them?"

"Some accusation. He could've objected to what she spent on her branch's activities—maybe unauthorized expenses. Your assumption's a big leap. What'd Mike say?"

"He's not sure. But he'd like to help the authorities get to the bottom of the kidnapping and Ray's house fire, if the supposed robbery is connected. You know Mike. He needs proof."

"So you *are* investigating. I knew it."

"Mom," Toni sighed. "I've got a vested interest here."

"I understand, and I'd like to help you. But this type of question isn't right."

"Neither is bank robbery."

"True. If I think of some way to ask the agent, I will. Anyway, I've got to get back to the office. My new buyers and I have several homes to see."

"Just be safe, Mom."

"I always am. That's why I meet them at the office." She hugged her daughter. "Bye, Toni. You be safe, too."

Okay, I set myself up for that one. Like mother, like daughter.

Chapter Forty

The block-letter note in the center of her desk caught Toni's attention. It read that today Peggy's title was office errand girl who'd gone to purchase tons of supplies.

Toni laughed at her associate's flair for exaggeration. Tons, sure. She opened the storage cabinet. Yup, out of printer ink.

With a mental plan for the afternoon, Toni sat at her desk with pen in hand, armed for agency business. Her cell phone ring cut into her deliberation. Brad again. She wondered what he'd need already. *Maybe Sue had been found and was safe?*

"Hi Brad."

"Hey. Sorry to bother you again. But I've had time to work on the posters we talked about for the children's event. I'd like your and Chloe's opinion before I go further."

"That's super, but I'm not sure this afternoon is such a good time to visit Chloe. I saw her this morning for other business. She's pretty tired."

"I get it. But this might brighten her day. It'll only take a few minutes. How 'bout it? You said you wanted to get a jump on these materials."

"True. But we don't need the posters yet."

"I understand. But you never know when new business will roll in and it'll be crunch time—for either one of us. And I like to be proactive. What do ya say? Just a few minutes. We're on a roll here, Toni."

Toni sighed. Brad did make a point. She hoped to land more clients, which would keep her busy. Chloe seemed to like Brad. *Maybe it would be a good distraction for her,* Toni thought. *Or not.*

"I don't know. She's not quite herself today because she's a little upset about . . . something."

"Then we can cheer her up. You saw how well Chloe and I got along, right? Come on."

"You're very persistent, you know. What were you, some strong-arm salesman in your past? Let me call Chloe and I'll get back to you. Okay?"

"Sure. Thanks."

And they used to call me a pushy broad. Hell, nothing like Brad's pushiness. He's right. Our visit might cheer her up.

Toni pushed the phone icon next to Chloe's name. After several rings, the woman picked up but sounded somber.

"Hi Chloe. Are you feeling better?"

"I wasn't feeling bad to begin with, Toni. I was scared. Now I've moved into mad as hell. Did you go to the police?"

"Yes. Detective Dietz took the letter to forensics and the FBI. And believe me he understands how delicate this matter is. He'll take care of your safety."

"Good. But if I see any law person on the prowl, a face that doesn't belong—"

"I know," Toni interrupted. "You'll sic Brutus on them."

She heard a small giggle from Chloe before the woman stated, "And they won't forget it, either."

Toni grinned. The real Chloe was back. Maybe a visit with Brad and a little fashion show distraction will be good for her.

"True. And I've got an idea to brighten your day."

"My ring?"

"No. Sorry. But a bright idea nonetheless. Brad just called me. Our diligent artist has been working on posters for the fashion show. They'd be a super addition to our materials. And I agree with him that stores will display them. Can we come over so you can give his design your stamp of approval? He insists that you sign off on his art as soon as possible. I guess he's anticipating a big surge in other work coming in. He's pretty conscientious about deadlines. In this case, he's being quite proactive."

"Humph. Finally someone smart and respectful . . . like you. Fine. We can have coffee in the solarium. That young man is delightful. What about three o'clock?"

"Excellent. We'll see you then."

Toni was quick to text Brad and confirm the poster appointment. He replied that he'd meet her in the parking lot. Parking lot? She wondered why he didn't say lobby unless he wanted more admiration for his fancy new car.

***

Waiting for Toni seemed to be Brad's specialty lately. Toni spotted him in the center of the lot as soon as she turned in. She waved and found a parking spot.

"Hi. You know the lobby is cooler," she said as she approached the man.

"I like the outdoors. Balmy breezes, sunshine."

"And eighty-five degrees. Well, you do have a nice tan. Thought you wanted me to gawk at your new vehicle again."

"Good idea. Feel free," he said. "I love it. If you're lucky, you might even get a ride."

"If I'm lucky? Imagine, when I spoke with Chloe, she called you smart and respectful."

"Did she? That's great. I think she's smart, too. Reminds me of my grandma. Chipper, happy, knows her mind."

"You got that right. For sure, Chloe does have her opinions. Called you delightful, too. I'm amazed," Toni kidded.

Brad opened the lobby door. "See how delightful I am," he said with a bow. He then extended his arm in a courteous gesture as Toni strutted by.

Several residents chatted in groups throughout the lobby. In the expansive solarium, only Chloe and one other person were present. Toni observed Brad searching the room as if he wanted to find someone. Then he smiled at Toni.

What was that about? Almost like he expected someone else to be here. I guess he just wanted to look around. Maybe I'm a bit paranoid. He's never been here . . . at least I don't think he has.

Chloe and Brutus were lounging in their favorite spot, nearly devoured by the overstuffed chair. Two white ceramic pots, along with a cream pitcher and bowl of sugar packets, waited on a silver tray centered on the rectangular glass table in front.

"Hi, Chloe," Toni said. From between large pillow creases, she could see the tip of Brutus' tail in a restricted wag. He grinned, as only Brutus could, so she figured he was, indeed, still alive amidst the folds of upholstery. Toni bent to scratch the dog's head.

"You're a good boy. Yes, you are."

Then she hugged Chloe and sat on the couch. Chloe looked up at Brad as he took her hand and bowed in proper ceremony.

"Nice to see you again, Chloe," he said with demonstrative fondness.

"Sit down, Brad. Want me to break my neck with you way up there?"

"No," Brad chuckled, "I don't want any broken parts. Is this coffee?"

"Yes. Help yourself. There's hot water for tea, too."

"I'm a coffee guy. Mmm. Smells good. And just what I needed this afternoon. Can I pour some for you?"

"No. All set here," Chloe responded.

"Toni?" Brad asked holding out a cup.

"Sure. Thanks," she responded.

Chloe didn't waste time. Before Brad completed his coffee duty, she began, "So Toni tells me you've been busy. Posters, huh? We didn't have posters last year. But you think the local stores will display them?"

"I'm confident the local businesses will cooperate. I'll take the posters to them myself. When I was in South Florida, I worked on a charity event. The merchants were very supportive. We had posters everywhere, which, I'm convinced, helped the turnout as well as the bottom line."

Chloe frowned. "I don't know. This isn't South Florida. And Seminole's turning ugly."

"You mean the robbery and kidnapping?"

"What else could I mean, young man?"

Toni couldn't hold back a snicker. Chloe glared at her. Brad maintained his serious expression.

"Chloe, this is the way I see it. Situations happen. Bad and good. We take care of them and do what we can to make them better, whatever it takes. After all, isn't that the reason you guys put on this charity event for the hospital? To make it better for the kids?"

Chloe stared at Brad for a minute. Then she turned to Toni.

"You bring me an artist and now he's a philosopher," she said.

"I like to look at the positive side," Brad said.

"Never would have guessed. All right, where's this art you're so dang-blasted eager to show me?"

Toni was pleased with the rest of the meeting. Chloe and Brad had become friends after a mere two encounters. With a little addition here and some punctuation there, the posters were on their way to production.

Five o'clock already? Didn't accomplish as much as I wanted to today. Or maybe I did. We're ahead of schedule for the fashion show. Tomorrow I can get back to client materials.

After a stop at the grocery store, Toni headed home to see what Bubbles had gotten into. And she wanted to get back to her suspect diagram. Not one bit of news about Sue was on the radio. Toni figured the six o'clock news must have some report on the case.

The case? Brad seemed cool about it. But why was he scouring the solarium. He examined the whole place. Swiveled his head on the way out, too. In particular, his eyes examined everyone and everything as he walked by the front desk. Could he be involved with Emily or Jesse, or that note for Chloe? He came from South Florida. But exactly how long ago? He's a good artist and people-person— talented, confident and smooth. Too smooth?

Chapter Forty-One

Toni pushed open her front door and noticed a round of fur in the corner of the couch. Bubbles' tail covered her eyes. A head jerk and simultaneous meow from the cat meant the human had probably interrupted a vibrant kitty dream.

"Oh did I wake you, Bubbles? Good, my papers are intact. Didn't get to the bottom of my case today, huh?"

Toni deposited her groceries on the kitchen counter. After all of the bags were empty, she sat beside the cat and flicked on the news. The Channel 9 anchor revealed violent conflicts overseas. No local news. Toni switched to Channel 10 and pulled the warm feline onto her lap.

"I need to find out what the deal is with Sue's search," she said. Toni didn't mind that the conversation with her cat was one-sided as long as she could express herself. And she was sure that Bubbles needed to hear all about her day.

"Not a mention of Sue on the news. And I got nothing from my visits around town. But Mike's a good listener," she continued as the cat settled in. "Okay, he's a great listener. I just wish he'd let me in on any up-to-the-minute scoop. Mike and Alan. Stone-wallers personified—both of them. Good thing you're a cat. No worries, huh?"

Bubbles purred her usual affirmative. At last, the local news declared that the search for the kidnapped woman continued. The fate of Susan Anderson was yet unknown.

"Man. That stinks. What in the hell did she do? I mean she didn't accuse Jesse of stealing, did she? And what reason would she have for doing that? Brad called me about the ring a mere thirty minutes before. And Jesse wasn't even in Plait when Sue left. Or was he? Did Brad mention his suspicions to her when he saw the ring? He seems brighter than to do a lame-ass thing like that. Oh lord, Bubbles. If Jesse was the thief, did he kill his wife? Where is Jesse? And Emily?"

Toni moved the ball of fur back to the cushion. The pampered cat squeaked her dismay. Nonetheless, Toni headed for the kitchen, determined to find her own crunch food for dinner. Chomping eased her frustration. Fortunately after a day like today, the freezer was well-stocked with comfort frozen yogurt, chocolate no less.

"What do you want for dinner? Huh? The usual?"

The cat sat near her bowl with wide-eyed attention, like any culinary-disciplined cat on-guard for dinner. Toni's cell phone interrupted the dining discourse.

"Stay there, Bubbles," Toni stated as she got her phone.

"Hi Mom."

"Hi. The agent who handled the Phillips' sale was in the office today. I figured out a way to get some information about their cash for the house. Since the bank's trouble and the manager's disappearance were in the news, I asked her if she had any information about the house being listed. I told her I researched it myself, but if she got the listing, it would make sense since she'd helped the buyers. She said those buyers, your Emily and her hubby, were pretty difficult to work with. In fact, she'd been glad to get the deal over with. Jokingly, I asked her just how difficult a large cash sale could be. And here's the good part. She said the money was a family inheritance. But no one was supposed to know because some relatives were angry about it. She was quizzed over and over about confidentiality and making sure the title company didn't question the source. She said the whole experience left her a bit nervous. What do you think?"

"Ya done good, Mom. I appreciate your efforts. We'll talk tomorrow, okay? I have to think about it. Bye and thanks."

Toni ended the call. But the phone rang immediately. .

Mike. Wow. Maybe he's worried about me, or he misses me.

"Eaten yet?" Mike jumped in before Toni could utter a sound.

"No. Bubbles and I were about to—"

"Good. Forget whatever you're about to concoct for dinner. I need to talk with you, and I'll deliver. What do you want on your pizza?"

"Um . . . ." Toni hesitated. Was this a date, she wondered?

"It's not rocket science, Jasper. I'll stop for food and we'll eat at your place. So the question is, what should I get on your half?"

"Mushrooms and spinach sound good."

The silence confirmed her choices didn't suit Mike's taste. "Fine," he said. "You get your own entire pizza and can have leftovers for lunch tomorrow. Or plant it. Doesn't that green stuff grow?"

Toni had to laugh. "For an educated guy, you amaze me. Spinach has terrific health value."

"Good. I like to amaze. Be there in about thirty. Okay? Be sure you're decent, too."

"What? I'm not indecent."

"You know what I mean. I'd hate to open the door and have the neighbors in for a rude surprise. I've heard what single women wear when they romp around home alone."

"Good grief. Did I actually agree to this dinner with you?" She could detect his soft laugh.

"It's food, Jasper. You never say no. Remember, don't open the door unless you know it's me. Promise?"

Toni hesitated. Mike went from fun to fearful in five seconds flat. "I promise. What's up? I haven't gotten any threats."

"Tell you when I get there. Bye."

"Bye," Toni said, though Mike gone. Now she was concerned. So she double checked the front door's deadbolt and slid the chain guard into place. After an examination of all windows, she felt relieved—for the moment. Then it occurred to her that some areas hadn't been examined since she'd been home. With pepper spray in hand, she combed the condo once more checking closets and even under her bed. All clear.

Maybe mom's right. I should get an alarm for the condo. I'll check them out tomorrow.

Toni gave the cat her meal, set two dinner plates and two forks on the table for the human diners and then headed upstairs to change. She figured that Mike at least deserved to see a clean t-shirt.

***

Toni eyed Mike's Jeep as it pulled into her driveway. An old compact car with shiny new paint followed right behind. She knew Brad used to have a car like that, but a different color.

Brad's driving? It's his old car with new paint. What the hell is Brad doing here? Thank God Mike's here. But they seem a bit chummy walking up my sidewalk. What the hell?

"Hi guys," Toni said as she opened the door. "Brad, what a surprise."

"I invited him," Mike said as he passed her with a waft of pepperoni in his trail.

"Come in." Toni tried to sound authentic. It wasn't that she didn't want Brad there, but she was confused.

She grabbed a third plate and fork and joined the men at the table. They'd brought beer. She poured water for herself. This situation called for a keen mind.

"Dig in," Brad said. "Mike's spoiling you with a whole pizza. It looks good. May I have a piece?"

"Certainly. As long as you explain the reason you're here," she said and realized the rude implication. "I mean, I'm glad you're here. I didn't realize you guys knew each other."

Brad stared at Mike who nodded in return.

"I saw that look. What gives?" Toni asked.

"I have a past, Toni, part of which you know," Brad began, "but most of which doesn't involve graphic design. In South Florida, I was with FDLE, Florida Department—"

"of Law Enforcement," Toni interjected. "You? What happened?"

"Yes, me. I was a pretty good cop, too. Several commendations for my undercover work. But I reached a point where I needed a change. Years of crime in and around the Miami area got to me. I'd had enough. Then I realized I had a knack for computers and design. When I visited my mom, who lives here, I liked the serene vibe. So, I relocated to have fun with a new career and enjoy life."

"Serene vibe? Is that law enforcement talk or design lingo?"

Brad chucked. "Good point. However, I'm still alert when a situation seems suspicious or the vibes are off. It's usually a bad deal. With hardened criminals, I've had to pay extra attention to my inner feelings, so to speak."

Toni eyed Mike, who calmly munched and listened. "A lot like my gut intuition."

Mike shook his head and raised a hand toward Toni.

"Don't go and think your instincts can fight crime," he added after a quick swallow.

"Mike's right," Brad said, "I'm in touch with both Alan and George Nelson on this case. And it's taken a turn for the worse."

"Taken a turn? It's been awful all along. But why are you involved?"

"Look, I wanted a new career when I came here. However, I'm also aware that the local detective can be stretched in a case like this. When I read about the explosion, I drove by and saw the arson investigators. Then I met with Alan and shared my background in case he or the department needed my assistance as a consultant."

Toni sat and chewed her pizza. At least it was comfort food, though not on her diet. Her mind struggled to process this different side of Brad. "Did Alan send you to Mike?"

"Yes. Alan's concerned about you." Suddenly, Brad's seriousness and vocal tone demonstrated an "I mean business" side, almost an about-face to the man she'd seen in their ad agency encounters. She couldn't even imagine the dark side of humanity that he'd witnessed.

Mike interjected, "I can't watch you all the time."

"Which is the reason," Brad continued, "I seemed like a— what'd you call me—strong-arm salesman. I told Alan I had a good excuse to check out Pine Oak Place. I needed to survey the cars in the parking lot. We know what type of vehicle Jesse Morton owns, and there's an APB out on it. Alan questioned him on Monday before the report came back regarding the pin in Debra Morton's arm. Since the body has been positively identified as her, the FBI regards Jesse as their main suspect."

"But the fracture information hasn't been released, right?" Toni asked.

"Not as far as I know," Mike said, "I haven't even shared it with anyone at the paper."

"So why would he run? Jesse was supposed to meet Sue at Plait on Tuesday. She was leaving work early specifically to meet him there. When I talked with her after you saw her, she mentioned your comment about her ring. If she told Jesse about the ring getting attention, maybe that spooked him?"

"Good point," Mike said. "Brad, do you think he's already on the run? Toni witnessed him cleaning out his bank account."

"But that was Monday morning," Toni said. "Chloe's dog, Brutus, practically bit his foot off."

Brad smiled with triumph written across his face. "I saw the incident. He's a tough little pooch."

"What? You were there?" Toni was annoyed with herself at her lack of observation.

"I'm a creative guy. Who needs Halloween to have a clever disguise?"

"You're my so-called bodyguard?"

"You're important," Brad's caring nature showed through his words, "as is this last slice." He reached for the solitary remnant of pepperoni and cheese.

"But you?" Toni realized her police tail had been right at her side most of the time.

"Yes, me. But yesterday, when I met with Sue," Brad continued, "and commented about her sapphire ring, in no way did I suggest it was stolen or even connected to the bank or Mrs. Ford. Perhaps Jesse got scared because she wore it in public."

"It doesn't make sense," Mike said. "Why call attention to himself with a kidnapping instead of just gettin' out of Dodge?"

"Have the authorities been to his house in Tampa yet?" Toni asked, not that she planned to confront the man.

"Yes," Brad answered. "FBI's had the place staked out since the kidnapping. Odd thing is no one's come or gone. They searched it with a warrant last night. Found no trace of Jesse or Sue. They did find suitcases. So if he left town, he didn't take anything except his car."

"What does he drive?" *Okay, I'm just curious.*

Brad described the details of Jesse's charcoal gray car. "Have you seen it?"

"No. Don't worry. If I do, I'll call you or Alan."

"Good." Both men shouted in unison. Toni jumped back in her seat. No doubt they meant business. And their business seemed to focus on her not snooping.

"Come on, guys, I want to solve the puzzle, too. See, I've connected some of the dots." Toni fetched her suspect diagram from the coffee table. After Brad and Mike moved the pizza boxes to the kitchen counter, she laid out her rough concept.

Brad examined it, fingering the name Carl Johnson. "Who's he?"

"The regional vice president of PinCo. I met with him in an attempt to save the account after the open house was cancelled and Emily vanished. Has anyone located her? Do you know she claimed that they used family inheritance money to purchase their home?"

"FBI confirmed that she left the country," Brad said. "Maybe her travel's tied in with more money. From what I've gathered, she and her brother don't have any immediate family."

"Her departure was kept well under wraps," Mike commented.

"Sorry, Mike. Alan told me he trusts you, but this bit had to stay top secret. I'm only sharing now because I know that crucial facts won't leave this condo. Port Authority and airlines around the state are on alert. She has to come back for her husband."

"Geez, Brad. Do you know how sick he is? I went to their house on Monday—or did you know that, too?"

"No, I missed that excursion."

Toni looked at Brad and raised her eyebrows in a blatant expression of surprise. She wondered how she'd gotten away from a watchful eye that day.

"Jon could be dying," she said. "He looked that bad."

"But he's not a suspect, so we can't help him. Only Jesse and Emily are on the FBI's list. The FBI has photos of Emily boarding a plane for the Cayman Islands."

"Then she did bilk the bank."

"What?" Brad's furrowed forehead let Toni know that she, at least, was one up on him.

"When I met with Carl Johnson on Monday, he asked me if I had anything to do with missing bank funds. Or 'bilking the bank' as he put it."

"That could explain the trip to Cayman. But we don't have proof yet."

"What about Ray Edwards from the bank? He called me." Toni hoped by now, Ray had contacted Alan or some law person.

"I know," Brad said. "Alan filled me in. He hasn't surfaced."

Toni was sad to learn Ray was still at large, but relieved to know Brad was, indeed, one of the good guys.

Though Mike offered to sleep on the couch, Toni sent him and Brad home. She did post a sticky note on the kitchen cabinet to check on the cost of a home security system.

"We need protection, right Bubbles?" Toni's question brought the usual feline stare.

The cat had observed most of the evening's activities from the top of the couch. Toni knew that Bubbles liked Mike. And he'd been allowed to give her a few behind-the-ear scratches. But the small animal had to check out the new tall man at a distance. When the newcomer came too close, the cat scooted up the stairs until she deemed it safe to return to her living room cushion perch.

Now as Toni cleaned up, Bubbles watched her human intently. Toni took it as a sign to continue vocalization of her thoughts. Of course, Bubbles is interested in my concerns, Toni mused.

"Emily's out of the country? She must have transferred money from the bank. Probably checking on her foreign account. But the house? What will she do about it? And Jon? Would she leave him? He needs help. And Sue? And where the hell are she and Ray? I wish Ray would get police protection. The FBI must be close to figuring this out. How close?"

After Toni sat in the middle of the sectional and clicked on the television, Bubbles climbed onto her warm lap. The cat was a comfort since the news was not reassuring.

Chapter Forty-Two

Toni hardly slept a wink. The eleven o'clock news had broadcast that an unidentified body was found in a car at Tampa International Airport's long-term parking lot. A car matching Brad's description of Jesse's vehicle had been parked there for two days. The license plate was missing. Toni's mind was a high-speed race of fact and conjecture. Now at almost four in the morning, her best options were pain reliever and another crack at her suspect diagram, even if it meant waking Mike, who had come over right after the news.

Toni hadn't been surprised when Mike showed up at her door around midnight, overnight bag in hand and concerned expression on his face. He had politely knocked., though she reminded him that he had made his own key in case of emergency.

"I know, but I'm a nice guy, and you need a watchman," he told her. "I'm sleeping on your couch, just a precaution. Brad's been called in to consult. They don't know where Jesse is or if he's the airport body or not."

Toni's mind had refused to slow down after she kissed Mike good night at about twelve thirty. Now a little over four hours later, she threw on a bathrobe, padded down the steps and stood motionless to observe Mike sleep. Some watchman he turned out to be. *But he was a comfort,* she thought, *even if not conscious.*

Toni turned toward the kitchen and heard Mike stir.

"I'm awake." Mike spoke without opening his eyes. "What the hell are you doing?"

"Hey, sunshine," Toni responded.

"If you want to roam around with that noisy shuffle, then please turn on the news."

"Okay," Toni said as she reached for the remote. "Breakfast will be served soon, my esteemed watchman." She could do this every morning—but without the sense of danger.

"Just coffee. Got any orange juice?" Mike asked while he struggled to prop up his head.

"Yup. Comin' right up."

The breaking news was a copy of what was reported the night before. The reporter droned on about an unidentified body in a car found at the airport. Toni had assumed the body was Jesse. Now she panicked. Could it be Sue?

"Mike, is it Jesse's car for sure?" she asked, placing the juice and coffee on the table in front of Mike.

"Brad hoped to find out," he said, "but that doesn't mean he'll tell me. The FBI has control."

"I understand. I just want to know whose body it is."

Mike stared into her eyes. Toni felt he could see her thoughts—her fear that Sue was dead.

"Come here," he said as he sat up and pulled her next to him. He wrapped his arms around her and kissed her forehead. "We'll find out. But why would anyone kill Sue? Not because of a ring? It's not enough of a motive for murder."

"Can you call Brad? Maybe he'll tell us who it isn't if he can't say who it is."

"Yeah. Good idea."

While Mike made the call, Toni tossed a prepackaged ham and cheese scramble into the microwave. She downed a small glass of orange juice and moved her mug of coffee to the dining table. She spread out her suspect diagram, now complete with notes from her conversation with Brad and Mike.

"Great. Thanks, buddy." Mike hung up and turned toward Toni with a look of satisfaction.

"The car was Jesse's. Apparently, the body wasn't a body, though. Some eager reporter jumped the gun. Just an empty rolled-up rug in the back seat. They also found brown wrapping paper and tape. So he must've shipped something."

"But why leave the rug in the car? Why put it in the car in the first place?" Toni asked.

"Good questions. But let's not jump to conclusions, especially so early in the day."

Toni paused to exhale, one of her small burdens of worry now lifted, "I'm relieved it wasn't Sue's body. Toni saw Mike's questioning eyes.

"Or Jesse's?" he asked.

"Yeah. Not Jesse either, as much of a creep as he is."

"Now," Mike reprimanded, "my former reporter wouldn't have made such a quick judgment until all of the facts were in."

"Right. I'm just tired. And still worried. And I need more coffee."

"And *I* need to get to the office. Maybe news has come in."

Mike grabbed his overnight bag and headed for the first-floor half bath. He emerged in clean clothes and with a smooth shaven face.

"I'm leaving a toothbrush. Do you or your cat object? I may need to be your night watchman again."

"Fine. If my mother comes over, I'll tell her it's Bubbles' new brush."

"Come on. Your mother loves me," Mike said triumphantly.

"Trust me. I know." Toni smiled and shook her head. "She's quite happy that we are . . . well . . . sort of seeing each other. Aren't we?"

Toni blushed. Was she overly tired? Or maybe she'd interpreted Mike's increased attention all wrong. Did he care for her as a girlfriend? Or was it his duty to protect? Brad had stated that others besides him were watching her. Was Mike her guardian as well?

"Yes, Toni. They were dates." Mike walked over to Toni, smoothed her hair and softly kissed her lips. "Don't worry, though. Chinese food has never been my first choice to woo any woman."

Toni found herself speechless as Mike left, locking the door behind him. *Guess that key is handy for you, Milner.*

Finally, the current dilemma returned to focus. Toni considered Jesse's car at the airport since Tuesday night, but no Jesse. And he wasn't at home, but his luggage was.

What the hell? Did this development mean that Jesse was or wasn't at Plait earlier on Tuesday? If it was Jesse who took his car to the airport, how did he leave—plane, taxi, rental, stolen car, Emily? But the FBI has Emily out of the country still, according to Brad. Oh no. Where's Sue then? If Jesse didn't kidnap her, then who did?

I have to give Alan hell for not sharing information about his so-called consultant. Brad's my artist. Okay, part-time freelancer. I don't own him or even employ him full-time. Alan needs him, too. I just want to know what's happening.

"Bubbles, let's make some sense out of this mess." The cat jumped to the top of the couch and settled into her usual pillow observation perch. The cat's job was moral support from a nearby cozy spot.

"You know, Bubbles, if Chloe hadn't gone into the vault last Thursday, what would have happened?"

Toni glanced over at her cat whose ears were erect, apparently listening.

Toni remembered seeing Emily and Jesse in a heated—and almost intimate—discussion outside of the bank the same afternoon as Chloe discovered her ring was missing. Was it a disagreement? A foiled plan?

"Bank officials had to have kept duplicate keys to some of the safe deposit boxes, rather than destroying them," she reasoned to Bubbles. "Was this Emily's plan for financial security? Are she and Jesse in cahoots on the theft with her master keys and his tech knowledge? But in addition to a palm print, a unique code was needed for entry. So how'd they manage to get past that?"

Toni remembered that she'd heard Emily ending a phone call with an almost punitive tone. She had been abrupt in her comment of "we'll talk about this when I get home." Thinking back, Toni wondered if Emily had been speaking with her husband Jon. Or with Jesse? Or were all three of them involved?

She paused to retrieve her now cooled breakfast from the microwave. Munching the ham and cheese egg concoction, Toni glanced at the content cat. "Well, you're my support, Bubbles, even though you're asleep over there." She smiled when the cat opened her eyes. Then it hit her.

"What if Jesse had devised a way to get into that vault and not be there? Did he have enough tech knowledge? No. Bank security would catch it. But he was bank security. And he had control. How much control? Emily was the manager, so she should have known what was happening. If she was stealing, how does embezzlement figure with the vault?"

Toni's one-sided discourse with her cat continued through her final cup of coffee. "Did Ray," she wondered out loud, "catch those two culprits doing something out of the ordinary? He said he saw Emily in the bank after hours. Did he realize what was going on? Does Ray have evidence about the vault or the embezzlement? Is that why they tried to kill him?"

Six o'clock already. Bubbles was fast asleep and not at all listening. Toni raced up the steps to put on makeup and get dressed. From her closet, she pulled on navy slacks and a red and blue flowered tie blouse. She secured her hair back in a ponytail.

Back downstairs, she hit Mike's number. "Any news?"

"No," Mike said. "The FBI's upping their search for Jesse and Emily. No reports of Emily coming back from the Caribbean. But Jesse should still be in the Bay Area. Maybe he's got another car—a rental perhaps, and he's travelling around, yet maintaining a low profile. We don't have any reports back from our car rental alerts."

"Wouldn't he be a fool to come anywhere near Seminole? Especially if he did kill his wife and actually robbed the bank? Will they maintain a watch on his Tampa house?"

"I believe so. They've got a travel alert for anyone resembling him, too. Just go to work, Toni. Better yet, get more rest."

"I will. Thanks for coming by last night. I was grateful to have you close." Toni could still feel Mike's soft touch as she spoke.

"Glad to be there," he said. "Let me get back to what I was doing. I'll text if I get any update. See you later."

"Good."

Mike had a point. She was tired. A few minutes on the couch would help, she figured. Then she could go to the office. Mike would be happy. Peggy, too.

Toni dozed off on the couch with Bubbles curled up as a warm compact ball of fur.

Chapter Forty-Three

A distant chime penetrated Toni's consciousness and jerked her to an upright position. *Damn. My cell phone. Geez.* Only half-awake, she grabbed the phone and noted the seven o'clock time.

"Hello." She hesitated to give her name since she didn't recognize the number on the screen.

"Toni. I'm sorry to call so early and I apologize if I woke you. It's Emily Phillips."

Toni blurted, "Emily! Are you okay? What happened? Is Jon okay?" Toni stopped, stunned not only by the voice of a returned Emily, but also by the realization that she sounded like her mother in inquisition mode. Though groggy, she remembered Emily was not supposed to be in the country. Was she back? Toni fought through her sleepy fog to make sense of this call.

"I'm fine. Jon told me you stopped by. I wanted to contact you sooner, but I've been so scared that I had to get away to think. I'm being framed for the whole bank fiasco when I was the one helping the FBI."

Really? That's hard to believe. Toni couldn't help herself. *Yes, inquisition mode wins. But one step at a time. Especially with you, Emily. What I want to know is why you would try to kill Ray? How did you get into that vault—if it was you? What do you know about Sue?*

"I heard about Sue's abduction, too," Emily said in a calm voice, almost as if she was hearing Toni's thoughts. "But I'm not sure if it's related to the operation."

"What operation?" Toni asked, confused about the unexpected word use.

"I've been kind of undercover. We've known for a while that someone was using this bank branch—"

"We?"

"The FBI."

"What?" Toni stopped to look around her. Was this a dream? Nightmare? She clutched her phone tighter. "Does Agent Nelson know?"

"Of course. But he had to play his role to protect me. Then I needed to get away and check out a few outside leads for him. After we learned someone actually got into the vault, time became critical."

Outside leads? What about Jon? Or Ray? Or what the hell is this woman smoking? Is she a functional drug addict? Genuine nut case? Or liar?

"Do you know how sick Jon is? He's home alone," Toni emphasized. The image of Jon's death-mask face came to the forefront of her brain.

"Yes. It's unfortunate. Ever since he was a kid, Jon gets sick every year. He has a poor immune system. I left him soup and other special food that normally helps him to snap back. Besides, he knew I was on an important mission."

Mission? I'm still on nut case.

"Emily, have you heard about Ray's house?" Toni asked. She hoped to pry as much as she could out of the woman while on the line.

"Yes. What a shame. Ray was one person we watched closely. We were about to question him, then the fire happened."

"Question him? At the FBI?"

"Of course. The next morning. Maybe he burned his own house down as a diversion? Poor fellow must have felt trapped. What a horrible way to go."

The fire? Okay, she knows that part. She doesn't know Ray's alive. He said she was onto him and his suspicions. Now she wants me to believe he was an FBI person of interest? No, I believe Ray. And what about Carl Johnson's accusation?

Toni was torn. She wanted to believe the former bank manager. But, she had faith in Ray since Chloe had leaned on his advice for a long time and he'd come through for her. Now, the knots in Toni's stomach urged caution.

Toni waited for more information from Emily. But Emily was silent, playing her waiting game. Finally, Toni asked, "Does Alan know all of this? You need to go to police headquarters and update him."

"Unfortunately, I'm not allowed to divulge all of my information to the local police. But I do have to share a few facts with Alan today. After I meet with him, can we talk? I know you're worried about your friends."

Worried? Damn right.

"Which friends do you mean, Emily? I'm worried about all of them. Where are you now?" Toni pulled on her years of reporter training to maintain a calm and even tone of voice.

"I'm in Port Canaveral. I had to touch base with another bank informant."

"On the East Coast? What's an informant doing over there?"

Toni's muscles tightened. She couldn't envision Emily assisting the FBI. *Only a terrific actor could manage this role for two years. No, she has to believe I'm gullible as hell. Or she's playing me? What exactly is her game plan?*

"It's complicated," Emily said.

Toni didn't know what to say next. Emily had rehearsed her lines. Or so it seemed.

"Toni, are you there? I'd like to explain the situation to you today, at least as much as I'm authorized to reveal."

"Yeah. I've got a couple of appointments, but I'll reschedule them. I want to speak with you, too. Any other help I can provide?"

Like turning you in? Or testifying that you're a lying criminal and horrible person? And I should never have fallen for your bullshit at the bank!

"How about if I call you when I get back into town? It'll be after ten or so. Okay?"

"That works." *Gives me time to hatch my own plan.*

"Good. See you then. And remember, we have to keep this quiet until we find Sue. You understand, right?"

"Sure. I don't want to jeopardize Sue's life."

Toni stood motionless in the center of her living room. *Emily mentioned Sue. Did that comment mean she's alive? Why the hell didn't Emily stay out of the country . . . if she is really back? Damn.* A "meow" from the top of the steps brought her back to reality—if it were real. She flopped back down on the couch and looked at her phone. Ten after seven.

The situation daunted her, but the choices were clear.

She needed to call Alan and tell him about the phone call. *After all, innocent until proven guilty. No, the creep is guilty. On the other hand, a good reporter considers every angle. No. Damn, she's a liar. And that's that.*

When Emily had said Jon got sick every year, Toni wondered if he also looked like death warmed over? The man appeared to be a walking ghost. Zombie at best. Toni added "check on Jon" to her due diligence list.

She realized Mike would be mad or just worried if she didn't touch base and bring him up-to-date on Emily's call. "I didn't pursue this lead," she rehearsed her own line, "Emily called me."

Her phone calls and the day's agenda planned, Toni knew that Peggy would have to handle most of the client list and any agency problems. *Mental note: take Peggy out for a nice lunch. Maybe dinner with her hubby and kids.*

She punched Alan's number. Voicemail. Toni decided to call Brad. No answer. Damn. She left an urgent message for Brad to call her as soon as he could. Seven-thirty. She called Mike, and he picked up on the second ring.

"You won't believe who I just heard from."

Toni summarized Emily's call. Mike told her to keep trying to contact Alan. He'd work on the call to Brad.

"Where now, Jasper?" Mike's tone was serious.

"I'll go to the office. Emily has to call me back."

"Good. Let me know when she does. I want to know more about her cagey FBI story. I'll find out if the FBI has eyes on her at all. If so, how'd she arrive back into the country? Port Canaveral sounds shady to me."

"I don't trust her either," Toni said. "Not anymore. She could be anywhere, but the area code was 321. That's Port Canaveral."

"Or it's a phone from there."

"True. Can't Alan get my cell phone calls traced?"

"Ask him. And soon, Toni. Keep at it until you get him. I'll try him, too."

"I will."

"Be careful," Mike added. "I mean it."

Wondering what the latest public information was on Sue, Toni turned on local news to find out. The reporter indicated that a large manhunt continued. "Shit." She then dashed upstairs to check her makeup and change into her new outfit. She needed to feel confident and comfortable. After a twirl in front of the mirror, she nodded in approval.

This may be a challenging day. I got bad vibes from Emily's call. Brad had better be on my tail this time. Hopefully he has his own bad vibes.

Chapter Forty-Four

The phone rang several times until the same unhelpful recording declared, "Alan Dietz. If this is an emergency, dial nine-one-one. Otherwise, please leave your name and number."

Damn. It's eight o'clock, Alan. You need to answer.

Toni left another message urging him to call her immediately. Then she grabbed her keys, locked the condo and took off for her agency to put in a quick appearance.

A few early workers followed her through the door of her office building. She tried to be vigilant with quick glances to scan her environment, a direct imitation of Brad's surveillance approach.

The ad agency's client list still had many on-hold items or need-final-approval status notes. She started coffee, and then turned on her computer to check the latest email. Toni perused the list and saw that one of the on-hold proposals wanted to schedule an appointment. Alleluia, she thought, this is good news.

"Hey" came a voice from the front of the office.

Toni hadn't heard or seen the door open. Peggy was standing just inside, a plate of cookies on the palm of her hand.

"Hi Peg. I see you've brought temptation," Toni stated after she recovered from being startled. *So much for today's vigilance. Maybe I'm still tired. Good, a cookie with more coffee.*

"Leftover chocolate chips from my troop. Don't worry. They've been in the fridge. Not stale yet. We needed the room for real food. The vultures in this building are easy targets for cookies. I'll make the rounds at lunchtime and get rid of them."

"What do you mean real food? These have chocolate, an essential food group. Man, do I need one today."

"So much for your healthy eating. You look tired. What's going on?"

"You wouldn't guess in a hundred years. Make that a thousand."

"Do I even want to know?" Peggy shook her head.

Toni forced a smile. *No, Peggy, you don't. Not yet.*

Toni waited for her associate to place the plate on the shelf. Then she snagged a large round cookie with another cup of coffee.

"This cookie is the best," Toni said, savoring a bite.

"Glad you like it. The girls made them. Nice outfit."

"Thanks. It's the one I got last weekend at Wiregrass."

"When you weren't a sleuth, only a mere shopper?" Peggy's cynicism seemed appropriate today. Toni decided she wouldn't share the latest detective news with Peggy. Not that she didn't trust her. Peg was on the top of the trust-and-friend-for-life list. But Toni needed her to focus on the agency's business. She'd fill her in with everything later. Toni required at least one person in her life who wasn't worried most of the time, especially about her. Since the day she was born, Toni was convinced her mother excelled at that. Her mom embodied worry. At least Peg knew how to go with the flow.

"I do have good news," Toni began, "we got an email from that large plastic surgery clinic in St. Pete. They want an appointment to review our proposal."

"Fantastic. Do you want me to set it up? We could go tomorrow."

"Sure. How about in the afternoon? I want to get with Bob Wolfe in the morning for the photo shoot schedule. And I'll check in on Chloe while I'm there."

Tomorrow? I hope I can. The FBI has to capture Emily today. She called from inside the country. She had to be.

Peggy cut into Toni's ruminations. "I didn't hear if Sue was found."

Toni finished her gulp of coffee and said, "No. I'm truly concerned about her. But I can't do anything to help. I'm sure you know how frustrating that is for me."

Peggy provided an eyebrow arch of empathy, a nod and a weak smile.

After Peggy left the room, Toni's phone beckoned. Alan's name and number. About time, she thought.

"Alan, did you get a call from Emily Phillips?"

"What? No. No one's heard from her. Did she contact you?"

"Yeah. She called at seven today. But she has a new phone number."

"Give it to me," he said with a brusque tone.

"I need to text it, Alan. Didn't write it down. But it's a 321 area code. As soon as we hang up, I'll send it. Are you aware of her being FBI? She told me she's been undercover for a couple of years."

Alan didn't respond. Toni felt uneasy on the line with a silent detective at the other end. She stood tall next to her desk holding her breath, on high alert for what might come next.

"No. That's bullshit. What else did she say?"

"She told me she'd call you for a meeting this morning. She claimed that Agent Nelson knew about her cover and what she was doing."

"The woman's delusional. Where'd you say she called from?"

"She said she was in Port Canaveral. She had to get a statement from an informant over there."

"Damn her. Hang up and text that number immediately. I'll contact the FBI."

"Sure," Toni said. Alan was off.

Toni texted Emily's number to him and sat down. So much for her morning momentum. She felt stuck. On her desk, the remainder of the cookie sat, ready for consumption.

"Emily? Did I hear right?" Peggy called from the other room.

"Yeah. You have big ears, you know."

"I need them for both of my charges, you and my kids. So what did Alan say?"

"Basically, he said bullshit."

After Toni finished the cookie, she grabbed her phone, tossed it in her purse and pulled out her keys. She was on a mission. Of that, she was sure. And if she was followed, all the better.

"I'm out of here, Peggy."

"So soon. I was on the verge of relief with you here, in my very presence. Where are you going? The paper? Mike? Not anywhere . . . wrong?"

"Where's wrong? I'll get with Mike, again. Already spoke with him this morning. He knows what's going on. By the way, Brad's a cop, too. So you're safe around him. Bye."

"Huh? What?"

Toni ducked into the stairwell. No time for the elevator. I can rescue at least one person, Toni thought. If Emily doesn't care to save a life, then someone has to do it.

Chapter Forty-Five

The drive was short, slightly over three miles to the Phillips' house. Alan's reaction, Toni deduced, indicated he was more than upset that Emily had contacted her before phoning anyone else, especially him. The question of whether or not she was a federal agent added to Alan's evident irritation. As a former reporter, Toni's instincts were in an uproar about Emily's reappearance and the still-not-found Sue.

She suspected that Emily didn't plan to call or meet Alan. She knew she was in trouble. Carl Johnson had alluded to—no, flat out stated—that Emily would not work in the financial industry again.

His term "bilked" could mean lots of things, as mom mentioned. Did Emily know I met with Carl? Is she on the run because she's an embezzler or a safe deposit thief? Or both? She's been busy somewhere, that's for sure.

Toni knew if she believed Ray's story about Emily's attempt on his life, then Jon might be in trouble unless he was in cahoots with Emily and Jesse.

As sick as he appeared, Toni considered the "he'll snap back" verbiage as fabrication. *Who the hell "snaps back" from a death-like illness? It should take Emily a while to get here from the other side of the state or wherever she is. She had to know I'd call the authorities. Perhaps she wanted me to send them on a wild goose chase. So my plan will work. If I'm wrong, no real harm will be done. I just hope I'm still being followed.*

The plan was to get Jon to a hospital. She had had it with Emily's self-centered disregard for her spouse. After digging out the address, she drove to the subdivision. Again, she didn't have a code to access the gated community. So she pulled over and pretended to check her cell. A car went by and the driver pushed buttons on the metal box a few feet before the gate. When the iron arm opened, Toni pulled right behind the vehicle to enter. She passed several streets with no activity. Not a soul in sight.

Toni turned onto the Phillips' street. The cul-de-sac was empty and the house looked deserted with window coverings blocking out the daylight. Only the front door glass provided visibility to the inside. Toni had been ultra-observant during her short ride through the community. No federal vehicles in sight. Brad had said the FBI was watching ports and airlines. She trusted they'd watch the house, too. At least, she hoped so.

She decided to ride around a few more streets to find out whether she or the house was being watched, or if any cars looked like they didn't belong. The manicured yards basked under the sun with no humans or vehicles of any type in sight.

To allow an ambulance to get close to the house, Toni parked in the cul-de-sac rather than in the driveway. She was prepared to call the paramedics and get medical attention for Jon. The house looked dark from the street, no apparent activity from inside. She wondered if he was asleep. And she prayed he wasn't dead.

Oh man. I hope he's not contagious. He hasn't been out of the country, or at least I don't think he has. Toni took one more peek at her phone inside her purse. No text message. *Alan, Brad and the FBI must be on some remote quest to find Emily. However, I'm not waiting for her to contact me. I'll let the authorities go after her. She must not care about Jon, but I don't want him to die. I'm here to save him—*

The familiar cell chime interrupted her mental deliberation. Mike's number seemed to jump off the top of the screen.

"Hi Mike," Toni said in her best innocence imitation.

"What are you doing?" His voice sounded like contrived friendship. Not his latest warm and personal approach.

"Well . . . I did go to the office this morning and got a few things done. Ask Peggy."

"I did. You left. Where'd you go?"

"Listen, Mike. I'm driving. Can I call you back in a little while?"

"No—" The man's tone had an edgy bark.

"Thanks for calling, Mike. But I need to call you back. Bye."

Ach. Hanging up on Mike feels worse than awful. I'll make it up to him. I can cook him a very romantic dinner. For now, time's ticking. And I'm here. I've got to get Jon out of that house in case Emily actually shows up.

The phone rang again. Alan? Toni hesitated to answer it.

"Alan." She had her own brusqueness for use in tight time frames.

"Where are you? Ray came in. He and Agent Nelson are here."

"What? Great." *Hooray for my belief in Ray.*

"Yeah, he's been so distraught about Sue's abduction and knew he had to show his face. He asked that you come and join us A.S.A.P."

"Sure, I can be there in a bit. I'm involved in a project right now. How about an hour? Will that work?"

"No. Where are you?" Toni recognized the FBI agent's voice, cutting in with a stern tone.

"Agent Nelson, I'm thankful and glad Ray is there. Most of all, he's safe. I'm sure you want to debrief."

"Toni," Alan came back on the line, "I never got that call from Emily. We've relayed her information to state police and every federal agency from here to Timbuktu. We hope our APB finds her—and soon. One more time, where the hell are you?" The detective was good at forceful communication. But Toni gripped her phone, determined to complete her one small mission.

"I'm helping a sick friend. I need to get him to the hospital quickly. Then I'll be right there, at your disposal."

"One hour. No more or an APB's out on you. Is that clear?"

"Yes."

Toni knew she sounded defensive in response to the men's demands. But she was convinced Jon had to get to the hospital. Then, she hoped that everyone would stop asking her where she was. Why weren't they focused on Emily and Jesse?

Her phone rang as she started to open her car door. Alan? Again?

"Al—"

"Ray wants to talk to you. Now, Toni."

She looked down the street and at the surrounding lawns, impatient to get on with her extract-Jon mission. No cars. No people.

"Okay," she said.

"Toni. Where are you? Emily's dangerous. She's not at all what she seemed to be at the bank," Ray said, urgency in his voice.

"Hi Ray. I'm so happy you're there. I've been worried about you."

"I'm very upset about Sue. Alan told me about Debra Morton. I think Emily's capable of murder."

"What about Jesse? I know they were both at your house."

"Never trusted the man. But Debra would come into the bank and have ferocious arguments with Emily. I could never make out the entire conversation. Emily kept her door shut. But I'm certain the topic was money. Emily and Jon were living high on the hog. Debra and Jesse were struggling, at least that's the way Debra sounded in the few words I could make out."

"But Jesse had the bank contract," Toni said, "and other work in Tampa. He should make good money."

"I tried not to converse with him. He didn't give me the time of day either. So I don't know. What I did observe was Jesse and Emily engaged in many a private huddle. That situation worried me." Ray sounded anxious. And Toni was amazed that she had never noticed Jesse and Emily together at any time other than once outside the bank. The pair did not even look at each other at chamber meetings.

"Ray, I met with Carl Johnson. He alluded that Emily stole from the bank. Specifically, embezzled. Did she?"

"I believe so. She kept the branch's financial reports close to her, stashed and locked in her desk. Guess she figured no one'd ask if the bank appeared to be financially secure and everyone was happy."

"Ray, what about Jon, Emily's husband? He's very sick. When I saw him on Monday, he looked like walking death." Toni waited.

"Sick?" came Ray's response after several seconds. "I don't know. He's in the medical field. You'd think he'd get treatment. He didn't go away with Emily?"

"Nope. Go where?" Toni asked. "Do you know where she is?"

"No. I haven't the slightest. Alan told me she called you this morning. I think they're trying to check that phone number and pinpoint her location."

"Good." Toni felt reassured

Ray continued, "Emily liked to take long weekends in the Caribbean. Maybe that's where the money is if it was stolen, as Carl believes. I didn't steal anything, Toni."

"I know, Ray. Did Jon go with her on those weekends?"

"I'm not sure."

Toni pursed her lips as she digested the latest facts. She was grateful that Ray was safe with Alan.

"You know, Chloe misses you."

Ray sighed. "Oh, she's a delight. I've been so concerned about her. You need to give her my best."

"You need to tell her yourself. I'll take you over to see her. She's already closed out her checking and safe deposit box at PinCo. She didn't know what to do about her investments."

"We'll work it out. Her funds should be safe. I would never cheat anyone, especially that wonderful lady."

***

Toni bid goodbye to Ray. He warned her to be careful. Obviously, Ray was the latest addition to the "be-careful-Toni" group. Though she was eager to facilitate a Chloe and Ray reunion, Toni had to complete her mission to rescue Jon.

After locking her car, she looked all around, with a focus on each driveway and each bush. She walked up the pavered sidewalk to the stately columned entrance and etched glass door. At least the outside met Emily's particular and lavish taste, she thought.

She peered through the glass after ringing the bell, but didn't see anyone, even with her face pressed against the glass inset. Man, she thought, what if he's unconscious. Toni tried to decide what to do next as she continued to stare inside and observe as much as she could.

Call the paramedics? No. What if he already went to the hospital? One of his co-workers could've taken him. Of course, the man could be dead by now. She doubted he'd bounced back as Emily stated he would. She tried to imagine what soup and other food could have been prepared by such a sick person. Emily had vanished in a day.

"Welcome." A hushed but firm voice jolted the quiet of the portico.

Toni jumped several inches. When she turned around, Emily faced her from beneath a blond wig and large hat pulled down over her eyes. The former banker stood close, with a gun jammed in Toni's ribs. How she appeared without a sound was a mystery in itself.

"It's open. Go in," she whispered in a controlled manner.

Emily didn't sound or resemble her banker manager image. In fact, Toni didn't know how to handle this version of Emily. Options flashed through her mind. But the woman's gun ruled. Toni understood her only choice was to step inside. The dangerous metal object thrust in her rib cage solidified the decision. So she moved with deliberate caution into the foyer.

Damn. Why the hell didn't I sign up for that self-defense class at the community center? Hope Alan knows my whereabouts. Good God! Did Emily kill Debra? Or is she protecting Jesse? Play it cool, Jasper.

Chapter Forty-Six

"Emily, what the hell? How'd you sneak up on me? And why in God's name do you need a gun? I'm not the enemy. We're both on the same side, right?"

Toni did her best to sound composed and confident. But a contrived and somewhat scary grin stretched the gun-holder's mouth. *This isn't what I expected. Not good at all.*

The foyer seemed dark, even after her eyes adjusted from the bright sun. The sliding glass doors at the far end of the living space had opaque sheets draped over rods. The only sound at the moment was the slight squeak of Toni's sneakers. With each step, the shoes gripped and bowed over the travertine floor. Her feet felt heavy and her gut was like an internal knot. Nevertheless, Toni turned to face her captor and look her squarely in the eye.

"Emily—," Toni said. The woman returned a cold stare, like sizing up her quarry for conquest.

"Sit. Over there," she commanded and pointed at a couch against a far wall. She punched a code into a small white alarm. "You're such a little do-gooder. I must say, Toni, you almost surprise me. Almost. I took a risk when I called you today. But you made it so easy . . . asking about poor Jon. I hoped you'd fall for my lame story of his recovery. And you did. Still, I'm amazed at how predictable you are. Just not surprised."

Emily's cackle of a laugh raised the hair on Toni's arms and legs. She'd never been in this position. The bad guys she'd written about for her investigative reports didn't have guns. At least they never pointed them at her. Furthermore, she never considered them her friends.

Toni continued her squeaky stride to the lone couch, the only furniture in the sizeable room adjoining the kitchen area. She turned and stood once again facing her captor and the gun. In slow motion, she lowered her body, noting that she was now out of view from the see-through door.

You win, for now. I have friends. They'll be here. Good God, they'd better be here.

"Where is he?" Toni asked from the edge of the old worn furniture.

"Who?"

"Jon. I saw him on Monday. He looked very sick. I know he didn't make a miraculous recovery."

Emily smiled and lowered the gun. "Oh, him, my unfortunate and dumb spouse. We'll get to him. You know, I had a backup plan. I always have a backup plan. My best plan today, though, was for you to come here on your pretty little own. One way or another, I wanted you where I'm in charge."

"But you were in charge at the bank. You had control."

In charge enough to steal money. What about those safe deposit boxes?

"Damn right. Those idiot executives in their lofty headquarters. They were so slow. Good thing, too. Gave me plenty of time to take a little out of this account, a little out of that one. Brilliant because it's not a new idea. But a concept those dumb bank execs thought they'd never see in their little community bank. 'Lots of security' they said over and over. Right, lots of vulnerability because of Jesse."

"So you did steal from the bank. Did you rob those safe deposit boxes, too?

"Steal? Absolutely. I was passed over for promotion. One I deserved." Emily almost spat the words. Her eyes widened and she waved the gun upward as if to assert her authority.

"There would have been another opportunity—"

"Shut up, you idiot. I wasn't about to wait for what I deserve. So I got those bastards good—right in their profit statements." The crazed expression with slanted eyes and bared teeth, a guise between a smile and a grimace, gave Emily's face a demonic appearance. Toni felt her back stiffen.

"What about the safe deposit boxes? Those people didn't misplace their items."

"Yeah, the vault and the old people's supposedly safe stuff," Emily said, "that *was* the ingenious plan. We were smart, no question about it. But stupid Jesse had to get greedy on our test run and blew it. Then that damn Ford woman had to come in."

"Chloe Ford didn't deserve to be robbed. What test run?" Toni asked and immediately regretted it.

Don't make the crazed woman any crazier, Jasper. Change the pace and the subject.

"Where's Sue? Is Sue here?" Toni continued.

If Sue's here, maybe Emily didn't kill Debra. Damn, I'd like to be right about that. Not that I'd be happy if Jesse murdered his wife. They're both nuts. Was Debra shot, though?

I don't remember anything about wounds in the victim. Who could tell? Wonder what type of gun this is? Maybe I need a gun . . . and an alarm. Or just Alan or Brad to be close behind. Where the hell's the FBI?

"Of course, she's here so I can keep a close watch on the little troublemaker. Once she wore that damn ring out in public . . . well, she sealed her own fate. Again, my stupid brother-in-law caused a problem. Such a jerk. Now, give me your purse."

"What do you mean fate? Where's Sue? I want to see her now. I want to know she's alive."

"My, my. Quite feisty today. You're supposed to be polite and accommodating. Remember, I'm your client."

"You can't kidnap and kill both of us. Every law enforcement official and FBI agent from her to Timbuktu is on your trail." Toni couldn't believe she'd uttered Alan's Timbuktu metaphor.

"Who said I plan to kill you? This situation's my stupid brother-in-law's fault, so I'll just make use of him. Now, hand over your purse."

Toni clutched at the bag, her arms stretched around it. "No. They're onto you. I just spoke with Detective Dietz and Agent Nelson with the FBI. You might as well turn yourself in."

"Ah ha, ha, ha." The woman's cackle bounced off the walls. Toni stayed perched and frozen on the edge of the seat.

"Well, Toni Jasper," Emily continued, "You're quite the risk-taker, aren't you. Look here, I'm the one with the gun. Hand over the purse. Trust me. I know how to use this weapon."

Emily pointed the gun at her motionless victim. Toni thought it looked pretty small for a gun. They looked bigger in the movies. But she wasn't willing to match mental power with firepower.

She wished she'd left her phone in the car. Maybe Alan or Brad had tracked her already. Any time would be good for them to slam on their brakes and line up around the cul-de-sac. Right now would be best. She knew her phone would be smashed once in Emily's clutches.

Slowly she lifted the handbag toward her captor. Emily snatched it. The handle's seam scraped Toni's fingers.

"Okay. You've got my purse. Where's Sue?"

"So impatient. Shut up."

Emily walked to the kitchen. She put Toni's phone on the counter and opened the drawer beneath it. With one fell swoop, she retrieved a hammer and smashed the cell phone.

Emily dialed a number on another phone. "Jesse, get the hell over here fast. Yeah, I'm home. This time, do what I say, got it? Take a cab. Then get rid of the car in front of the house. Get back here in a cab from a different company. What? Don't think, you idiot. Just do it."

Emily banged her hand on the counter after setting down the phone. Toni had listened and watched with eyes wide and brain open to any backup plan enlightenment.

"Come on, you little busybody," Emily ordered. Toni dutifully got up and followed.

Around the corner from the spacious kitchen and one-couch room, Sue sat in the corner of an empty bedroom, just past a guest-pool bath. A loose chain extended from one ankle to the other. Her terrified eyes looked up from the floor as Emily pushed Toni in. Toni stopped herself from falling and stood in the middle of the room.

"Now girls, play nice. Remember, this weapon can discharge easily. So don't be heroes. Stay put. Especially you," she said as she pointed at Toni with the gun. "And Sue. Tell your friend if she behaves, she might even get lunch. If I'm still here by then. You know the drill. Bathroom here is as far as you go. Don't mess up my rug. We've got a lot of equity in this place. Any questions, ladies?"

In unison, Sue and Toni shook their heads. Toni was glad she wasn't chained. And both of them could walk, sort of. Toni didn't want to dwell on what would become of them if Alan and the FBI brigade didn't get here soon.

Get out of here, you fake bank manager. I'm smarter than you. Crooks get caught, especially ones like you who make far too many mistakes.

Emily waved her gun back and forth at the pair one more time. A wicked sneer revealed a human far removed from the open house planner-banker of less than a week earlier. Sue cowered even deeper into the corner. Toni stared into Emily's eyes, shocked that she had never detected this evil side of a person she considered a professional colleague. Emily had been undercover all right. But undercover took on a whole new meaning with this criminal.

I know Alan's figured you out. That fake FBI tale must've made him realize what you are. For sure, Brad's on to you. He knows your type. Just another bad criminal idiot out to bilk a lot of good people. By now, the real FBI's ready.

Emily laughed again and turned away, ending the staring contest.

Chapter Forty-Seven

"Sue," Toni whispered a few minutes after Emily had disappeared around the corner.

"Wait," Sue said, "I'm so sorry you're involved. I was a dummy to fall for Jesse. Me and a man like him? I shouldn't have accepted the gift. But I never thought, for one second, he was a thief. I had to give the ring to Emily. She said he stole it and it was hers now. But why am I still here? I don't know what she wants from me."

"She may think you know more than you do. Is the ring Chloe's from the bank vault?" Toni asked.

"I don't know. What do you mean Chloe's ring?"

Toni realized that the newspaper had never specified what had been reported missing from the alleged bank robbery.

"Brad asked about it, didn't he?"

"Yeah," Sue said with a surprised look, "how'd you know? Men don't usually comment on women's jewelry, do they? My ex never gave me jewelry."

"Did you tell Jesse someone commented about the ring?"

"Before I left, Jesse called, just to be sure nothing had come up and I'd be at the gym. I did say that maybe I shouldn't have worn it to work because a lot of people admired it."

"I bet he got spooked. That's why he kidnapped you."

"No. He was never there. I waited on a stool near the snack bar and then got a text saying he couldn't make it after all. I was leaving when she pulled me into the SUV."

Toni's eyebrows arched in surprise at the pronoun.

"She? Emily grabbed you? We saw you but couldn't identify the plate or the driver."

Sue nodded. "Yeah. Her. What do you mean 'we'?" she asked, apparently astonished and a bit too loud in her last syllable.

Toni put her finger to her lips and watched the doorway. No Emily. No sound. Eerie quiet.

Emily wouldn't leave. She just told Jesse to get here fast. She also told him to move my car. Damn. I wish I could peek around the corner to see what she's up to. Better stay here. I don't want Sue to have a coronary.

Toni nodded for Sue to continue.

"Yeah. She's got one hell of a grip. And the car was moving. I had to get in. She chained my ankles after we switched vehicles. Then she blindfolded me before she drove a long way. I think we were near the airport."

"Did you see Jesse or hear him?"

"No. She climbed out and then jumped right back in. We drove a little more. She got out for a bit longer. Finally, she drove back here. She put me in this room before leaving the house. About thirty minutes later, she was back. We've been here since Tuesday night."

"No one thought to get a warrant for this place?"

"The doorbell did ring the next morning. I remember Emily saying she was a nurse and her patient was quite sick. I don't know who was at the door. But . . . why *are* you here? You're alone?"

Toni eyed Sue, her fear and anger about being a captive swung to guilt and regret since both of them were subject to the whims of a mad woman.

"I came to help Jon, Emily's husband. I saw him through the front door on Monday and thought he needed medical attention. Is he here?"

"I don't know. Maybe he's the patient she mentioned to whoever came by."

"If he's alive," Toni mumbled.

"What? Did you tell anyone you saw him?"

"Alan said the FBI had questioned him from outside the front door last weekend, but wanted to focus their manpower on the search for Emily and Jesse. Evidence proved that Emily left the country. This morning, Alan was surprised I'd heard from her."

"She called you?"

Toni nodded while she listened for any sound. She understood that being scared was the easy part. To sound self-assured, not so easy.

It was too quiet. And where the hell are Alan and the FBI? I might even hug George Nelson if he shows up. When he shows up. Be positive, Jasper. Think.

Toni made a mental note about Emily, strong as well as deceptive. *If the cavalry doesn't come soon, I have to come up with my own plan.*

Toni continued, "But that was a mistake even though she counted on my contacting Alan. The phone number was an east coast area code. She said she was at Port Canaveral, but Alan didn't believe that or other lies she told me. I figured she had what she wanted—money from the bank—so she wouldn't dare come back to her house. I dove right into her deceitful trap."

Sue's panicked eyes reflected her inner fear. "Do you think she'll kill us?"

Toni struggled to appear confident. "What would she gain from it?" The truth was if Emily made it out of the country again, she'd be home free. Witnesses wouldn't be a concern. Or would they?

"I don't know," Sue said in a forlorn voice.

"Look, Alan called when I was in the driveway. He said he'd put out an APB on me if I wasn't at his office in an hour. That was forty-five minutes ago. Remember Ray Edwards, the guy whose house exploded? He's alive. That's why Alan called. Ray was there. He told them that Emily's out of her mind. I hope Alan traced my phone before Emily smashed it."

"Me, too," Sue said with a sigh.

"At least, he'd want to find me to chew me out," Toni added with a smirk. "He's been quite annoyed with me."

Toni figured she'd need to apologize to Alan and promise to be good for the rest of her life if he rescued her. If anyone rescued both of them.

"With you?"

"Yes. He thinks I snoop too much. I told him I care for my friends and want to help. Mike's been on the lookout, too. Trust me, you weren't abandoned."

"You said Brad's a former cop?"

"Yeah, when he lived in South Florida. For this case, he's a consultant for Alan."

"I see," Sue said, her voice unenthusiastic.

"Brad was supposed to be my watchdog. So the FBI must be around here by now. I can't believe Jesse wouldn't be spotted coming here. Emily told him to get here fast by cab."

Sue sounded weak, almost hopeless. "I want to go home to my kids."

"I know. The sooner we get out of here, the better. Whether the police arrive or not."

What the hell did I just say? I don't have a plan. Think, Jasper, think. There's always a plan. It needs to be discovered. Oh shit. This time, I don't know what to do.

"How? We can't escape. Look at these windows. When do you think they were opened last? Emily would hear us."

"Good point. But we'll think of something. We're two smart women. And that witch out there is one dumb criminal."

"With a gun and good muscles," Sue said in a hushed but firm manner, emphasizing the obvious. Toni chose to ignore the potential consequences.

The quiet atmosphere was destroyed by the firm close of a door.

"You idiot. Can't you even shut a door? The neighbors might notice." Emily's strong insult came through loud and clear, though not quite as loudly as the sound of the door.

"What the hell is Toni doing here? That was her car, right?" Toni recognized Jesse's voice. She glanced over at Sue whose pained expression became streaked with tears maneuvering over her cheekbones.

"Look, you dummy," Emily said, "both of those women are pains in the ass."

"But we've got plenty of money now. Let's get the hell out of here. I don't want the police all over me again."

"Oh sit down and be quiet."

"Don't point that gun at me. Why'd it take you so long to get back?"

"Hey, flights to Caymen Islands with forged documents don't exactly fly on my schedule."

"Jon told me that Debra is dead. Did you know? They found a body in Land O'Lakes. It was hers."

"How'd they figure that out? And when'd he have the strength to tell you anything?"

"I called him yesterday. Man, he could hardly speak. "

"Just what'd he tell you, damn it?" Emily reacted with defensive intensity.

"The medical examiner noticed the pin in her arm, where she broke it as a kid. Since it had a number, they got a positive I.D."

"Shit. It's always one thing."

"What the hell do you mean? My wife is dead and that's all you can say? Maybe she was on her way to see me. Some pervert must have forced her over and—"

"Stop," Emily cut in. "That nosy, angry wife of yours had to go. Kept after Jon about where we got our money. Of course, he's such a poor money manager, he told her I did well enough at the bank to buy this place. I think he believed it, too."

"Emily" Jesse's voice was tense, "what happened to Debra? Tell me."

Toni and Sue didn't have to strain to hear his question.

"Sit still or I'll have to shoot you, too."

"What? YOU shot my wife? She was my wife, for God's sake. What the hell did you do? And her postcards? She didn't leave me?"

"No, I got rid of her. She divorced you, according to the papers I forged. For God's sake, she was pushier and pushier. Admit it. Your marriage wasn't that great. She bitched about the slightest thing. So I took action. That 'peace-making' shopping trip to Tampa last year worked out pretty well for her and me. At least for me." Emily ended on a forceful note.

"You forged her name on those divorce papers? What about the postcards?"

"Oh Jesse, you're such a naïve jerk. They were easy to mail. I took a couple of road trips when Jon thought I was away on bank business."

Toni and Sue listened without a move, not even a hair—except for those standing on end. Then they heard a scuffle.

Jesse shouted, "You killed my wife? How could you do that?"

Toni imagined Jesse had lunged at Emily.

"Get back," Emily shouted.

After hearing a pop and a painful cry from Jesse followed by a thud, the captive pair shuddered.

Emily's dictate rang out with freakish control. "I don't need you anymore. So be good if you want to live." After a moment, she continued, "Here's a towel. It's a flesh wound. Such morons. All of you," she shouted, assuring her entire audience heard the message, followed by a contemptible laugh.

Toni and Sue exchanged terrified expressions.

Emily probed, "Why'd you come back so soon? I told you to get on that damn boat with the machine. You *did* ship it out of the country? I mailed the other stuff you left in your car."

"Yes. After I saw it load onto the ship, I decided to stay here. I didn't want you to get caught 'cause of me or what I did with the ring. I was gonna get it back. I told you that mousy newspaper woman didn't mean anything. It was a diversion tactic so no one would know we were in this together."

Oh no. I can't even look at Sue. Trust me, Jesse scoundrel, you'll be crying real blues before long. At least I hope you will.

"Oh terrific. You thought I cared for you?" Emily said, in obvious disbelief. "Good lord, you're dumber than ever. This deal was business, no matter what you may've conjured up in that little brain." Though they couldn't see him, the prisoners could hear Jesse's sobs.

For several minutes, no sound skipped around the corner from the front great room to the small back bedroom. No shouting. No gunshot either. Sue and Toni held their breath.

Then Jesse angrily asked, "I was questioned by the FBI about the bank thing. What if they think I killed—"

"Oh stop. You ruined it. Should've left that ring, the bonds and everything else in the vault as we planned. You had to get greedy and sneak out a few little souvenirs from the test run. Now, since the old lady needed her ring for some shindig in the middle of September, we're running around like clowns. And I had to find a way to cover your ass. Should've let me hide the ring. But no, you had to have it. Just hope my nasty note shut that old woman up. If I'm lucky, she blabbed about it to her friends."

"What note?" Jesse asked, his voice shaky.

"I had someone deliver a threat so she'd back off."

"Who? Who else is involved? It was us, Emily, only us. What the hell have you done? The damn note didn't have my name on it, did it? All they can get me for is robbery."

"Right, dummy. That's all. It's a federal offense, you jerk. No, I didn't sign my threat 'Love, Jesse.' I swear, for someone with such computer smarts, you're pretty damn dumb."

"Don't call me dumb. You know how hard I worked at getting that hand scanner to work. And the tests were viable most of the time. If the old guy hadn't come back that night . . . ."

"Yeah, Ray. Well he's out of the picture now."

"I heard his house exploded and burned down," Jesse stated.

If only I could record this, Toni thought, the whole case on a platter for the FBI.

Emily laughed. "With a little help, it exploded. What'd you think? I was such a marvelous guest and toted our glasses back to the kitchen just to be nice?"

"What do you mean?"

"Oh, a little gas and a little candle worked wonders. You didn't know? The house blew not long after we left. I couldn't let him blab to anyone."

"You killed him, too?"

"He was another nuisance and too much trouble."

Sue and Toni could hear every word, loud and clear. With a unique brand of morbid fun, the sound waves bounded from room to room. Toni turned toward Sue whose eyes were the size of cherry tomatoes and about the same color, with streams of tears creating mini roadways down her face.

"She tried to kill Ray." Sue's whisper was so low that Toni had to lean in to hear.

"Yeah. But Ray was smarter."

Chapter Forty-Eight

Toni and Sue were startled by the sight of Emily's face at the edge of the doorway. Not her full body. Only a face attached to an elongated neck stretched around the corner.

"What now?" Toni used the deepest voice she could. Intimidation was not her specialty, but she wanted to sound resolute.

"Nothing. Glad to see you're good at your new job. Sue's easy. Make sure you stay easy, like your pal."

Emily flashed a cynical smirk and left.

Toni looked at her watch. It'd been more than an hour since Alan's APB threat. Toni prayed he followed through.

They have to find us. Would they think to come here—to Emily's house? Would Brad? They're pretty darn good at their jobs. One of them would've seen my car if anyone came by before Jesse moved it. Or they'd find it at the mall. Don't they have observation cameras there?

The sound of a cell phone caught Toni by surprise. Who'd be calling here? Emily's response from the kitchen was cryptic.

"Yeah. Yeah. You know what to do. Do it. Get me later, you fool. They won't find me, you moron."

Who else is involved? Not Carl Johnson? I can't believe it. Who could have phoned? If only I can get Jesse to help overtake Emily. If he hasn't lost too much blood. If he hates his sister-in-law enough for killing his wife.

Toni's succession of "ifs" was interrupted. Tap. Tap.

She looked at Sue. "Hear that?" she asked in a low voice.

"Yeah. Oh my God. Look." Sue pointed at the window on the adjacent wall. "It's Brad," she whispered.

Brad waved and held up a sign: "Sh. FBI's here. Come to pool door in bath. Cops see everyone with infrared cameras. We know where you are."

Sue couldn't stop staring at the window, even after the sign disappeared.

"Don't look at the window," Toni warned Sue. "We have to pretend nothing happened. I trust Brad. If he said the FBI's here, they're here. He's a man of his word. I know. He hasn't let me down yet."

"Okay." Sue's shaky voice concerned Toni.

"Take a deep breath," Toni coached. "We'll be fine. Believe me."

"I want to believe you, but—"

"Listen. I'm going to the bathroom, and I'll slam the door. Don't say a word if either one of them comes. Though I don't think Jesse's moving around."

Sue nodded, but her eyes and drooped shoulders demonstrated less than an affirmative. Toni snuck into the bathroom and firmly shut the door. She heard footsteps on the hall's tile floor.

"She had to go to the bathroom," Toni heard Sue confirm.

Toni pivoted to see Brad through the window. He seemed to be crouched or kneeling outside of the pool door, only his eyes visible. She mouthed a thank you and held up her hands in prayer mode. Then another paper sign from beyond the door read, "Unlock this door. Go back to bedroom. Stay there."

Toni nodded with excitement and gave him a thumbs-up.

After he pointed to the door knob, Toni unlocked the dead bolt simultaneously flushing the toilet. She turned on the faucet to validate the mini expedition. When she looked back at the door's window, Brad was gone.

Toni opened the door to a not-so-patient Emily. She blocked Toni's exit.

"Come on, little miss perfect. I need you to complete an easy project. And fast. Think you can handle it?" The serious mockery in Emily's voice brought an involuntary head shake from Toni.

And what do you mean fast? Okay, creep, enough is enough. Very soon, you'll be sorry.

Emily waved the gun in the direction of the family room. Toni felt she had to comply despite Brad's command to go back to the bedroom. Slowly, she edged into the room. At the same time, her eyes roved to see what tools could help with a plan—any plan.

She was concerned that the thermal-image camera didn't know which person was which. Could the FBI decipher that she might appear to be one of the bad guys in the room? Maybe the detection device had registered one person standing. Now there were two. Toni wasn't sure if the rescue squad realized that Jesse was injured, or if they even knew he was there.

Crumpled on the floor, Jesse looked totally dejected. He sat beneath the breakfast bar with his knees under his chin, a veritable heap of misery. The blood-stained towel wrapped around his upper right arm and his deep-lined forehead completed a pathetic new image.

Jesse raised his sad, dark eyes toward her in a sad attempt to gain sympathy.

"Toni, I didn't kill anyone. I mean it. I would never kill a person. I certainly wouldn't kill my wife."

"Save it for the jury. You're hardly the role model or even a decent entrepreneur. What you did to Sue was despicable."

"Look—" Jesse wasn't allowed to finish. Emily had enough chit-chat.

"Shut up. This isn't old home week," she interjected, her impatience obvious. "Here, hold this." With a plastic-gloved hand, she extended a small narrow bottle to Toni.

"What is it?" Toni asked without taking it.

"Just a little end to my failure of a husband. Yeah. I told you we'd get to him. He needs this and you *will* give it to him."

"End? You have to murder him, too? This is why he's sick. Poison. What the hell did Jon do to you?"

"He married me for starters. First mistake. I should've known he'd amount to nothing after he flunked out of medical school and settled for a dumb job at that clinic. Well, I don't settle. And I was honest with you, Toni. I expect to make it big. I deserve better. And my marriage has, well, irreconcilable differences." Emily snickered but continued to hold the bottle out toward Toni. Her face and arms motionless, Toni stared at the bottle. She hesitated to take the vile liquid, whatever it was.

"We can help you," Toni said. "This situation doesn't have to get any worse." *Oh man, why the hell did I say that*, Toni thought.

Emily laughed harder. "Right. Now you're a psychoanalyst. I must say I never saw this hysterical side of you. See, the problem with most people is that they don't know how to control their fate. Jon didn't realize we had to help ourselves to get what we wanted. We wouldn't have this house if I hadn't gotten a little creative with a few of the bank's large accounts. Those stupid rich people. They don't even stop to count their pennies."

"Pennies? It must've been a lot more."

"And to think you run a business. It all adds up, dummy. I told you I deserve it, every damn dollar. Now, take the bottle or I'll shoot you."

"That'd be helpful. I can't do your dirty deed if I'm dead."

"Good point. But your fingerprints will be on this bottle."

Toni needed a minute to think. How could she stall? How could she get back to the guest bedroom?

"They'll know you killed him. And Debra."

"Nope. This might go undetected as a heart attack. Or better yet, they'll think that you did the old boy in. People have seen you talking at the chamber. What might they suspect? And Debra? Hell, Jesse's as good as convicted. They'll never figure out who did what to her. No way they'll prove how she met her sad demise. No blasted evidence."

Toni knew that since she and Sue overheard her confession to Jesse, they were as good as dead. But how would Emily escape? What'd she mean on the phone when she told the caller to "get me later?"

"Go." Emily pointed to a door on other side of the family room. "Open that door."

Toni walked with calculated heel-to-toe steps, turned the knob and pushed open the master bedroom door to see a long lump on the bed. Jon.

"He's thirsty," Emily said, "and you'll pour this into his fruit juice cup. See the one with the straw?"

Toni took the small bottle after a rib jab from the small gun. The label said "Liquid Nicotine."

As she walked around the bed, the sight of Jon's ravaged face made her sick. She empathized with the poor man. Being married to Emily must've been no picnic. But Jon didn't deserve to die. She glanced past Emily toward the guest room, gauging the distance.

216

Thank God I wore sneakers. This has to work.

Toni's hand flew to her face. "Emily," she blurted as she gagged, dropped the bottle and turned away from Jon. "I'm going to be sick."

The bottle's fall was noiseless on the carpet. Damn, it didn't break, she thought.

"Shit, we haven't got all day." Emily picked up the bottle. Toni stayed in place, bent over in her best demonstration of agony.

"I'm gonna throw up," she said with deep throat sounds, the performance of her life.

"Damn it, go puke," Emily growled as she picked up the bottle. "I've got your prints here anyway. Don't leave a stinking mess."

Chapter Forty-Nine

Toni raced across the family room, slammed the guest bedroom door and locked it.

She grabbed Sue and pulled her across to a corner of the room, just in case Emily felt a need to shoot through the door. The captives heard quick steps approaching. Then a scuffle in the hall.

"What the hell—" Emily's voice was choked into silence. But a gunshot broadcast loud and clear.

"Gotcha." The sound of Brad's voice was welcome relief to both women. Seconds later, a loud crash signaled the front door glass had been smashed. Shouts of "get up," "call an ambulance" and "how the hell did you get in here" told them that the cavalry had, indeed, arrived.

Sue looked at Toni, still apprehensive and frozen in her spot.

"We're safe," Toni said, "The FBI is here. I caught Brad's face out of the corner of my eye when I ran past the bathroom."

A few minutes later, the pair heard a call from outside of the door.

"Sue, Toni. It's Brad. I'm coming in. Okay?"

Toni leapt to her feet and unlocked the door.

"You need an invitation?" She threw her arms around his neck, hugging him. At that moment, he was her knight in absolute shining armor.

Sue stood up, but remained in the corner of the room, uncertainty in her eyes and chains around her ankles. Brad opened his hand to her. "Come on. You've been through enough. Let's get you to the hospital."

The distraught woman reached for him as she moved one foot forward. Overloaded with emotion, she started to collapse. Brad rushed forward to catch Sue before she hit the floor.

"I've got you. Trust me, I won't let you down." He pulled her close and began to walk her out of the room, with a nod for Toni to go ahead. "By the way, your kids are fine. I went with Detective Dietz and somehow he convinced social services to let them stay with my mom." Sue pressed her face against Brad's chest, her emotion releasing a steady flow of tears. Brad led her out of the house.

A paramedic approached to take Sue to the ambulance, but Brad shook his head. He wanted to be with her all the way. Toni watched them with satisfaction, realizing that now Sue had a good man. And he likes kids to boot.

The cul-de-sac had become a veritable parking lot of police cars and emergency vehicles. Flashing red and blue lights cut through the sunlight. Neighbors gawked and lined the sidewalks as if the parade had come to town. And in a sense, Toni mused, it had in the form of Emily Phillips and Jesse Morton, a criminal team who failed to jump through one last hoop. What had Emily said, "Running around like clowns?" Toni chuckled at the irony.

An FBI agent protected Emily's head as the handcuffed woman entered the back seat of a shiny black four-door vehicle. Soon she can show off a new shiny bracelet, Toni considered, and couldn't imagine better jewelry for the former bank exec in a prison jumpsuit.

But who was the creep she'd asked to come and get her later? And from where?

Jesse's handcuffs and ankle shackles kept him secure. Paramedics were treating his wound inside an ambulance. If I were the reporter on this case, Toni thought, the word dejected wouldn't even begin to describe his look.

Then she watched a gurney emerge from the house with gaunt Jon atop. Paramedics pushed him into an ambulance, ready to whisk him away for recovery.

"Excuse me," she called to the EMT, "did you find the bottle of liquid nicotine in the house? It may be important."

"No," the woman responded. "We'll look for it. Thanks."

Toni began to walk away from the house, not quite sorry she'd come, but not about to linger for police questioning either.

"Toni." Harry came up next to her, pen and pad in hand.

"Hello, Harry. You're here. Where's your boss?"

"He's around. Not sure where. I just arrived so I want to get your side of this story, okay? What happened in there?"

I'll try to be nice today though I don't like you.

"I appreciate your diligence, but I'm not ready to talk. Not today. Get the FBI's information for now. Maybe tomorrow. Sorry. Good luck, Harry."

He stood in place, reluctant to accept the decline or move. Toni pondered how to evade the man's block. She wanted to go home.

"Hello, Ms. Jasper." Toni turned her head as she recognized the voice. Special Agent George Nelson approached and his timing couldn't have been better. Smiling, he handed her a bottle of water.

"Hi. Thanks. I knew you'd be here, Agent Nelson. And I am glad to see you."

"Are you all right? Can I get you anything else?"

"No. I'm fine."

"I need to get a statement from you. Can you come to the police station tomorrow? It can wait until then."

"Absolutely, I'll be happy to give you my statement and cooperate in any way. What about nine o'clock?"

"Fine. I'll make sure I'm there. Detective Dietz wants to speak with you, too."

"I bet he does." Toni cringed. More extreme chewing out, she thought. "By the way, I believe when you search the house, you'll find Mrs. Ford's stolen ring. Emily Phillips had it last, as best as I can ascertain. Sue Anderson had received a sapphire ring as a gift from Jesse Morton. Mrs. Phillips took it from Sue when she kidnapped her. Since it caused quite a stir among these thieves, it has to be the ring stolen from the bank vault.

Toni continued, "I can provide more information on the bank robbery as well as the embezzlement tomorrow. Hopefully afterwards, you can help my friends who had other items stolen from the bank."

"We can pursue the case. However, I can't promise we'll recover the other items. Not if they've been shipped out of the country."

"Okay. Just please talk with the Pine Oak residents, Agent Nelson. They're good people. And they told you the truth."

"Yes, ma'am. I can do that."

"Thank you. I'll see you tomorrow."

Then, Toni realized her car had been hijacked.

"On the other hand, Agent," she said, "I'll need to rent a car first thing. My car made it to the mall parking lot without me."

"Yes, we found it."

"Toni," called Alan as he strode toward her. "You okay?"

Toni nodded a farewell to the FBI agent. Then, with apprehension, turned toward the detective. "Yes, thank you. I know I—"

"I'm just glad you're safe. And you did help us. Believe me. I'm biting my tongue as I say that. Just promise—never, never again."

"Got it, Detective. I promise. I know I should've listened to you. And I should've informed you I was here. Mea culpa. But I worry about my friends when they're in trouble."

Alan raised a hand in defense. "I realize that. We'll talk later. By the way, your car's evidence. FBI found it."

"I'm glad no one considered that I'd gone shopping," Toni quipped. She needed a laugh. Any laugh. Alan didn't see the humor.

"No. We knew you were snooping—alone. As I walked up, I heard that you'll be in the office tomorrow morning. We can talk more then. Right now, I'll have an officer drive you home."

"Thanks. And one more thing."

"Only one, Toni?" The detective's exasperation was a familiar sight.

"My purse should be in the house. I suppose my wallet is evidence, too? But I need my credit card to rent a car."

"I'll look for it myself if you, for sure, promise to listen next time."

Toni's face brightened. "Next time?"

"Damn it, Jasper. That's not what I meant." He gestured toward a uniformed gentleman. "This officer will take you home. I can arrange for someone to pick you up in the morning if you need a ride. But I suspect Mike'll want to pick you up himself."

"Great. Have you seen him? I thought he'd be here."

"He was earlier. He knows you're fine and happy about it, too. He said to tell you he had some critical deadline issues. They must have been important."

"Yeah. Must have been." Toni's heart sank. She expected Mike to be by her side, expected she'd be important enough for him to be with her when she needed him the most. She tried to not show her disappointment.

Toni followed the officer to the patrol car, pleased to get away from the house, the people, the neighborhood and the crime scene. She felt lonely on the ride home and didn't converse with the officer. Empathetically, he didn't ask her any questions, which she appreciated. He just drove.

Why didn't Mike delegate to someone else to handle his crisis? Like Harry? Or could I be wrong about Mike's affection? Is he too angry to face me? Damn. I blew him off with the last phone call.

Toni held back tears most of the ride. Her mind flooded with emotion and confusion, she simply wanted to cuddle with Bubbles and cry. Sue had the right idea. Break down and let it out.

The police car rounded the corner into her driveway. Lights shone out of Toni's condo window. She sat straight up in her seat, fearing that someone had broken in and panicked that Bubbles hadn't hidden in a secure cranny. As the car slowed to a stop, the front door opened. Mike stood under the transom with a look of relief spread across his smiling face.

"Is that your place, ma'am?" the officer inquired.

"Yes it is. Don't worry. I know that man. He's the editor of the *Woodlands Gazette* and a friend. Thank you for the ride," she said with sudden glee.

As Toni approached the front door, Mike stepped back and gestured inward. Toni crossed into her living room. She gasped at the sight on her coffee table, two dozen deep red roses tucked into an elegant ten-inch crystal vase. Lit votive candles glowed in front of the arrangement. Last and not least to the famished former captive, a large plate of veggies and lush, chocolate-covered strawberries completed the welcome-home display.

Toni was stunned. "Mike—" She stopped. She didn't know whether to gawk at the gorgeous bouquet on the table or the even more gorgeous man beside her. Both took her breath away.

"Thought you'd be hungry for health *and* comfort food," said a grinning Mike, breaking the silence. He closed the door behind her, turning the deadbolt.

Toni reached around Mike's shoulders and faced him with a loving gaze. He pulled her close.

"Toni Jasper, I need to tell you. Don't ever chase criminals again, at least by yourself. I know you're smart and clever and independent. But . . . you're stubborn, annoying and, at times, frustrating as hell . . . and I love you."

"Oh Mike. I love you, too."

Their lips met in a powerful kiss. She didn't want to cry. But tears of happiness or gratitude or both began to flow. Black mascara streaked through bold berry blush. Today, she didn't care how unfashionable she looked. For the moment, Toni was taken out of this world. She was suspended in time, cloaked by Mike's tight embrace. Until . . . .

"Meeooww."

The humans had to laugh.

"Bubbles approves," Mike whispered.

"Indeed," Toni responded as they walked arm-in-arm to the couch.

Chapter Fifty

By eight-thirty Friday morning, Emma Jasper, Peggy, Chloe, Paul Delaney and even Carl Johnson had phoned Toni. They all wanted to check up on how she felt. She told them "great, marvelous, couldn't be better," but revealed no other details in spite of a mystified silence on the other end of each call. Her mother demanded to see her later.

Peggy also wondered if, after more than a week of super-sleuth heroism, Toni remembered her agency clients.

"Oh them," Toni joked, hardly containing her inner exuberance at the positive turn in her love life. "I'll be in tomorrow. Promise. Unless you need me today?"

"No," Peggy said, "I've tamed those who growl the most. Just take care of yourself."

"I will. Thanks, Peggy."

Mike and Toni arrived at the police station promptly at nine o'clock. The normally drab white walls and brown desks were surrounded by men and women in blue, applauding as she and Mike entered. Even Alan wore a pleased expression, one Toni hadn't evoked lately.

After motioning the pair to his office, Alan said, "Have a seat."

"Thanks, again, for being there, Alan," Toni said. "I was actually praying you meant it when you threatened an APB."

Alan's half-serious glare confirmed that Toni wasn't totally off his watch and "be careful" list.

"Ms. Jasper," the detective began, "Toni. I am personally grateful that these two cases are solved. But, on the other hand, I'm also responsible for everyone's safety, even yours. Is that clear?

Should I ask if there's any glimmer of hope that you'll no longer risk your life as a crime solver?"

Toni picked up a slight twinge of a smile from the tough man.

"Yes, sir," she responded with a smile of her own and a nod. "Lots of hope."

Alan shrugged. Toni grinned more.

Special Agent George Nelson appeared at the door.

"Good morning, Ms. Jasper, Mr. Milner," he said, shaking their hands. The agent handed Toni a legal pad and pen.

"Ms. Jasper, I need your statement," he continued. "Then we'll move to the conference room and convene with the others."

"Others?"

"Correct. For now, please write," he instructed, pointing at the blank paper.

Mike sat beside her in protective mode while she penned as many facts as she could in chronological order. Her reporter skills afforded her the ability to complete the report in a logical and comprehensible fashion.

Alan had offered to fetch coffee and returned with a cup for each of them. When Toni completed her account, Agent Nelson surveyed her statement with an official stern expression.

"Very good. Your statement has plenty of detail. The D.A. will be pleased."

"If only I had been wearing a wire," Toni added.

"Don't even think about it, Jasper," interjected Alan, who had been standing off to the side of the room next to his framed awards. "I would never send you into any suspicious location with a microphone." Alan turned toward Mike. "You're in charge of her now. I give up," he stated, shaking his head.

Mike smiled. "No problem."

"We're ready to move to the conference room," George said. He led the way down the narrow, linoleum-floored hallway. Mike, Toni and Alan followed suit. Stopping under the transom, Toni eyed those standing around the oval, solid-wood table. The conference table may not have been genuine mahogany, but the warmth of the people behind it was the real deal.

"Ray. Thank God." Toni ran to hug him.

"Hey," Ray said, "you're the last person I would've expected a hug from."

"Don't get used to it," she joked. "I'm so happy you're alive, and I'm glad you trusted me."

She moved along the group. "Brad. You deserve another hug. Thank you for what you did yesterday. You are Sue's and my hero."

Brad grinned and nodded.

"Take a seat." Agent Nelson motioned toward the seats opposite the others.

He faced Toni. "Ms. Jasper, we did have your back. You, on the other hand, made it quite difficult at times for us to follow your trail. The regional vice president, whom I believe you know, Mr. Carl Johnson, contacted the FBI when he noticed unusual figures in the branch's monthly statements, including items that didn't add up and funds that were unaccounted for. Mr. Johnson couldn't confirm who was diverting the funds. He had trusted Mr. Edwards for many years and, therefore, believed he was innocent and could help us."

Toni looked from Agent Nelson to Ray. The light bulb went off in her brain.

"So Ray and Agent Nelson already knew each other," she said in Alan's direction.

She saw Ray and the FBI man nod with a glance between them.

"The twist came," the agent continued, "when Mrs. Ford reported that her sapphire ring had been stolen. Her insistence of theft and the other irregularities, including the threatening letter Mrs. Ford received, were taken seriously and given a great deal of consideration, whether you realized it or not, Toni."

Good. Guys, if I'd only known . . . .

George Nelson went on, "But the critical issue was the disappearance of over a half a million dollars from the bank's key accounts. Emily Phillips had been with the bank long enough to have diverted this large sum in small doses. The embezzlement started before she was in management and went undetected for a long time."

"The missing money explains how Emily and Jon paid cash for their house," Toni injected.

"Yes. Mrs. Phillips also carries three passports and established a bank account in the Cayman Islands. We knew she left the country as Mrs. Morton, not wanting to use her real passport. But that third one tripped us up when she landed in Sarasota on Tuesday."

"Three passports?" Toni asked.

"The third is an excellent fake. We also suspected that she worked with Mr. Morton on the embezzlement. When Mrs. Morton's body was found in Pasco," the agent stated, "we knew we had to close in soon. Thanks to the cooperation of the press," he nodded toward Mike, "the fracture and pin in the body's left radius bone weren't released."

"Yeah," Toni commented, "Emily didn't even think that the body had been identified. And she called me the dummy." Toni looked at Mike and Alan with a pleased-with-myself expression.

"Hmm," Alan responded with a scowl.

"Was Emily's house under surveillance?" Toni asked.

"Until we saw she left the country," Agent Nelson answered.

"No one suspected her re-entry?"

"It's unfortunate. Not only did her third passport go undetected, but also her sophisticated burn disguise makeup fooled our detection devices."

"Burn disguise?"

The agent nodded. "The makeup on her face looked as if she had covered over large burn scars. You know, the theatrical stuff used in the movies. She even singed her eyebrows. We found colored contact lenses in her possession, too. We can't fault Mrs. Phillips for some talent, at least in the covert area."

"And her acting ability for the past couple of years. She fooled many people. The bank's top executives believed she was a decent, ethical person." Toni shook her head. "Have Carl Johnson and the rest of the bank's executives been given this news?"

"Yes. We'll meet with him later today. Ray will go with us for that debriefing. Thank you—"

"One more question, Agent Nelson," Toni said, "what'll happen to Emily and Jon's house? I assume Jon will recover."

Toni glanced over at Alan. He rolled his eyes and added, "She always has one more question."

Toni widened her eyes and stared at the detective, a visual challenge to his comment. He ignored her and tilted his head back to the FBI agent.

"True." George Nelson continued, "Mr. Morton will be fine. Tests revealed that small doses of liquid nicotine had been given to Mr. Phillips over time. The paramedics found the vial you told them about. The dose in that cylinder, by all indications, would've been fatal. They're keeping him for observation over the weekend."

Toni felt a chill in her blood.

"As for the house, it's owned as joint tenancy with rights of survivorship. As unfair as it may seem," the agent shrugged, "Mrs. Phillips retains her half of the ownership in prison unless Mr. Phillips divorces her. Of course, if Mr. Phillips had died, she would have been the sole owner and could've disposed of it if she desired. The big concern revolves around stolen funds used for the original purchase. The bank may make a claim if they can confirm the money trail."

"Emily took more than three hundred thousand, which was the sale price of the home. So other funds are still missing. What about the contents of the safe deposit boxes?" Toni asked.

Okay so I have one more question after the one more question. And maybe more. I've worked hard on this caper and dealt with a mad woman. I want all the facts.

"Regarding the vault, we found what appeared to be keys to safe deposit boxes in the bedroom. Though we haven't confirmed them, there's a strong possibility they'll provide a clue to how the valuables were taken. By the way, Ms. Jasper," the agent's face brightened, "we did recover Mrs. Ford's sapphire ring. As soon as it's processed, we can return it to her."

Toni thought that was the best news of this meeting. Mike reached over and hugged her when he saw her moist eyes.

"Thank you so much," Toni said, holding back tears. "Mrs. Ford will be thrilled. I'm thrilled. And I hope you can locate Walter's bearer bonds."

Mike forced a smile. Toni knew he'd be happy when Walter didn't hound him like a gruff Labrador Retriever on a serious quest.

"Might the bonds be on the Cayman Islands? In a bank vault there?" Mike asked.

"Good thought," Agent Nelson said. "We don't know. For sure, the bearer bonds have not surfaced."

Toni's brainstorm jolted her in the chair. "Oh," she blurted and all eyes shifted toward her, "What about that package that Jesse shipped for Emily. She presumed he'd gotten on some boat with it."

The agent nodded. "We're checking into it. Thank you, everyone, for your cooperation. Ray, I need to see you. The rest of you are free to go . . . for now."

Toni wanted to be free and run away with Mike to some exotic and private destination, as long as it wasn't the Cayman Islands. But the mental and physical drain of the week's events left her feeling weak all of a sudden.

"I guess it's time for lunch," she said, ready for a break.

Mike took her hand. "How about a little cafe on the beach?"

Chapter Fifty-One

Mike pulled his Jeep in front of a stylish café on North Redington Beach. He sat back to observe Toni. Her eyes rotated toward him while her head stayed on the seat's headrest as if reluctant to relinquish the comfort. Her long ponytail hung in gentle brown waves down her right shoulder.

"You're exhausted," he observed.

"True," she replied softly.

He wrapped his long fingers around her relaxed left hand. "Come on. You'll feel better after a good meal." He leaned over to kiss her. Toni raised her right hand to caress his neck.

"Is that the appetizer?" she asked.

"Let's go," Mike chuckled as he opened his door. "One more thing," he added with a smirk as he pulled open the restaurant's door. "Just because this place is also a boutique doesn't mean I want to go shopping after we eat."

Toni couldn't resist a cheery smile that lit up her face. "You *are* in such trouble, Milner."

Seated on the patio, they enjoyed the well-shaded area and a slight breeze that added a welcome touch on a still-warm September day. The hostess had led the couple to a maple-laminate round table situated under the curved, reaching limb of a gnarly old tree. Lush green ferns surrounded the patio, tucked between other vegetation. Toni liked the ferns best. She considered them graceful yet strong, much like her own self-image. Maybe not today, though, she surmised.

After perusing the menu, she decided to hell with any diet restriction. Smothered with strawberries and bananas, the Belgian waffle shouted celebration in the menu photo. Toni asked the waitress for raspberry syrup as well. At least I've got the fruit groups covered, she rationalized.

Mike ordered apple crisp French toast and specified extra butter. "See, fruit for me, too." His proud yet mischievous expression drew a loud laugh from Toni.

"Oh Milner," she sighed, "you're hopeless."

Mike grinned and pulled both of her hands into his. "Good. And don't you forget it, Jasper."

Toni had to admit Mike was right. After waffle carbs and berries, she recovered almost to her normal energetic self.

"Hey, I just remembered something weird yesterday. And I didn't think of it when I wrote my statement this morning. When I was in Emily's house, she got a call. I wondered who would call her. She told the person 'You know what to do. Get me later.'"

Mike's eyebrows arched.

"Now I realize that someone, we don't know who, must've known where she was. I mean, Jon was half dead, and Jesse was a slimy coward on the floor. So who called?"

For the moment, Toni hadn't a clue. She pictured her suspect diagram in her mind's eye. All characters had been accounted for, but some person had to be missed.

Mike's face morphed into a pensive façade. Toni liked that look. To her, it was the outer manifestation of the intellectual side of her man.

"Someone else from the bank?" he asked. "I can't see Ray as able—or willing—to play both sides. Do you think the bank's regional VP was in on the heist, pointing blame toward Emily?"

"No. If he is, I'd be super surprised. Why jeopardize his career? Besides, he's the one who contacted the FBI and enlisted Ray's help. No, not Carl."

"The fact that you're on a first name basis with the guy doesn't rule him out."

"I'm on a first name basis with lots of people, smarty. Emily also said 'they won't find me.' Clearly she didn't know Brad was ready to pounce." Toni restrained her tears at the memory of Brad's heroics.

"About Brad," Mike stated in his official business tone, "he's in hot water with the FBI and Alan. They didn't know he intended to break in. Luckily, no one got hurt after his stunt. Alan told me Brad had an obligation to you and to Sue. But I don't think his loyalty plea got him off the hook."

"Everyone's okay." Toni sounded her own plea. "Shouldn't they be relieved at the outcome? I'm not losing my terrific artist, am I?"

"I don't know. Talk to Alan . . . on the other hand, wait and see. I don't want you in hot water any more than you are." Mike's engaging grin stopped Toni in mid-thought. However, in less than a minute she was back on track with Emily's cryptic words still front and center in her brain.

"If Emily had an escape plan, she'd go back to the Cayman Islands. Unless she didn't stash the money and bonds on that island."

Mike stroked Toni's slender fingers with his thumb as they rested across his palms.

"I don't know, Toni," he said. "I do know that I have to get back to work, as much as I'd like to stay here with you all day."

Toni's heart leapt as her face relaxed in a warm gaze.

"Me too," she admitted. "I'll see if I can get Ray and Chloe together later. She'll be ecstatic to see her ring and her investment banker. I have to stop by my mom's, too."

As Mike paid the bill, she held up one of the appliquéd denim handbags that hung on the wall near the register. She twirled it in admiration. I need a nice remembrance of this lunch, she thought.

"Oh no," Mike groaned when he noticed her in shopper mode.

"This is cute," she said. "New purse, new outlook."

"Who the hell came up with that line?"

"Your former reporter," she whispered as she looped her arm around his elbow.

Chapter Fifty-Two

The goodbye kiss was long and passionate.

"I'll come by later," Mike whispered.

"Great. I can cook if you want," Toni said as her hands glided down his shoulders.

"I feel adventurous. Why not?" He attempted to restrain a lovesick giggle.

Toni slapped his arm. After unlocking her front door, she turned and blew a kiss.

After closing the door, she felt alone in the all-too-quiet condo. But she had to keep busy. First, hunt for Bubbles, who was soon discovered in deep slumber in the center of Toni's bed. In true midday mode, the cat had snuggled between bed pillows. Toni retrieved her new cell phone to rent a car and call Ray. He'd finished the FBI and bank executive debriefings, or what he had called not-brief-at-all meetings. Therefore, he could meet her at Chloe's. Toni hit Chloe's number on her cell and felt nervous.

"Hi Chloe."

"Toni. I didn't think I'd talk with you again today. Are you okay?"

"Better than okay, Chloe. Are you sitting down?"

"I'm usually supported by my posterior. Out with it."

"First, you'll get your ring back. I'm so excited for you."

"Oh Toni! How do you know?"

"Agent Nelson, your FBI friend, found it. As soon as he can, he'll bring it to you. See, he's an okay guy."

Toni heard a whimper from the other end of the phone. She knew it reflected Chloe's emotional display of happiness. Before she hit her with another shocking pleasantry, Toni debated whether Chloe needed more time to process the first one.

"Chloe," Toni said softly.

"I'm okay. You said first. Is there a second?"

Toni chuckled. Chloe was fine.

"Yes," Toni said. "I know you heard on the news that Ray's alive. So how about if he and I come to visit at about four o'clock?"

Toni heard a sound, of what she wasn't certain. It ranged between a screech and the precursor to a faint.

"Chloe?" Toni held her breath.

"In a little over an hour? That's hardly enough time to put on the right outfit and fix my makeup," Chloe huffed.

Toni laughed. "Good," she said with a grin. "We'll see you then."

***

Toni appreciated the little blue compact car rental. However, she'd be happier when she got her own car back, especially since some of her fashion show notes were still on the back seat. For the moment, the Chloe visit turned into a reunion of the most surreal type.

"Hi, Ray," Toni called as she strode in from the parking lot. They exchanged a quick hug and proceeded through the lobby.

"The solarium is Chloe's favorite room. Have you been here before?"

"No. Chloe always came to the bank. It's not a bad idea, though."

"What's that?"

"For me to come here. House calls from the investment banker," he said with pride in his voice. "I think I should suggest it to Carl Johnson."

"I like it, and the residents will love it. Tell Mr. Johnson that my artist will design a special ad for your personal service."

Ray beamed.

They stopped at the portico of the wide, window-walled room. The greenery of the exterior garden appeared as an extension of the inner environment. Chloe and Brutus were entrenched in their usual overstuffed seat. The requisite white ceramic pot, with complementary cream pitcher and bowl of sugar packets, was ready on the table.

"Ray," Chloe called as she wrenched herself from the deep cushion and stood with open arms.

"Chloe, so good to see you," he said as he rushed toward her. They embraced briefly. Chloe graciously waved them to their seats. "I'm pouring," Ray announced as he reached for the coffee pot. "Chloe? Toni?"

These two have picked up as if nothing had happened. High society and suave genteel are back together again. Chloe trusts Ray, and Ray believes her investments are safe. And he'll keep them secure.

Toni sat back and sipped her coffee while she watched the duo reunite. For over an hour, the pair chatted of past times and future earnings. They laughed, planned, assessed risk and set a date for their next in-bank conference.

"Toni, what do you think?" The sound of her name whisked her back to reality and out of her daydream of a luxurious vacation with Mike.

"Sounds good to me," she responded, though she had no concept of the question. The two just smiled at her. She stood and hooked her new denim purse over her elbow.

"Thanks for the coffee, Chloe. I have to run."

"Oh, so you *can't* stay for dinner?" Chloe asked. *Ah ha,* Toni thought. *How could I have missed a question that concerned food?* She made a mental note to tell Mike about the amusing slip-up.

"No, I need some rest. But you guys have fun. Ray, the menu's fabulous here. And you'll see a number of the bank's customers."

They hugged and bid farewell. Toni peeked into the dining room as she passed. A few seats were filled. No Walter.

Toni maneuvered the rental car out of the parking lot. As she was about to turn left onto Seminole Boulevard, a car sped past her through the yellow light.

Damn. That was close. Harry? What the hell's he up to?

***

Armed with jumbo sea scallops, large organic potatoes and low-fat sour cream, Toni juggled her way to the kitchen.

"Hey, Bubbles," she called.

"Meow," came the response as the furry pet descended from the loft.

"Guess what? Your pal Mike's coming for dinner. He might even give you a big round fishy treat if he doesn't like scallops. We'll see."

With two chocolate brown placemats, dinner plates and silverware, the dining stage was set. A bouquet of yellow mums added just the right festive touch. She turned to admire the deep red roses still gracing the center of her coffee table.

Toni bounded up the carpeted stairs and slid open her closet door. Definitely red and silky, she thought. Or maybe hot pink?

Chapter Fifty-Three

The click of the deadbolt didn't surprise Toni. She'd seen Mike drive in and watched him amble up the walkway. In a split second, she greeted him with open arms. The now familiar embrace lingered as did their passionate kiss.

"I've missed you," Mike admitted.

"Good," Toni said. "Work must be boring, huh?" She couldn't hold back a slight giggle.

"Not exactly."

"The story's difficult to edit or—"

"No." Mike cut her off as he released her from his grasp. He started to pace back and forth in the kitchen, watchful and puzzled. Toni frowned, bit baffled by Mike's sudden demeanor change.

"The story will be written," he continued, "even if I have to do it myself. I've got a couple of days until deadline. The reporter is the concern. Harry didn't show up for work today, and I didn't find out until I got there after lunch. No answer on his cell. And no one's heard from him."

"Harry? I saw him at the crime scene yesterday."

"Yeah, so did I before I left."

"Did he seem nervous or jumpy to you?"

"No . . . well, now that you mention it, maybe a little on edge. I told him to research the facts and we'd get together today. He hasn't been out one day in the six months he's been at the paper."

"He sped right in front of me this afternoon like on a mission." Her stomach began to tighten with the all-too-familiar gut instinct alarm.

Mike's puzzled expression jolted Toni's memory.

She began with caution, "What references did you check before you hired him?"

"References? Okay, I only called one."

"Just one?"

"The position had been open too long. I needed someone. And I knew Harry's former editor. He vouched for the guy."

"You're sure you talked with him?"

"Yes. I remembered his voice even though we hadn't spoken in about eight years."

Toni's mind raced as she sprang from the couch. She ran to the loft bedroom and retrieved her laptop. Mike observed in silence.

"What's Harry's last name? And what paper did he come from?"

"Murphy. *The Arizona Weekly*."

Toni searched Harry's name with the paper's title. A photo and biography popped onto the screen. Both of them leaned in, wide-eyed, to scour the information.

Toni broke the silence. "That's not Harry. This guy died in a car crash last year." She sat back and gazed at Mike whose cheeks were royally flushed.

"Who the hell did I talk to? It sounded like Don." Mike's narrowed eyes and tight lips alarmed Toni.

"Are you thinking what I'm thinking?" she asked.

"Jasper, far be it from me to ever understand what's in your brain," he retorted.

"The call Emily got in the house. Could it have been from Harry? Did he say he knew anyone when he moved here?"

Mike sat back and sank into the couch. His eyes fixed on the computer screen. After several minutes, Toni had to break the man's brain spell.

"You know, when Harry sped past me, he was headed in the direction of Emily and Jon's neighborhood."

"You're sure it was Harry?" Mike's interrogation tone was at full throttle.

"Yes. He turned right in front of me."

"Damn."

Mike's firm one-word response spoke a multitude of worry and irritation. He reached for his cell phone.

"Hey, George. Sorry to bother you this late, but a new detail's come up in the Phillips' case. I believe one of my staff may be involved. Can you call me back as soon as you get this message? Thanks. I appreciate it."

Toni forced a smile. Trouble hadn't subsided, but she and Mike were here, together. She moved closer and hugged him.

"We should still eat dinner," she whispered in his ear.

He kissed her in response.

***

"I confess," Mike said, "I never would've ordered scallops. But these little devils were pretty darn tasty. You can make them again."

"Oh, you presume I'm going to cook on a regular basis?" she asked.

"Not at all. You haven't checked out my awesome, world-class culinary skills." Toni recognized Mike's light exaggeration meant his tension regarding Harry was on hold.

"Do I have to give in to beef?"

"No. My pork barbeque ribs are out of this world, if I say so myself."

"You can say what you want. I need proof," she said.

The couple lingered over chocolate chip cookies. Toni had enjoyed Mike's presence during the years they had worked together. But their new loving relationship was better than she'd imagined.

Startled by the ring tone, the editor reached for his phone. Mike proceeded to give George the details concerning their suspicions regarding Harry and thanked him for his help.

"He said they would try to locate Harry immediately. Meanwhile, I should go to the paper and check out Harry's desk. Who knows what unauthorized material he's squirreled away in those drawers."

Toni stood still as Mike pocketed his cell phone and reached for his keys.

"I've got a better plan," she announced with a straight face. "Who's minding the crime scene tonight?"

"What?" Mike stopped in his tracks. "You think Harry'd go there? Why?"

"You just said it. 'Squirreled away.' Emily also told the caller 'they won't find me.' She had to know the FBI would soon catch on to her fabricated story, and figure she was in Seminole or at least in the country. That caller alerted her to something."

"But, I don't understand. What could be at the house? It's been searched."

"Maybe those bearer bonds."

"Where?"

"Oh Milner," Toni said with satisfaction, "I bet planner-Emily installed some secret closet. Her safe room. The FBI might not find it. But if Harry's one of her minions, he'd know about it."

Mike shook his head. "Sounds far-fetched, Jasper. Let's go."

***

The white Jeep glided past lush green lawns as twilight settled over the area. They'd easily slipped into the gated community behind another vehicle. Toni felt like a pro at that maneuver. Mike turned onto Emily and Jon's street. The home driveway and cul-de-sac were empty.

"Let's go to the next street, Mike." Mike glided around the corner one block north.

"Stop," she said. "See, in front of the last house. That vehicle looks a lot like Harry's."

"That's his license," Mike said.

After parking several houses away, he hit autodial. "George. We've got him. He's parked at a house behind the Phillips'. Is anyone at the Phillips' residence? No? Then I suggest you get someone over here ASAP. We'll stay put in case he tries to leave."

Toni beamed. "We make a good team."

"Always did," he said with warmth and certainty.

Chapter Fifty-Four

The bustle was uncharacteristic for a Friday evening in Seminole's modest police station. Mike and Toni watched as Harry was led past them in handcuffs.

"Guess I'm the reporter and editor for the weekend and who knows how many weeks," Mike said with a decided lack of gusto.

"Don't worry about eating," Toni said with cheer, "those leftover hot dogs are still waiting in my fridge. Bubbles refused to eat them."

Mike had little time to throw her a disconsolate look before Agent George Nelson stepped in front of them.

"I don't know how you guys did it," the agent started, "but thanks. We caught Mr. Murphy inside the Phillips' home clearing out a secret closet in the guest room. How ironic, Ms. Jasper. You and Sue were a few feet away from those bonds and more stolen jewelry. And as weird as it seems, Mrs. Phillips even stashed food and incontinence pads in her safe room. She imagined her way out of several scenarios. Just not the one that got her caught."

"Glad we could help," the couple said in unison.

The agent smiled. "Mr. Murphy admitted he was also supposed to rescue some scanning machine Mr. Morton had shipped to the Cayman Islands. They'd wrapped the machine along with a few other computers and printers in a rug to carry them out of the house without arousing the neighbors' suspicions. Mr. Morton didn't want anyone to think he might be moving, just replacing carpet. Then he figured his car wouldn't be noticed in Tampa International's long-term parking. Emily retrieved incriminating documents left there for her. When Ms. Anderson said they'd been near the airport, she was right. "

Toni looked pleased. "That's my pal. She's sharp for sure. Agent Nelson, will you please tell her about this development? She needs some encouragement."

"Yes, I will. She's agreed to testify against Mrs. Phillips. This group won't be up to their shenanigans again. Oh, by the way, Mr. Murphy's real name is Don Sudall. He's Mrs. Phillips' cousin. He claims that she wanted him to fake an AP release reporting she'd fled to Mexico. The misdirection would give them time to get away. And, Mike, he did work for *The Arizona Weekly* in the newsroom. At least he didn't lie about everything."

"That explains it," Toni said.

"Explains what?" the agent asked.

"What happened to Mike when he called the *Republic* for Mr. Murphy's reference." She turned toward Mike. "When you asked for Don, you got Harry instead. He must've told the operator to send the other Don's calls to him."

Mike stood speechless, shaking his head.

George Nelson extended his hand. "See you both next week. I've got work to do. Go have fun for the weekend. Ms. Jasper, no more detective work."

"I've learned my lesson, Agent Nelson," she said with a penitent smile, though the agent's countenance remained somber.

Mike and Toni strolled hand-in-hand toward Mike's Jeep.

"Fun?" Mike asked in a rhetorical way. "I have to get to the office. Who knows what damage that character did that I didn't catch."

"I'll come with you," Toni offered. "I can help. I once had a job just like Harry's," she kidded.

"So I can't get rid of you, Jasper?"

Mike pulled her close, his arm wrapped around her waist, as they strolled past the few cars parked in sporadic form on the lined asphalt.

"Nope," she said with levity.

Toni's gleeful expression was focused on the tall man who gazed down at her, pleased with her company. But her cell phone chime broke the tender intimacy of the moment. She fumbled in her new denim bag for it and viewed the caller ID.

"It's someone from PinCo Bank," she proclaimed reading the caller identification. "Hello, Toni Jasper. How can I help you?"

"Ms. Jasper. Carl Johnson here. I apologize for calling so late on a Friday, but I'd like to get you on my calendar. Can you come to my office Monday morning?"

Toni's heart skipped a beat. She replied, "Absolutely. What time?"

"How about nine o'clock? And Mr. Ray Edwards will be joining us. He has an idea to help recoup our somewhat tainted image. I want your input and assistance. Perhaps we can schedule a *true* open house and not a criminal diversion. Is that alright with you?"

"Mr. Johnson, a meeting with you and Ray is more than alright. Thank you."

Toni hung up, jumped with delight and landed in Mike's arms.

96907069R00155

Made in the USA
Columbia, SC
08 June 2018